SMALL TOWN WIVES

A Novel

Eugenia A Haisley

2014

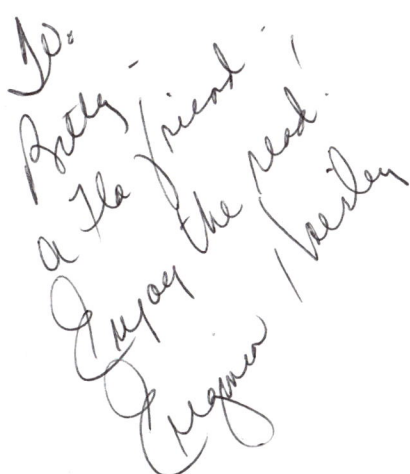

Small Town Wives is a work of fiction. Names, characters, places and incidents are the products of the author's imagination or are used fictitiously. Any resemblance to actual events, locales, or persons, living or dead is purely coincidental.

Copyright © 2014 by Eugenia A. Haisley

ISBN-13: 978-1500324018

CHAPTER 1

July 4, 1967

The town of Creviston was bustling with activity. Local entertainment was minimal, so it seemed as though most of the town's population of 2,300 had turned out for the annual Fourth of July festivities. A medley of John Philip Sousa's marching songs, being played by the high school band, could be heard as the annual parade rolled down Main Street. Town dignitaries, perched aboard the fire engine, led the parade with lights flashing, followed by the band major strutting his stuff as he led the majorettes and members of the band. Tractors pulled patriotically-decorated floats, painstakingly created by members of local fraternal organizations, including the Lions Club, American Legion and the VFW. Horseback riders dressed in red, white and blue brought up the rear of the parade.

The rolling, tree-lined park was decorated with flags, banners and lots of balloons. Almost fifty antique-car owners had arrived to show off their restorations. A flea market with craft tables, garage sale items and baked goods were popular attractions; children stood in line waiting for the sack race to begin; men were drooling over the old cars and discussing politics; while their wives simply enjoyed browsing the items for sale and having a day out.

It was the late sixties, a rebellious time for the USA. A

segment of young people on the West Coast, otherwise known as hippies, talked of peace and love, smoked pot, wore tie-dyed clothing and pinned flowers in their hair. The hippies were looked upon by polite society as social misfits and had coined this season their "Summer of Love." Lyndon Johnson, half way into his second term as president, having inherited the office when John F. Kennedy was assassinated, was at the helm of the country. His biggest program as president was the creation of his "Great Society", but he was spending most of his time mired in the promotion of two wars, his controversial "War on Poverty" and the one which would prove to be his downfall, the Viet Nam War, a fight against communism in Southeast Asia.

Creviston was a pretty town with wide, oak-lined streets, Victorian homes with lots of gingerbread trim and front-porch swings, dormered Craftsman houses from the Catalog Department of Sears & Roebuck, various retail business including grocery stores, gas stations, a hardware and drug store, post office, banks, the Town Hall, several churches and one school system. Children rode their bikes everywhere, played outside until dark, walked downtown to buy ice cream cones and their parents never worried about their safety. The local police department consisted of the town marshal and one deputy; crime wasn't an issue in Creviston. Everyone knew almost everyone else in town and the gossip mill ran day and night. While anti-war demonstrations were taking place across the country, Creviston was only grazed by the war-time climate; a few young men were drafted, while others chose to enlist in the branch of their choice. Children raised in Creviston usually graduated from high school; a few continued on to college, but the majority labored to make a living; guys finding jobs at either the automobile factories in nearby cities or Dillon's, the local construction company.

Getting married and raising a family was the main objective of the girls. Occasionally, after marriage, a girl would go to work in a local bank or dress shop before having her first child, but once that event occurred, most became stay-at-home moms. Life in Creviston seemed innocent, until you peeked below the surface.

Teresa Farris, a petite blonde with a turned-up nose was cute in a tomboyish way. A popular cheerleader in high school, she met and married Ted after a short romance and within seven years, they became parents of two daughters, Rose, age six and Colleen, age four. Teresa was taking classes to become a realtor and liked to stay busy. She loved to read, decorate, garden and dabbled at cooking. Ted was dark haired, muscular, not much taller than his wife and was well known in the trades as one of the best at finish work. He spent a lot of time on the job and Teresa nagged him frequently about being a workaholic. They were renovating an old two-story, built in 1905 with its' own carriage house, beautiful in its day, but deteriorating in recent years, however; Ted and Teresa were beginning to restore some its' original splendor. Teresa was creative and had decorated the home in Victorian colors of rose and emerald with lots of antiques. She scoured the yard sales and used furniture stores for bargains. The couple had been struggling to come up with enough money to build a new home, while Teresa was experiencing her own struggle; often daydreaming about Doug Jones, her high school sweetheart, who dumped her in their senior year for Linda Norris, who he married. Speculation around town had always been that Teresa had married Ted on the rebound.

Janet Steele, Teresa's best friend, returned home from college to find all her friends married. Out of desperation and afraid of not finding a husband, she rushed into marriage with Robert, an afternoon-shift factory worker. He moved into her bungalow on a downtown side street, which she had decorated in a cottage style, with a floral over-stuffed sofa, white-washed walls and floors, bright accent colors and lots of pillows. Her friends called it "Janet's doll house". She was a perfectionist, both in her home and her first job as a bank teller, because at the end of the day, she wanted everything to match. Earning her degree in Accounting; numbers became her passion. Robert was a secretive guy, not very ambitious and extremely jealous of her and of the riches of others. He enjoyed taking weekends away on hunting or fishing trips with his buddies and his favorite pastime, poker. Janet was unaware of Robert's major reason for proposing to her; he happened to overhear a conversation between his mother and one of her friends that Janet would be able to access her sizeable trust fund when she turned twenty-five, which was just around the corner. Janet's parents, who felt that she had married beneath her, owned and operated the local tomato-canning plant, which shipped products all over the country. They lived in a fenced-in estate by the river and were considered the wealthiest family in town. Janet was a tall brunette with a sexy figure, looked upon lustily by many of the local men, but her beauty and intelligence intimidated them. The average guy assumed she wouldn't be interested in him; consequently, she ended up with the good-looking guys who depended on their looks to carry them through and lacked in the personality department, therefore, the relationships had little chance. Then, along came Robert, five years older, tall, blonde, and sexy; unfazed by her looks. He was arrogant, but insecure, a complicated combination. His jealous streak had begun to create problems in their marriage; he often questioned her on how she spent her evenings while he was working. Actually, she was quite lonely and of late, was wondering if she had mistakenly rushed into marriage, just for the sake of having a husband.

Dianne Powers, another close friend, had to get married at sixteen because she had "given in" to Mike and now at twenty-five, was becoming restless in her marriage. She had recently seen the movie "The Graduate" and went away asking herself if life was passing her by. Their son, Phillip, was eight and ready for third grade. Dianne, a pretty girl with long, dark hair and icy-blue eyes, was warm and affectionate, but no longer felt much passion for her husband. She had returned to high school after her marriage and earned her diploma; her high school yearbook said she would be remembered for her courage. The next several years were spent at home, raising her son, cooking, cleaning, getting hooked on the soaps and becoming bored to death. She needed an outlet. Becoming obsessed with decorating, her home became her chief project. Currently, her central theme was shades of neutral, a cream-colored velvet sofa, light, off-white, airy curtains, comfortable wing chairs covered with a taupe brocade, a fireplace with a white mantle, plus lots of books and music. The decor was peaceful and she loved being there, just not all the time. Mike, at age twenty-eight, was the youngest crew foreman at Dillon's, a non-union company and worked long hours. He spent numerous evenings at the local tavern with his cronies, drinking beer and talking to other women. He was a handsome man, dark hair with a thin physique, somewhat of a Latin look, egotistical and rumored to be a womanizer. Dianne was past being seduced by his looks, growing tired of the situation, she was contemplating her options.

Jill Hines, age twenty-seven, was the oldest in their little circle of friends. She had married Johnny, a wiry guy with sandy-colored hair and a ruddy complexion, after a two-year relationship. He worked as a plumber in his Dad's business and was secure in the knowledge that the business would one day be his. They had three sons, ages six, four, and a baby of nine months. She had little control over the older two and even though Johnny was a good father; he left the lion's portion of child rearing to his wife. Jill had become increasingly depressed and frustrated since the birth of her last child, turning to food as a comfort and alternating between dieting and overeating. Her friends suspected postpartum blues; Johnny didn't know such a malady existed. Jill was cute with auburn hair and soft blue eyes and possessed a saucy disposition with a quick temper, Irish roots probably, since her maiden name was Mullins. Johnny was a carefree guy; quickly adapting to most situations without becoming angry. They lived in a Craftsman-style house, which was perfect for their family. The upstairs worked for the boys; the dormers added extra room for all their toys, which left the downstairs relatively free of clutter. Merely keeping the house straightened was a formidable task, one which Jill seemed unable to accomplish.

The town had hired a small band to play for the evening festivities. Food vendors hawked hamburgers, hot dogs, soft drinks and lemonade, the usual picnic fare. Due to daylight savings time; fireworks were delayed until nine. It was a beautiful evening, mid-eighties, normal for a July day in Indiana. The circle of friends stood out in the crowd, wearing the new skorts, a cross between a mini skirt and shorts. Flowered halter tops and bright tees in hot pink and orange completed their outfits. Jill was wearing a turquoise headband, which matched her skort.

Teresa and her friends placed their lawn chairs in a good spot for the fireworks and the music. Everyone brought their own bottles, customary in their circle, and soon the beer and mixed drinks were flowing freely. The kids inhaled their hot dogs and the music grew louder. The band played "Brown Eyed Girl" and the dancing began. Out of the corner of her eye, Teresa spotted Doug and Linda. She hadn't seen him for a very long time and he looked wonderful to her. Linda looked ready to deliver any day and appeared very tired. Teresa knew her in high school, but after she started dating Doug, there was no further conversation between them.

"Linda, you look as though you could use a seat; take mine." She then walked over to say hello to Doug. "Haven't seen you around for a while; how've you been?"

"Okay, I've been spending a lot of time at the office; summer is a busy time for me, what with people buying and selling houses and needing new insurance policies, plus I've started doing home inspections for the banks."

She chuckled. "That's interesting; I'm studying to become a realtor; maybe you'll be doing some of the inspections on my deals."

"That would be ironic, us working together. By the way, you look fabulous; life must be treating you good."

"Thanks Doug, you always did say just the right things to make me feel good; I don't hear many compliments these days" she said wistfully.

"Damn, you're kidding me; doesn't Ted realize what a lucky guy he is?" He flicked his cigarette away in a show of exasperation.

The band broke into "Smoke Gets in Your Eyes" and Doug yelled "Hey, Ted, care if I dance with your wife?" Ted, who, by this time, had had several beers, could not have cared less. Doug pulled her close and they both felt that old sexual attraction.

"Wow, this takes us back" and she murmured "Yes, it does." The song ended way too soon for both of them. Neither noticed the hurt in Linda's eyes.

The fireworks finale lit up the sky, then everyone began packing up their things and saying good night. Teresa looked around at the crowd and thought, we do this every year; it's always the same, too much beer, too many Tom Collins, but for me, tonight was different; Doug held me in his arms, not nearly long enough, but just enough to make me want more. She wondered if any of her friends were feeling this heavy burden of routine and searching for an escape.

Too many beers had affected Ted and an argument ensued about who would drive. Teresa finally snatched the keys away from him and drove home. Ted staggered to the door and she didn't offer to help. He plopped down on the sofa and was asleep within minutes. Disgusted, she went to bed; knowing she'd have to be up early to pick up their daughters, who were spending the night with their grandmother. Lying there, she wondered how their dance had affected Doug; she knew her own feelings were both scary and exciting.

Jill packed up the baby; Johnny herded their other two sons toward the car and they headed home. The boys were fighting in the back seat and Johnny was oblivious as usual. She couldn't wait to get them to bed. They were so wound up from all the excitement; she was afraid this was not going to be easy. When they pulled in the driveway, she was surprised to see the little guys almost asleep. Heaving a big sigh of relief, she and Johnny carried them to their beds and she went straight to the refrigerator.

"Haven't you had enough to eat tonight, Jill?" Johnny asked as he lounged in his recliner.

"Oh, I just want a little something to settle my tummy before I turn in; besides, what difference does it make to you?" she replied.

"Nothing, Jill, but aren't you dieting again? It's hard to keep up with your eating habits and your mood swings. I wish you'd go see old Doc Landers. Maybe he could give you something to put you back on track."

"That quack, I'd rather go see a medicine man than him, but I might make an appointment with Dr. Nelson. I've heard good things about him. Anyway, I'm drinking this glass of milk and going to bed; it's late and we have lots of work to get done around here tomorrow."

Dianne and Mike had hardly spoken to one another all evening. He had been late the night before and Dianne wasn't interested in talking to him. Mike had tried to put her in a better mood by spending time with Phillip, but she was not going to be bribed by his actions. She had waited up until after two, finally gave up and went to bed, pretending to be asleep when he finally came home. Lying there, Dianne had made a decision; she needed to find a job. If things worsened between the two of them, she would need an income. She hated the thought of a separation or divorce, but she wasn't willing to resign herself to an unhappy marriage. Times were changing and women now had choices, where in the past they had little hope of supporting themselves; therefore, they remained trapped. She was not a believer in "Father Knows Best" families; they only existed in the land of television.

CHAPTER 2

Since the early days of their marriage, Janet and Robert had made a habit of going out for breakfast whenever possible. With his late nights and her banking hours, it was a good time to catch up. For her, it was one of the few pleasant aspects of their relationship; they enjoyed the leisure time and lingered over their coffee. Janet had become ambivalent in her feelings toward Robert; she cared for him, but was it love? When they married she wanted children, but suffered two miscarriages; now she saw that as a mixed blessing. Was it wise to bring children into an uncertain marriage? Mother Nature had taken the decision out of her hands. It didn't seem to bother Robert, one way or the other...

"Robert, what did you think of the evening? Did you have a good time?"

"Sure did, Janet, but something I noticed last night; what's going on with Doug and Teresa? He seemed to be really digging her, especially when they were dancing."

"Well, you didn't know them in high school, but they went together for almost three years. Everyone thought they'd get married for sure, but they broke up in her senior year because he started seeing Linda. Maybe they just felt drawn to each other last night; I really don't know."

"I'm telling you right now, Janet; if that had been you

dancing with an old boyfriend; I would not have been happy. No way, no how, just you remember that."

"Oh, Robert, don't be paranoid. You have absolutely no reason to doubt me." If only I really felt that way, she thought to herself.

As they drove home, Janet was thinking about Robert's jealousy; she wouldn't want him to know that the president of the bank had been quite attentive to her lately. Dave Brown was a handsome guy, much taller than she; his dark hair tinged with gray. He had piercing blue eyes and a great body for forty-two. He worked out, played golf with his father at the local club and had been married to his wife, Debbie, for almost twenty years. They had three teenagers, a boy and two girls. Being a banker, Dave had become a very powerful man in the community and with his wife threw lavish parties at their estate a mile outside of town. Debbie golfed, played tennis and shopped. Being an only child from a wealthy family, she had been very spoiled and expected the same from her husband. Still attractive in a Grace Kelly kind of way, she valued her figure and worked hard to keep it. With household help, she found lots of time to dawdle in the things she enjoyed, which included spending lots of time with Jake, the tennis pro. She served in various positions in several organizations, chaired numerous charitable events and obsessed over her beloved passion, bridge. Debbie had grown into the position of society wife quite easily. Janet had only slightly responded to Dave's flirting; she knew his reputation and felt he wasn't being serious, just having fun.

The ringing of the phone shattered Dianne's thoughts and she hurried to answer it. "What are your plans for the day?" asked Teresa, hoping they could get together later.

"Oh, I'm sitting here checking the employment ads; do you know of any jobs available right now?"

"Someone mentioned the other day that Mrs. Morrow at Molly's needed help in her dress shop. She wants to hire a manager trainee and cut her hours to as few as necessary to keep the business going.

"Do you think I'd qualify for that? I've had no experience in retail other than the drug store, if you can call that retail. But I do love clothes and have sewn several things for myself."

"Dianne, you're a smart girl, a quick study and how hard could it be? Go over there this morning and then stop by afterwards and fill me in on the details."

"Okay, a pep talk was just what I needed; see you later today. Thanks."

Teresa washed the breakfast dishes while Ted was in the shower. She was afraid Ted was upset with her over dancing with Doug and she had no idea how to defend herself. There was no defense; she knew she was in the wrong. She would not have liked it had Ted been dancing with another girl and holding her close.

"What is it?" she said. To her, he looked angry.

"Nothing, Teresa, nothing at all," he said, pouring himself a cup of coffee and sitting down at the formica table. He was still very angry over the way she had hung on Doug the night before, but he didn't have time for a confrontation this morning; instead he told her "I'm headed over to the job to see how the guys are doing with the drywall. The kitchen cabinets are coming in tomorrow and they need to be ready.

This is going to be one beautiful house when we're finished; it would be nice if we could afford it." He didn't know what it would take to make her happy, maybe a new house; he felt like he was letting his family down because they were still living in this old, drafty two-story house. They had made progress on the downstairs, removing old wallpaper and sanding the hardwood floors, but more work needed to be done; next on his agenda was redoing the kitchen. He thought he could make the upgrades with a contractors' discount at a good price. His plan was to complete the remodeling of this house and sell it; thereby putting them into a position to build their own. Of course, they'd have to find a place to live in the interim, but he'd think about that later. For now, this place would have to do. Hopefully, the new kitchen would appease her for the time being; now he just had to get her out of the house in order to do it.

"Oh, I thought you weren't working today, but it's just as well; Dianne is coming by later and then I have errands to run. Will you be home for dinner? I hate to fix a big meal and then you're not home to enjoy it."

Ted felt like she was nagging him, but said, "I'll be here before six. Plan on that and we'll have a quiet evening at home with the kids." He refilled his coffee cup and hurried out to his truck.

Teresa watched him go, thinking Ted's a good family man; what am I doing with Doug on my mind all the time? Maybe I'm only imagining Ted was peeved at me. She got the girls dressed and sent them outside to play. She had showered, dressed, fixed her hair and applied makeup before Ted got out of bed. He rarely noticed how she looked; she never went out of the house without looking her best. She had seen women lately at the grocery store with their hair in curlers. What were they thinking? She felt like Ted should show some appreciation for her efforts. How would it be if I were with Doug; I wonder if he'd appreciate me. Teresa, she said to herself, what are you doing? Doug dumped me; Ted has always been here. Am I losing my mind? I have to quit this fantasizing.

Jill and Johnny arose early; they needed to tackle the garden while the air was still cool. They had planted a small plot and were growing an abundance of vegetables. Tomatoes, green beans, squash, okra, even two rows of sweet corn. Weeding was the worst; green beans were ready to be picked, snapped and canned for winter. Corn was close to picking and the boys were really excited about having corn-on-the-cob. Johnny was showing the boys how to weed. Thank God he's doing that, she thought; I'd never have the patience.

"Johnny, I've finished picking beans; I'm going inside."

He thought, to do what, lay on the couch? "Why don't you clean that messy house? I know the boys and the baby take a lot of time, but you've got all day and nothing gets done. I have no clean clothes and I work six days a week. Something's got to give."

Chastised, she looked down at her feet. "Okay, okay, I know; I'll get started on the laundry and mop the kitchen. Maybe the boys can help you snap beans. I'm sorry Johnny; I just don't have the energy to do anything lately. I know you're right about what you said last night; I do need to make an appointment with a doctor. I'm as tired of feeling this way as you are of having a lazy wife."

"I'm glad you're beginning to recognize that; we'll get through this weekend. I'll take care of the kids and you can clean the house; then maybe you'll have time to wash your hair." All the hints he had dropped just seemed to fall on deaf ears. Her hair looked as though it hadn't been washed for two weeks and she didn't seem to notice it or care. He was beginning to feel scared, a real departure from his usual, nonchalant attitude.

Dianne changed clothes for her interview. She was very nervous as she stepped into the dress shop. The only time she had applied for a job before was at the drugstore and then she was only fifteen. Mrs. Morrow was with a customer, so she browsed for a while. Some of the clothing was a little outdated, but there were a few new styles, such as the mini-skirts that had become popular because of Twiggy, a waif of a model from England, who had taken the fashion world by storm. There was also a rack of stirrup pants, which she loved and a few pair of the brand new look, bell-bottom pants. This could be interesting.

"May I help you dear?" said Mrs. Morrow, who was in her sixties, but still quite attractive. Her hair was naturally white and she wore it in a chignon, quite becoming on her tall figure. Her sincere demeanor put Dianne at ease instantly.

"I hope so, Mam; my name is Dianne Powers and I'm here to apply for a job. I love coming in here and one of my friends mentioned that you might be looking for someone."

"Yes I am. It amazes me how fast news spreads in this town. Have you had any experience in retail?"

"I worked at the drugstore, doing stock and ringing up

customers. I love clothes, am familiar with fabrics, do a lot of sewing, have lots of free time and would be very willing to learn. Also, I live nearby; which would be convenient."

"Dianne, tell me a little about yourself. Are you married? Do you have any children or plans to have a child? I can't afford to train someone and then lose them right away. I'm sure you can understand that."

"Mrs. Morrow, I'm married and have one son, Phillip, who will be a third grader and have no plans to have any more children. My mother will be taking care of him during the day and after school this fall.

"That sounds perfect; you may be exactly who I need. The starting pay will be the minimum wage of $1.40 per hour; you'll receive a 25% discount on clothing and the hours are 10:00 AM till 5:30 PM Monday through Saturday, with one day off during the week. We can establish a firm schedule for your day off when you start, which I would like to be Monday at 10 A.M. There will be a trial period of ninety days and at the end of that time; we'll know if you're a good fit for the store."

"Thank you, Mrs. Morrow. I appreciate your willingness to give me a chance. I'll see you at 10 AM Monday."

Dianne was thrilled. She couldn't wait to get to Teresa's to share the good news. Finally, she would have a little independence. Mike would probably not like the idea; he wanted her home, in much the same way the other men in this town felt about their wives. Men wanted to be the sole provider, thereby, keeping their wives dependent upon them. But things were changing; the women's movement in this country was gaining strength and she wanted to be a part of it. Birth control pills and wives working with other men were making husbands all over the country feel insecure. They would have to accept the inevitable, because now that women were becoming more independent; she doubted the pendulum would ever swing back the other way.

"Teresa, you're such an inspiration. I got the job; thanks to you. The owner is very nice and I start Monday. Can you believe it? I can't wait."

"Dianne, I only told you about the possibility; you took the initiative. Congratulations! Let's sit out front on the porch swing and have a cocktail to celebrate. How about we have a gin and tonic?" Dianne nodded and as Teresa made the drinks, she continued "I thought you and Mike were fighting last night because you hardly said a word to him. Now that you have a job, you'll gain self-confidence and feel better about yourself. That could improve your marriage in time. Who knows, if you have other interests, he may start coming home earlier."

Dianne shrugged and sipped on her drink as she watched people strolling down the wide sidewalk. She was not optimistic about her situation. "I doubt it, but only time will tell. He knows how I feel and that I'm about at the end of my rope with him. So, if he has any brains at all, or cares anything about me; he will have to make some changes. Now, how about you, I was really surprised to see you and Doug dancing last night. Is the old spark still there?" she teased.

Teresa lit a cigarette before answering. "Yes it is, but I could never act on it. I have two girls and I'm afraid of the repercussions. I've always had feelings for Doug and I think he feels the same way, unless that's just wishful thinking on my part. I'm really confused about things; my head tells me to leave it alone, but my heart says go for it."

"Well, Teresa, you can't go with a guy for three years and just forget it. He was your first love and that's hard to get over. It looks to me like the attraction goes both ways; never say never. If you spent time with him; it wouldn't necessarily mean a divorce, would it; no one would have to know, except me of course. That does not mean I am encouraging you to have an affair, quite the opposite. You need to look at this from all angles."

Teresa laughed. "You'd be the first to know, or at least one of the first, depending on who I see first, you, Janet or Jill. Dianne, I know these things happen, but to me? Nothing exciting ever happens to me. Anyway, their baby is due next month and that always changes things."

"Okay, but mark my words, something is going to happen between you two, somewhere down the road." She finished her drink and said "I've got to go, get supper started and all that. I'll call you tomorrow."

As Dianne drove away, she felt a bit envious of Teresa. She wished she had some excitement in her life, maybe just not that kind. She hoped beyond hope that this job would fill some of that empty space.

CHAPTER 3

Doug Jones was an independent, insurance agent with a fairly flexible work schedule. He was a tall, lanky guy with sandy-colored hair and hazel eyes and exuded a lot of charisma. He was a basketball star in high school and still yearned for the adulation of the crowd. His small office was located in one of the old, brick two-story buildings on Elm Street in downtown Creviston. Next to him stood a Murphy's Five & Dime and a Handy Andy Hardware store. Across the street was the United Methodist Church. His agency insured a lot of homes, automobiles and businesses in the county. There were few claims, unless storms blew through the town or there was an occasional auto accident. Commissions were good, overhead was low and he had only one employee, a girl named Joanne Howard. She typed up the policies, invoiced the clients, filed, maintained his appointment book and attended to other items as needed. Joanne respected her boss and liked his wife Linda, who was due to give birth any day now; it was extremely important for her to know where Doug was at all times, but on this particular day, she couldn't locate him. He had run into Teresa at Millie's, an old, aluminum, railroad dining car at the edge of town. The diner had a big counter with chrome stools and roomy booths, both covered in red vinyl. A huge jukebox stood in the corner belting out "Heartbreak Hotel" by Elvis Presley. The menu offered a full breakfast complete with fried potatoes or grits; favorite lunches were hamburgers, breaded tenderloins and BLT's. There was a dinner special each evening for eighty-nine cents: meat loaf, roast beef, fried chicken, spaghetti and the usual all-you-could-eat fish on Friday. The place stayed busy with locals and a few travelers coming through on the main highway. Mid-morning was slow in the diner; the streets were empty, with most of the population ensconced in either their homes or their jobs.

"Teresa, I saw your car outside and thought I'd take a chance you were here alone. I had a client nearby and needed some measurements. Are you meeting someone?"

"Oh, hi Doug, no, I've been here for a while. I'd been having coffee with a gal who's taking the realtor course with me. We were comparing notes and she had to run; I was just finishing up my coffee. Sit down for a minute; since you stopped to see me, the least I can do is offer you a seat. How's Linda? The last time I saw her she looked very tired."

He sat down and motioned to the waitress for coffee. "Yeah, she's exhausted; the baby is due any day now; I'll be glad when it's over. I'm trying to stay in close touch in case she goes to the hospital. It wouldn't do for me to miss that, would it? But, enough about myself; how are things with you?"

"Oh, busy with the realtor course. I'll be taking my test soon, but other than that; it's the same old routine, raising kids, going through the motions; I guess you could say I'm in a rut. I think lots of couples get into that situation. How to get out of it is the question."

"I know exactly what you're saying. Even though our first

child is due any time; we're experiencing some of that same syndrome." He laid his hand on hers. "Plus, I've been thinking about you since the Fourth; I can't get you off my mind. I still feel bad about the way things ended in high school; I never meant to hurt you. I was a stupid kid; I ended up hurting myself as much. I know I have no right to say these things to you now; after the fact, but I'd still like to see you once in a while, for old times' sake."

"You've been on my mind too, Doug. It's hard being married and thinking about someone else. It definitely takes a toll, especially when life has become so monotonous. I'd love to see you occasionally, but how can we justify that? I'd have to think about it, a lot; it makes us both seem very selfish. I don't want to end up in a messy divorce and I doubt you do either."

"You're right; maybe it's selfish, but that's not the way I feel when I'm with you. I don't want to lose my family either; we'd just have to be very careful. Let's give it some thought and I'll call you. What's a good time?"

"Mornings are usually best" she tentatively replied. As Teresa rose to leave, Doug squeezed her hand and smiled. Her spirits soared. "I'll be seeing you" he said as he watched her walk away.

Teresa was still confused. She loved her husband, but Doug was so exciting to her. Did she dare see him? How would she feel afterwards? What if Ted found out? Would he hate her, or try to take the girls away from her? Life was so easy at the moment and she supposed she was happy. With the exception of this fantasy, she was satisfied. Why do I want to risk my marriage for a fling?

Toni Blake, the waitress at Millie's, stood watching them from behind the counter. She knew who the guy was because Joanne, her boyfriend's sister, worked for him, but Doug hadn't recognized her. She didn't know the woman; only that it wasn't his wife. Toni was friends with Melanie, Linda's sister; although she hadn't seen her for a while. Recently, she had run into Linda at the drug store and she looked like her baby could come anytime. He was being a jerk, she thought. It's no wonder I'm not married; this is ridiculous. Toni was divorced with a son and was very cynical about men. The fact that she was now dating was miraculous, but he was a good guy. She wondered if she should call Melanie. Then again, what good would that do? Maybe she'd better stay out of it.

That afternoon, Linda began having labor pains. This being her first child, she didn't know what to expect. She timed the transactions and they were even, ten minutes apart. She called her husband's office and left a message with Joanne, his secretary. It wasn't time to go to the hospital yet; her doctor said to wait until the pains were five minutes apart. She checked her bag, changed clothes and waited. The pains got closer. Where was Doug? She called the office again and Joanne said he was on his way home. When he got home; it was time to go. They arrived at the hospital; the nurse whisked her off to the labor room and he went to the waiting area. The pain was mostly in her back and nothing made her comfortable. Her mother was there, trying to comfort her. The contractions were almost unbearable and the doctor wasn't even here yet. She thought to herself, "Girl, this is one thing you're going to have to do for yourself; your mother can't do it for you." At last, he arrived and immediately ordered pain medication for her. Soon, she was out like a light.

Three hours later, she woke up and was wheeled into the delivery room. The lights were blinding. Her contractions were coming fast and the nurses were telling her to breathe deeply. The doctor broke her water and it felt like a flood. The nurses were replacing some of the sheets under her and the doctor was telling her to push. Her daughter was born an hour later, so tiny, six and 1/2 lbs., 18 inches long with lots of black hair. She wanted to name her Beth. The doctor went to the waiting room. "Mr. Jones, you have a baby daughter and she and your wife are doing fine. You'll be able to see them in about thirty minutes. A nurse will notify you when they're ready."

Later, Doug walked into their room and looked down at his wife and baby girl. "She's beautiful, Linda and you are too. Are you feeling okay? Do you need anything?" This rush of emotions took him by surprise. This is a new human being, totally dependent on us. God help me; I want to be a good father to her and a better husband to her mother.

CHAPTER 4

Dianne started to dress for her first day at Molly's; she wanted to look like she had some knowledge of the fashion world. Should I wear a casual summer suit or a simple dress? She chose a coral print dress, added coral earrings to match and beige low-heeled shoes. She added a beige shoulder bag and packed a sandwich for lunch. Mrs. Morrow had not mentioned a lunch break, so she would go prepared.

Mrs. Morrow was there when she arrived, a little before 10 AM. She noticed a coffee pot and a small icebox in the back room. Mrs. Morrow was dressed in a casual turquoise paisley skirt and short jacket with a yellow tee. She wore a large silver brooch on her jacket and small silver earrings. The jacket had a little rolled collar with a scarf attached. Dianne thought she looked very classy. She put her sandwich in the fridge and went out to see what Mrs. Morrow would have her do first. As she looked around, she thought the store needed to be a lot brighter. Maybe she could do window displays soon; they needed a fresh touch, maybe even flowers.

The morning went fast. She spent time learning the cash register, waiting on customers and learning how to write out sales slips. Straightening racks and getting a feel for the merchandise took the rest of the morning. There was a half-hour lunch break, which they alternated. After lunch, a delivery of jewelry arrived. She learned how to unpack, price and tag the pieces. They were then ready for display.

Mrs. Morrow told Dianne, "The eye buys; do your displays to appeal to the customer. With the new fashions, women are uncertain how to put them together, so that's our job."

Dianne left at the end of the day feeling exhilarated. She was having so much fun and learning new skills. She arrived home to find Mike already there. He didn't look too happy.

"Where's dinner, Dianne?" he roared. "If this job is going to keep you from getting your work done around here; you may just have to quit."

"Mike, dinner is in the oven; don't be so mean. You could at least ask me how my first day went. "

He snorted. "Damn it to hell, just get dinner on the table. I'm starved."

She was so disappointed. He really knew how to take the wind out of her sails. But, never mind; nothing he says is going to change my mind about this job. I love it and I'm keeping it.

Teresa had been studying non-stop for her realtor test. George Ross, of Ross Realty, had offered her a spot in his office after she earned her license. The realtor commission stood at 7%: 4% for the sales person, 2% for the listing agent and 1% for the head of the agency. She couldn't wait to get started; her nights and weekends would be busy and there would be one to two days floor time each week, plus a tour of new listings on Tuesday and a sales meeting. Finally, the morning of the test was here. She hadn't gotten much sleep the night before, but she felt ready. It would be a few weeks before she received the results, by mail.

CHAPTER 5

Dillon's Construction Company had finished their latest spec house. Ted had agreed to host an open house in celebration of the event. Guests attending would tour the home, receive a party pass and continue on to the festivities. The guests were very impressed with the house. They loved the new L-shaped floor plan with the central foyer. Bedrooms were down the hall at the front of the house; kitchen to the left with an adjoining family room, large living room off the left-hand corner of the foyer. There was also a utility room, plus a one-car garage. The exterior was used brick, a new look in the industry. The interior had lots of wallpaper, sculptured carpeting, floor-to-ceiling windows in the living room with a white brick fireplace and wedge-wood blue carpet. The kitchen boasted pecan cabinets, a drop-down bar and the new color for appliances, avocado green. The price was $15,900. The average income for town folks was $7,300 a year, so this was top of the line. Dillon's hoped this promotion would sell some homes and create good will in the community. They were pouring lots of money into this party. Ted was in charge and Teresa was helping him with the planning. In anticipation of a large crowd, the event was being held at the local Lions Club Building.

"Teresa, are you going to have time for coffee this

morning?" asked Janet when Teresa picked up the phone. The girls met once a week at Millie's for a quick breakfast.

"No Janet, I can't, I'm swamped with this party. Would you be available to give me a hand later? I know what I'm serving for appetizers, but honestly, all these drink recipes. You'd think this was a high-class affair. Ted wants everything to be just so, but he's too busy to help."

"Sure, Teresa, I can help. But, don't blame Ted for not helping out; men look at entertaining as women's work and besides; he knows you're capable and has confidence in you to carry it off."

"Janet, I suppose you're right; I'd rather do it myself anyway. We'd probably be arguing about everything and nothing would get done."

"Yes, this way you make the decisions. Anyway, I need to ring off now and get in touch with the other girls to see who is coming for coffee. Call me if you need my help."

Teresa sighed. There was so much to do; if only Ted hadn't agreed to host this party. He was always taking on more than he could handle. Everyone will show up, eat, and have way too much to drink. Her mind wandered; hopefully, Doug will be there. She had not heard from him since the day at Millie's; although since then, their daughter had been born and Linda had suffered some minor complications. Rumor had it that everything was now back to normal, so they might attend. Maybe he's had a change of heart since the baby arrived; that would be the best thing for me, she thought, and probably for him too. Okay, enough of that; I need to make a list. Sliced ham and turkey for tea sandwiches, lots of cheeses, Chex Cereal for party mix, chips and dip, mixed nuts, bottles of vodka, gin and bourbon, plus mixers for those crazy cocktails. At least, Ted was getting a keg of Pabst Blue Ribbon and lots of extra ice. Paper plates, plastic cutlery and glasses had been picked up from the Five & Dime. Maybe I will get stuff for Sweet Old-Fashioneds. They will get the party started. Then there's me; I have to do my hair and nails, schedule a pedicure and get my dress out of the cleaners. I have to look fabulous. And the list goes on....

Somehow, the party came together; she hadn't needed Janet's help after all. Sandwiches were made, hors d'oeuvres were ready; the bar was well stocked. Rose and Colleen were happily staying with their grandmother. Ted loved her new mini dress in bright orange; the dress had big gold buttons down the front and bell sleeves. She had found a little pair of black pumps with low heels and a gold necklace with big earrings to complete the outfit. As their friends arrived, Ted hugged the wives and glad handed the guys.

Dianne looked around at the clothes being worn to the party. After working at Molly's for only a short time, she recognized the trends. There was a wide assortment of casual and dressy; some women wore cocktail dresses, while others wore simple, floral sundresses. She had chosen the new Johnathan Logan black knit, wide-legged pants with a tiny, silk halter top. Her platform shoes were pinching a little, but she wanted to look good, which would be a good advertisement for her employer. She noticed Debbie Brown wearing a mini cocktail dress in white; it looked dynamite with her tan. Dianne walked over and complimented her, "Debbie, that dress is fabulous, very chic. I've started working at Molly's; you'll have to stop by."

"Thank you Dianne. I've never shopped with her. I thought the store was more for the older women here in town" she said haughtily. "Besides, I wouldn't want to buy something there and see myself all over town."

Undeterred by her snobby attitude, Dianne contradicted her; "Debbie, that wouldn't happen, because she only buys one or two of each item. The jewelry is all exclusive to this area and lots of younger looks are arriving. These pants, for example, also come in white."

"Yes, those pants are stunning. Well, you've certainly piqued my interest. I'll try to stop in next week. Nice to see you again, Dianne." She walked away to join some of her country club set. Dianne smiled to herself.

Cocktails were flowing, hors d'oeuvres were quickly disappearing, the music was soft and low, dancing had begun.

Doug walked over to Teresa and touched her elbow, "Want to dance, beautiful?" Linda was watching from across the room and she was fuming. She saw Doug take her into his arms as the DJ played "Could This Be Magic" by the Dubs.

Teresa looked up at Doug and said "Do you remember dancing to that song years ago? It always reminds me of you when I hear it." He smiled and held her closer. Linda, sitting with her younger sister Melanie, whined, "How dare she, married with two kids of her own; she has a great guy, but now she wants mine back."

Her sister agreed. "I'm really surprised at this; she was crushed when he started seeing you. When she married Ted, everyone said it was on the rebound. You need to make him jealous."

"You're right; two can play that game. Hmm, there's Robert, he's always had a thing for me; I'll go talk to him. As she walked toward him, he met her halfway. "Good to see you Linda, I was going out for a cigarette, want to join me?"

"Sure" she replied, taking his arm and flouncing past Doug on her way out the door. She was not the least bit interested in Robert; but his longtime interest in her could come in handy at times.

"Linda, your husband is a jerk. Every time he sees Teresa; he's all over her. Girl, I don't know why you put up with it."

"Robert, he's probably had a little too much to drink. I know that's no excuse, but I have a new baby. What am I supposed to do?"

"Well, for starters." He pulled her close and kissed her. At first, she started to pull away, but then she responded. Maybe Robert wasn't so bad after all. They made out for several minutes, but broke apart when they heard people approaching.

Doug saw Linda go outside and immediately grabbed Teresa's hand and hurried out the other door. His goal was to be alone with her and they headed out through the parking lot. As they walked, he commented "I've wanted to call, but I've been leery. What if Ted answered? Where would we meet? It's been driving me nuts."

They reached the rear of the parking lot in a dimly lit area near his car. He took her in his arms and caressed her, kissing her deeply just as she remembered. He raised her dress and held her close to him. "I want you so damn bad." She could only moan softly. His hands were probing and she was unbuckling his belt. He lifted her onto the hood of the car and entered her. She held on tight; her brain was exploding. When he released her, they looked at one another and both said "Wow!" They rushed to straighten their clothes and he said "You go ahead; we don't want to be seen coming in together." Hurriedly ducking between the cars, she rushed inside and made a beeline for the restroom. Her lipstick was smeared and her hair mussed. She quickly repaired the damage and stepped out to rejoin the party.

"Robert, this is fun, but we'd better get back inside. They'll be wondering where we are." When they returned to the party, Teresa and Doug were nowhere in sight. Linda decided to investigate. As she walked toward the parking lot, she saw Doug coming toward her.

"Where have you been?" she asked. "I haven't seen you for over half an hour."

"Oh, honey, I was taking a walk. I got too hot in there and decided to come outside to cool off." Little did she know he was speaking the truth.

Linda was still suspicious. After her steamy experience with Robert, she wasn't sure whether to believe him or not. He looked a little sweaty, but it was humid and he was alone; so she decided to give him the benefit of the doubt.

As the hour grew later, the music got louder and soon the Town Marshal, Ed Bates, walked in the door. He told Ted they'd have to quiet down or break up the party. This put a damper on things and people began to leave. Teresa had been making plans with Jill and Janet to meet for lunch. "I'll call you the first of the week" she told them and excused herself to say good night to the rest of their friends. They thanked Ted and Teresa and praised the party.

As they reached their car, Ted asked "Where did you and Doug disappear to tonight? I looked around and couldn't find either one of you."

"Well, we stepped outside for some cooler air. It was very hot in the club. I came back inside after a few minutes and he went to his car for a cigarette."

"Oh, how nice is that; first you dance, then you're taking a walk together. What's next? Some secret get together?"

"Ted, for God's sake, don't be so petty; it was nothing."

They arrived home and Ted said curtly, "I'm going to bed; I can't continue this conversation right now." Teresa sat down on the sofa and thought back over the evening. The thrill of their lovemaking was still breathtaking to her; it was a memory she wanted to cherish forever. What am I going to do, she thought; I don't want to lose my marriage, but being with Doug is what I've wanted since he broke my heart back in high school. I've done some risky things, but is this too much? Deep down, she knew the answer, but she wasn't ready to face it.

Linda tore into Doug as soon as they reached the car; alcohol and jealousy were a volatile mixture for her. "You and your girlfriend were sure having a good time tonight. Do you wish you'd stayed with little miss Teresa and never met me? I couldn't find you for at least a half an hour. Where were you anyway? Out in the dark showing her a good time?"

"Linda, please don't do this; every time you drink, we end up in a fight about someone. Don't you realize what this does to me? If I'm continually accused of something, I might as well be doing it, and what were you doing with Robert?"

"Well, this isn't just any someone, this is Teresa, the old girlfriend, the one you can't seem to forget; not that she'll let you. She's always hanging around, ready to talk, ready to dance, what else is she ready for? And you can leave Robert out of this; he means nothing to me and you know it."

"You need to settle down and quit screaming at me. I'm not answering any of these silly questions. We'll talk when you sober up."

"Maybe I'll just take the baby and go stay with my mother for a while. That would suit you fine, I'm sure" she wailed.

Doug didn't reply. There was no use trying to talk to her when she was in this condition. It seemed like this was happening a lot; her drinking was getting out of hand. Does she know something or did she see us? How could she? It was too dark back there.

CHAPTER 6

Later that night Debbie Brown paced the floor, waiting up for her oldest daughter, Dani, short for Danielle, to come home. She and Dave named their children starting with "D", their son David Jr., age 19 and Dottie, short for Dorothy, 15. Dani, now 17, was out past her midnight curfew with a group of new friends. Debbie was kicking herself for allowing her to go out with Larry Howard. Dani said she'd be fine; plans were for a drive-in movie, followed by hot dogs and root beer at the local A & W. I know the root beer stand is closed by now; so where is she? Dani hadn't been a problem until recently. She'd started hanging around with some different kids, of whom Debbie was skeptical. Their parents were not exactly the towns' most upstanding citizens.

Meanwhile, Dani and her friends were out on a deserted country road with another carload of kids, watching two guys getting set to drag race. One was behind the wheel of an old '55 Chevy Bel Air and the other guy was running a '56 Ford Fairlane. Both had three speeds and the competition was tight. They lined up and at the signal took off with tremendous power; the tires spun and smoked, burning rubber down the road. Within seconds, it was over; the guy driving the Bel Air had won. They both hopped out of their cars and shook hands, "Hey, we'll do this again sometime" said the winner. The other guy yelled "Yeah, I'm going to beat your ass the next time." They laughed, jumped back in their cars and spun out, giving the kids another thrill.

"Wow" someone said "that was tough" as they piled into their cars and headed back to town. The adrenaline was high after watching the drag race and both drivers were feeling it. Larry Howard was Dani's date and he blew past the other car doing over eighty miles an hour. Suddenly, the car went airborne as they came around a curve. Dani and the couple in the back seat were thrown clear of the car as it came to rest upside down in a culvert. The kids in the other car stopped to help; everyone was screaming at once "What do we do", "We need help", until one boy took off running for the old farmhouse they had just passed. The couple was awakened by the noise and quickly answered the door. The farmer called the Indiana State Police; then hurried outside to see if he could be of any help. Soon, you could hear the sirens cutting through the silence of the night. Judy and Chuck, the girl and boy who had been in the back seat, were dazed, but walking around.

Chuck yelled, "Judy, my God, look at Dani; she isn't moving."

Judy was sobbing, "Oh, Chuck, what should we do?"

The police car screeched to a stop and the trooper jumped out. He looked at Judy crying and Chuck stepped in and said "Sir, the girl over there may be hurt bad and we're not sure about Larry, the driver." The officer immediately went to Dani, took her pulse, which was very weak and got a blanket out of his trunk to cover her. He then looked in at Larry, who was obviously pinned in the car. He went back to his car and picked up his mike. "Redkey, 25-4. We've got injuries and a possible 10-0. Need transport to the hospital and some equipment to remove a pinned-in victim."

The fire truck arrived and the firemen started working to

get Larry out. After twenty minutes, Larry was free, badly injured, but alive. The funeral director arrived and transported both Larry and Dani to County General.

Meanwhile, Debbie said to Dave "I can't stand this any longer; we have to go look for her."

Dave, looking askance at her, asked "Where would we look this time of night?" They were angry with each other over letting her go out with this guy and they sat there in stony silence. This was just another incident in a long litany of issues between the two of them. The ringing of the phone startled them both.

"The Browns" Dave said in his usual forceful voice. On the other end, someone replied "Mr. Brown, your daughter has been in an automobile accident and we need you to come to the hospital right away."

"How bad is she?" Dave asked, wanting to know, but afraid of the answer.

"I'm sorry, sir, we can't give out that information over the phone. Please get here as soon as you can."

"Debbie, let's go, she's been hurt in a car wreck; I don't know how bad she is." They dashed to the car and sped quickly to the hospital.

When they arrived, the doctors had stabilized her and were waiting for consent to perform surgery. They suspected a ruptured spleen and possible other internal injuries, plus a broken leg. She had lost a lot of blood. Dave signed the necessary papers and Dani was whisked away to the OR. As they sat down in the waiting room, Dave knew his wife was not handling this well; so he called their family doctor to see about some kind of medicine for her.

Dr. Nelson received the message from his answering service, came in and gave Debbie a shot of sedative to calm her down, plus a prescription. He told them he would check on Dani during his morning rounds.

One of the nurses came to notify them that the surgery was complete and the doctor would be there soon. When he came to the door, Debbie and Dave both started asking questions at once. Dr. Morrison said, "Mr. and Mrs. Brown, your daughter came through the surgery okay; she's lucky to be alive, she is due in part to her youth. We removed her spleen, which means her immune system will be compromised for a time; she is currently receiving her second pint of blood, the leg has been set and other than some cuts and bruises, there are no further issues. She is now in recovery and as soon as she is brought back to her room, you can see her. Her prognosis is good; now she needs to heal." Both parents were clearly relieved.

The relief on their faces was evident as they walked into Dani's room. She looked small lying there. Her eyes were open and she was smiling weakly. "Hi princess" said Dave. "You gave us a real scare, but you're going to be okay. We'll be taking you home in a few days. We don't need to talk about what led up to this right now; but we will be talking about it."

Debbie tried giving her a hug, but Dani winced. "Oh, I'm sorry, sweetie; I wasn't thinking; I'm just so glad you're okay. I've been so worried."

"Yeah, Mom, that's all you ever do is worry. I wish you'd let me lead my own life. I'm seventeen, old enough to know right from wrong. You're always interfering; I don't need that!"

Her Dad stepped in, "Dani, calm down; don't talk to your mother like that. Show some respect. She has been beside herself over this."

"Okay, Dad" Dani frowned "How is Larry? Was he badly hurt?"

"Yes, he was pinned in the car and has a broken pelvis and some other injuries. He's here in the hospital on another floor. We ran into his parents and they said he feels very guilty about the wreck and what happened to you. We told them it was an accident, nothing intentional.

"Do you think I could see him?"

"No dear" said her mother "not right now, you'll not be out of bed for a few days and when they put you on crutches, we'll be taking you home".

Her parents left the room, promising they'd be back later in the day. The pain medication was working; Dani was soon sleeping.

CHAPTER 7

Jill and Johnny had gone to her parents for Sunday dinner. Fried chicken was his favorite and her mother enjoyed cooking for him. The little boys loved the chicken legs and the baby was able to eat mashed potatoes and a few green beans. Jill took a small portion of each dish. "Jill," said her mother "you're not eating enough to keep a bird alive. You look like you've lost more weight since I saw you last week. Are you feeling okay?"

"Of course, Mom, I don't have much of an appetite lately. Maybe it's the heat, or it could be running after these kids. That would take weight off anyone." She didn't want to worry her mother by telling her she had finally, after weeks of putting it off, gotten an appointment with Dr. Nelson.

Johnny and her dad were talking baseball on the front porch. She helped her mom with the dishes and listened to the story of the wreck that had happened down the road from their house on Saturday night. The sound of screeching tires had awakened them, after which there was a banging at the door. Her Dad had phoned the State Police and then went out to see if he could be of any help. Her mom said it was a miracle anyone lived. Jill had heard there were two kids in serious condition; she felt sorry for the kids and their parents.

Her folk's farm was a beautiful place, eighty acres with seventy-five of those planted in soy beans and field corn. The house was old, but in good condition, a traditional two-story, built at the beginning of the twentieth century, around 1902. Gingerbread trim, a large front porch with a turret, ten-foot ceilings, thick plastered walls, beautifully carved woodwork and original hardwood floors all combined to create a charming place. The staircase and chandelier at the front door set the stage for the remainder of the house. Jill had one sister, who lived in California and had no interest in the property, so she knew it would be hers one day. For now, she was content to visit.

The boys were getting tired, her stomach was cramping and Johnny had a big job starting the next day, so they left early. She couldn't wait to see the doctor, maybe then her family would quit harping on her and she could feel normal again.

Joanne Howard had an older brother named Kris who was home on leave after a year as an Army Medic in Viet Nam. His job took him into the war zones as part of a chopper crew, risking their own lives to pick up the injured or dead. He felt like one of the lucky ones, having come home with only a shot-up leg; but now the Johnson administration was escalating the war. There were now over 475,000 U.S. soldiers fighting the Viet Cong. Thousands of others were in various stages of deployment. There had been many anti-war protests in D.C. and other areas of the country, young men who fled to Canada to avoid the draft, and countless, "conscientious objectors". Kris loved his country and felt deeply about the war; he hated knowing his buddies were still there. He wouldn't be going back to Nam due to his injury, but he had two years remaining to fulfill his commitment to the military.

Unlike some of his fellow servicemen, he had not left a wife and kids behind. Recently, he had started dating Toni, a cute little waitress from Millie's. She was divorced with a two-year-old boy, fun loving and a breath of fresh air. Kris liked her, a lot, but he wasn't up for a ready-made family; besides, she was older than him by a few years and his buddies were giving him a hard time about it. Toni was fun to be with and he enjoyed fooling around with her son, Matthew. She was easy to look at, auburn hair, big brown eyes and very petite. They were quite a contrast, he with blonde hair, green eyes and a foot taller than her. His mother thought they would have cute kids. Why did mothers always think like that?

He pulled up in front of her house. She lived in a small, light blue, cottage-style home with white shutters. Lots of flowers surrounded the house; he recognized some of them as ones his mother grew, daylilies, coneflowers, zinnias. He knocked on the screen door and she yelled from the back of the house to come on in. He went toward the kitchen and she met him halfway with his favorite drink, a Manhattan. Toni was fixing dinner for him this evening and he was looking forward to it. He figured she was a good cook from working at the restaurant, but who knows? She gave him a quick kiss and headed back to the kitchen. "Hope you like shrimp jambalaya" she said.

"Love it", said Kris, sipping on his drink. "Can I help with anything? I've been known to cook a little too."

"No, everything's okay. The rice is on, the shrimp is cooked; let's enjoy our cocktails."

He sipped on his Manhattan as she enjoyed her vodka and grapefruit, a favorite among the younger women in Creviston. "So, how was your day? Were you busy at the diner?"

"Yes, but speaking of the diner, I want your opinion on something. You know Doug Jones, your sister's boss. He was in a couple of weeks ago; it might have been the day their baby was born; anyway, he was having coffee with another woman. I couldn't hear what they were saying; but they looked real chummy. He was holding her hand and I saw him squeeze it when she left. I didn't know her; she had short blonde hair, about my size. What do you make of that?"

"Hmmm, that could have been Teresa Farris, his old girlfriend from high school. There has been some talk about them, according to my mother. She always knows what's going on around town."

"Well, I decided I'd keep my mouth shut and not mention it to Linda's sister. Do you think you should tell your sister?"

"Are you kidding? I'm staying out of that one. I've got enough to think about, such as how do I get a refill around here?" Toni laughed and went to top off their drinks.

Doug was late getting into the office on Monday morning. The baby had cried most of the night and there was little sleep to be had. He was thinking about Saturday night after the party. He and Linda had argued most of the night about Teresa, whose name might as well be a dirty word around their house. She was threatening to go home to her mother and take the baby, but he wasn't taking her seriously. What disturbed him the most were her accusations; he couldn't figure it out, did women have some kind of sixth sense about this kind of thing, he wondered. ESP or not, this wasn't going to stop him from seeing Teresa again; he'd just have to be more careful. His agenda this morning was clear cut. He needed to check out Larry Howard's car and pick up a police report of the accident. Hopefully, Larry's parents had a good hospitalization policy, because standard auto insurance only took care of the first $500 on the driver. The coverage for Danielle Brown should be sufficient, so he didn't expect a law suit against the company. Both kids were still in serious condition and would remain in the hospital for several more days. His secretary, Joanne, was Larry's older sister and they both still lived at home. The family was not in the same league as the Browns', but they were still well liked in the community.

Jill was sitting at Dr. Nelson's office wishing she was anywhere but there. The nurse called her in and ran her through the normal routine; getting weighed, having her blood pressure and temperature taken. Jill weighed 110 lbs. Shortly, the doctor came in.

"Jill, what brings you here today?"

"Dr. Nelson, I hope you can help me, I don't have any energy and it takes me all day to do what I used to do in an hour; I'd rather curl up in a chair. My two older boys are running wild and the baby needs to be weaned. I've tried to diet to lose this baby weight, but that isn't working either. My house is a mess and I've lost interest in my appearance; I simply don't care.

"Jill, first off, let's forget the diet; for your body type and height, you are much too thin. Now, when did you start to feel this way? Also, I need you to tell me how you are sleeping and if you're having headaches."

"Not long after my last baby; I have no headaches; but, I haven't been sleeping much at all. I toss and turn at night and then can't get up in the morning because I'm exhausted."

"Jill, you have a classic case of depression. I believe it stems from postpartum blues. This happens frequently after childbirth and can last for several months. It can be very debilitating, but it is easily treated with medication. I am going to prescribe Valium for you to take daily and you should see some improvement in about three weeks. Now, with the Valium, I don't want you to drink; the two can be a lethal combination. The other avenue I recommend is counseling. I can give you the names of two counselors who specialize in this type of disorder. I'd like you to get in touch with one of them as soon as possible."

She drove to the drug store to pick up her prescription. While she was waiting for the pharmacist, she sat down on one of the chrome swivel stools at the counter and ordered a cherry coke. The wooden counter was original as were the stools, which were bolted to the floor. Their seats were covered in black vinyl. She loved the atmosphere; the wide, wooden boards that creaked when she walked, were warped and worn. The building had been here since shortly after the town was founded in the late 1800's. There was an odd odor about the place, like a combination of tobacco, coffee, and cooking oil they used to prepare the daily lunch special. A man at the end of the counter was smoking a cigar and having a cup of coffee. The girl behind the counter was making ice cream cones for a mom and her little girl. Once her prescription was ready, she walked over to the dress shop to see Dianne. Maybe a new outfit would perk me up.

Dianne was glad to see Jill and gave her a big hug, "Oh Jill, I hate it that you're not feeling like yourself; is there anything I can do to help?"

"No, just be my friend. This is something I have to do on my own, but that's not why I'm here; I need something new."

"OOH, that will be fun. Casual, dressy or in-between? There are lots of new things coming in right now. "

"I just need something to perk me up; I've been so down in the dumps. The doctor says I have postpartum blues. Apparently, it's gradually worsened since Mark was born. He gave me a prescription and the name of a counselor to call. The medicine is supposed to help with my depression."

"Okay, we need to find something to brighten your day. Look at this cute dress from Patty O'Neil. It's short and flirty and the fabric is perfect for right now. The new olive green would be great with your red hair; or, if you'd rather get a pair of slacks; these black Junior House pants with the wide legs are the new thing."

"So, how much is the dress; is it a price I can afford?" Jill always tried to be careful with their money; jobs for Johnny came and went quickly and they never knew when their budget would be strained.

"It is $10 and the pants are $8. Things here aren't cheap, but they're worth it."

"For me" said Jill, "I would get more use out of the pants. They'd be more practical; please put them in the dressing room, but," she mused, "I do love the dress."

"Try it on too, you can always lay it away and pay a little each week." Dianne was dying to see Jill in this new style.

"Dianne" she said as she modeled the dress, "you are becoming quite the saleslady. Now, what do you have that will look good with the pants?" Several blouses and sweaters later, she chose a turquoise, V-neck sweater in soft acrylic, a very yummy fabric. "Oh, what the heck, put the dress on layaway and I'll take the pants and sweater with me." Either the new outfits or a possible resolution to her problem had made her feel a bit better. She headed home to cook dinner and share the good news with Johnny.

Dianne was happy she'd been able to help at least one friend. It seemed all their lives were in such turmoil lately. She stopped by the grocery to pick up bread and milk. Having those items delivered to her front door was one thing she missed by working. Even though her milk box was insulated, milk could spoil when the weather was hot and freeze during the winter. Now, she wasn't home to give the Omar Bread man her order and she really missed those little cakes he delivered on Fridays, especially the banana crème. There were definitely pros and cons to having a job.

Phillip was glad to see her; he had lots of exciting things to tell her about school. She loved her son dearly; it was just too bad he didn't have a better role model; if only Mike spent more time with him. Arriving home, she started dinner, glanced at the evening paper and read the mail.

While dinner was on the stove, she threw a load of clothes in the washer. What did she ever do before the automatic washer and dryer? She had hated that old wringer washer and having to hang her clothes outside on a clothesline to dry in all kinds of weather. It's no wonder women didn't work years ago, they never had time. As she arranged the table for dinner, she hoped Mike would come home early.

CHAPTER 8

Dani arrived home a week after the accident and the whole family was celebrating; even her sister and brother, who were usually bugging her, were thrilled to have her home. Since it was a Saturday, some of her friends were stopping by to see her.

A couple of tutors had been hired until Dani was able to return to school, which could be Thanksgiving or later. One of Dave's employees from the bank, Janet Steele, had offered to tutor Dani for two hours each evening in Bookkeeping and English. Another tutor would come during the day to assist with other subjects. Janet was to start right away. This was perfect for her, with her husband working nights; she had lots of time to spare.

"How is Larry doing, Dani, asked Amy, one of her oldest friends.

"Amy, it's sad, his pelvis was broken and the doctors said he would be in a wheel chair for several months; then he will be doing physical therapy to learn how to walk again."

"Will you go see him?" Amy thought Dani seemed very nonchalant about Larry's condition. How could she be so selfish?

"I don't know, it was only my second date with him."

"Dani, there is Mrs. Steele, your new tutor."

"Yes, she's nice; I hope she won't be a slave driver; she works for my dad at the bank. We start this week trying to catch up with my classes."

"Dani, I've got to leave, some of us are going to a movie tonight; wish you could go. I'll see you in a few days and I'm so glad you're feeling better."

Dave and Janet were talking about Dani in the hallway when Debbie walked up to join them. "Janet, do you remember Debbie, my wife?"

"Of course, I do; I'm looking forward to working with Dani, Mrs. Brown."

"Oh, please, Janet, call me Debbie. We'll be seeing a lot of you and I want you to be comfortable here. Dani can be difficult at times; hopefully, you won't have any problems with her."

"Well, if I do, I'll cross that bridge then. Right now, I am excited about getting started."

Janet left the Browns hoping she'd be able to get through to Dani. There seemed to be a lot of tension between the mother and daughter. Rumors were swirling around town that Dave and Debbie were having serious problems since the accident. Each was blaming the other for not being a better parent. Both spent a lot of time away from home; that was common knowledge. But, she had been married long enough to know that problems built up over time; they didn't come about as a result of one incident.

Doug hated Mondays, but this morning he had a specific reason for getting to the office early. He hadn't been able to get Teresa off his mind since the night of the open house and he was very anxious to see her. Making up his mind over the weekend to call her was difficult and he had no idea if she even wanted to see him again; maybe this was a one-time thing. There was only one way to find out. His secretary wasn't in yet, so Doug had a little time to himself. He went into his private office and picked up the phone. Teresa answered after the second ring. "Hi, can you talk?"

"No, I won't be there today." Ted was sitting there eating his oatmeal and toast; she had to come up with something quick.

Doug got the picture. He hung up the phone and wished he'd left it on the hook. She was probably in hot water at this moment.

"Who was that?" Ted asked. He noticed she seemed shaken.

Teresa pulled her robe tighter as she shivered. "It was Janet, wanting to know if I'd be free for coffee this morning." Teresa hoped she sounded casual. She certainly didn't feel casual. Afraid to look at Ted, she busied herself with the breakfast dishes.

"Well, you're acting squirrely. For some reason, that phone call really upset you. What's going on?"

"Nothing, Ted, I may have hurt her feelings. That's all there is to it."

"Alright, I have a late meeting; don't wait supper for me."

As soon as he was out of the driveway, she dialed the phone. When Doug answered, she said "Doug, I'm sorry I couldn't talk, but I was so happy to hear your voice. I wasn't sure you were planning to call; I was surprised."

"I just wanted to see how you're doing, you've been on my mind and I really want to see you again. I'm going to Fort Wayne later today on business and wondered if you could meet me. I found a little motel out on State Road 3 that could work for us. It's about thirty minutes from here."

Teresa hesitated, considering the situation. "That could work; Ted has a meeting after work and won't be here for dinner. I could drop the girls off at my Mom's and be on my way. What time are you thinking?"

Doug was ecstatic. "I'm getting together with a client for lunch. How does 2:30 work for you?"

"That should be okay; tell me where it is and I'll see you there." She wrote down the directions, hung up the phone and could barely hide her excitement from the girls. She needed to call her mom, fix her hair, should she take a small bag? This was all new to her; it wasn't like she could consult Emily Post for the proper etiquette when having an affair.

Rose looked at her and asked, "Where are you going, Mommy?" Flustered, she told Rose she was meeting a friend to go shopping.

She poured the milk on their cereal and sat down with her coffee. Her head was spinning. I'm not sure I can handle this, now I'm making excuses to my little girl. What kind of a person am I becoming? Am I capable of the deceit and betrayal this affair could cause?"

Janet had some extra time at lunch, so she dropped by to see Teresa. They went to the kitchen for coffee and a cigarette. Her friend seemed a bit preoccupied and she asked "What's wrong with you today?"

Teresa was having problems looking Janet in the eye. "Oh, Jan, I've really gotten in over my head. I want to tell you; but you absolutely cannot tell anyone else and once you hear it; you'll understand why."

"Teresa, you're scaring me. Are you sick? "

"No, no, it's not that. I just need to talk to someone about this or I'll go crazy. Doug and I are having an affair. It's been in the works for a while and it finally happened the night of the open house."

Janet was stunned. "Teresa, how could that be? The place was packed; where did you go?"

"This is so hard to talk about, even to you. We were out back by his car. No one saw us, but I think Linda and Ted are both suspicious."

"Teresa, I don't want to burst your bubble. Look at the timing. His wife just gave birth a few weeks ago. You know how doctors are about sex when you're in the last month and then you're not supposed to do it for six weeks after birth. I'm sure the guy has feelings for you, but don't you think his sudden interest in you could be because he's horny?"

"I don't believe that. I know he has feelings for me; he wouldn't be saying the things he does and taking the risk of Linda finding out if he didn't care for me. Plus, I've made plans to meet him this afternoon."

Janet hated hearing the denial in the words of her friend. "You'd better take it slow, Teresa; try to figure out where his head is, and by the way, where is yours? I don't want to lecture you; but you need to consider where this is going."

Teresa took a long drag on her cigarette, exhaled slowly and said, "Obviously, I've been living for the moment; it's hard to think straight. When we're together today, perhaps we can figure out where we go from here."

Janet sighed out of frustration. She felt like her friend was heading for a fall. "Okay, I've got to get back to work. Call and let me know what happens."

CHAPTER 9

Teresa was so nervous. What if someone saw them? She showered and dressed very carefully, putting on her sexiest lingerie. She had chosen a simple, pink-floral dress with silver accessories. Her hair was easy, but her makeup took a little more time. She wanted to look perfect for him. She hurriedly packed a cosmetic bag and threw it in her purse for use later. She fed the girls their lunch and packed a small bag for them to stay the night with her mother.

She stopped by the Shell station and Gary, the owner, came out to see what she needed. "You can fill it up for me, Gary." She gave him a five and he gave her back $1.60. The car had taken just over ten gallons. Dropping the kids off, she kissed them goodbye and headed out of town. She didn't mind the drive; she loved her '65 navy blue Tempest, a good car, easy on gas, especially with a manual transmission.

Doug had given her excellent directions to the Hi-Way 3 Motel. It was a one-story, brick-trimmed building with rooms to each side of the center office and a row of rooms at the back of the building. His car was parked next to room 12, a spot not visible from the road and as she pulled up next to his car, he came out the door. Grabbing her purse, she rushed to meet him.

He took her hand and led her into the room, closed the

door and wrapped his arms around her. "You smell wonderful" he said, "I've been so anxious to see you; I can't believe you're actually here."

"So, you like my perfume. I wore it just for you, Chanel No. 5." She looked up at him teasingly and he pulled her down on the bed. He slowly undressed her, removing her dress and kissing her breasts as he unhooked her bra. "That is one sexy bra, but I like what's in it better" he whispered. Straddling him, she unbuttoned his shirt, unbuckled his belt and put her hand inside. "Ooh, I think you're ready for me." He hooked his thumb in her panties and pulled them off. "Honey, you're ready for me too" and he pulled her to him. She spread her legs and enveloped him. They moved in unison, coming together as their passion soared to new heights. Afterwards, they laid there quietly and looked into one another's eyes. "I don't want to leave here, Teresa; I just want to be with you."

She wanted to hold onto this moment. "Doug, I can't lose you again; it would be too much for me to take. I have dreamt of this moment for so long and now that it's here; I'm scared to death."

"My sweet, sweet Teresa; I'm not letting you go, not this time. I was such a fool back then and I won't let it happen again." He made love to her once more, though much slower this time. They kissed and caressed and too soon; it was time to leave.

They showered together, got dressed and she repaired her makeup. They kissed furtively. He checked to see if there was anyone in the parking lot and sent her on her way. Fifteen minutes later, he took off. Damn, he thought, I'm back in love; I can't get enough of her. What the hell am I going to do? Right now, he knew he had to get back to the office and see if anyone had called; he needed to cover his tracks. This affair would take a lot of juggling, but he wanted it, even though he had no idea where it was going.

Everything at the office was humming along. He had taken care of the Howard accident, having turned it over to an adjuster. The kid was still in the hospital in critical condition. His parents were devastated and scared. The doctors were not telling them much. It was a day-by-day situation. He gave Joanne the details of his client meeting and the necessary information for her to type up the policies. He looked at his messages, saw nothing of much importance and left for home.

Linda was feeding the baby when he got there. He leaned over and kissed them both, "How was your day?" he asked.

As Doug leaned over to kiss her hello, she thought, something isn't right; what is that smell, is it perfume? Trying to place the scent, it finally came to her, Chanel No. 5. It wasn't hers, she preferred Shalimar, but one of her old friends used to wear it. Did Joanne wear Chanel? She hesitated to say anything; she didn't want to start another argument; they were just recovering from the last one, over Teresa, of course. She wondered what perfume Teresa wore. Am I getting paranoid? Surely, he hadn't been with her. "So, what did you do today?" She was having a hard time remaining calm.

"I had a client meeting up in Fort Wayne this afternoon. I had to spend a few hours with the guy, but I managed to get some good business out of it. He has several rentals and I sold him fire insurance with wind and vandalism on all of them. I can only hope he doesn't ding me to death with wind claims, but, he gave me some good leads for the area as well. This should prove to be a profitable contact."

"That's good" she said, wondering if his afternoon had included Teresa. I may be too suspicious, she thought. I need to relax and enjoy my little girl. "Doug, there is a pot roast in the oven; I hope you like it. I'll get it on the table as soon as she's done eating or you can finish feeding her if you want and I'll finish dinner."

"I'd love that" taking the baby and sitting down in the rocker. Can I reconcile what I did this afternoon with my little girl, he wondered.

When Teresa got back to town, she stopped off to see Dianne. As soon as she walked in the store, Dianne knew something was going on with her. She looked a little flushed and was not in her usual casual clothes.

"Teresa, are you going somewhere or coming back? You look so cute in that dress, it's very flattering on you."

"Thanks, Dianne. I chose this dress for my first meeting with Doug. That's where I've been, with him in a cheap motel out on State Road 3 this afternoon. Dianne, I am so mixed up about all this; what I need is to sit down with you and talk this out. Can you come over tonight? Ted won't be home until late; he has a dinner meeting; do you think you could manage that?"

"Let me see, I'll have to cook dinner and then, it depends on when Mike gets home. If he's real late, I won't be able to make it, but right now, I've got to get back to my customer. I'll let you know later."

Teresa walked slowly back to her car. She was still in a daze over the events of the afternoon. What's next, she thought, will I see him again and do I even want to see him again? Well, of course I do, I'm just scared. This whole thing could really screw up my nice, orderly life. I don't even have an income right now; real estate is not lucrative in the beginning. If I end up divorced, I will have to go to work in some other capacity just to support myself. I certainly can't depend on our meager savings to tide me over. Oh, My God, what am I doing?

That evening, the phone rang at Teresa's, "Mike isn't here yet" complained Dianne, "we'll have to talk later this week." She hated letting Teresa down, especially when she sounded so worried; but she needed to learn not to make plans around Mike.

After dinner, she covered the food for Mike and did the dishes. She tried to read her latest copy of "Good Housekeeping", but couldn't concentrate. Phillip's bedtime was 8:30 and afterwards; she took time to soak in the tub. As she was getting out of the tub, she heard him come home. She threw on her robe and walked into the living room.

"Why are you so late tonight?" she said angrily. "Your dinner is on the stove, but it's probably ruined. Just once in a while, could you please have a meal with your family?"

"Get off my ass, Dianne, I stopped to have a beer with the guys and time got away from me."

"What is the big attraction at the tavern? I can't believe it's just the guys. Is there some woman catching your eye up there?"

"You dumb bitch, I am sick of being accused of something all the time. What if there was, it would serve you right; you're so high and mighty these days, with your fancy job."

Dianne was standing there with tears running down her cheeks. "Mike, I'm tired of this; Phillip and I eat alone every night. Don't you see what you're doing to our family? You never spend any time with us and when you're here, you're drunk. That's not what I want for us."

"I know, I'm such a bad guy, but you don't mind cashing my pay check, now do you? I work hard and I deserve to cut loose a little after work. What do you want, a divorce? Are you trying to get rid of me?"

"Mike, if I thought you meant that, I'd be gone tomorrow. Is it the booze talking or am I being a fool?"

He picked up the plate from the stove, threw it across the kitchen and slammed out the door. She couldn't believe what had just happened. He had never reacted like this; something else was going on, she was sure of that. After cleaning up the mess, she went to bed. Sometime during the night she heard him come home; but he didn't come to bed. He was asleep on the sofa when she got up the next morning. She didn't wake him; she told Phillip his dad was not feeling well. She put him on the school bus and decided to drive by Teresa's before going to work.

She saw Teresa in the kitchen as she pulled in the drive. Very relieved to see Ted was already gone, she hurried in through the back door without knocking. Teresa welcomed her with a cup of steaming coffee and they both sat down at the kitchen table and lit a cigarette.

Dianne looked at her friend, "I need this talk as much as

you do; Mike and I had a huge fight last night; he left and didn't come back until sometime this morning. I don't know if he'll even come home tonight. He was madder than I've ever seen him. I'm not sure I want him to come home; his temper scares me and I don't want Phillip seeing that side of him. This is no way to live. I'm wondering if he has a girlfriend; he never approaches me. It's been months since we've had sex."

"I'm sorry to hear that; Ted is moody and spends far too much time working, but I'm not afraid of him. Have you asked him about counseling? I know the minister at the Methodist Church does that sort of thing."

"I've mentioned that; he says he'll be his own counsel. Maybe a short separation would help things; then he could see what life would be like without me and Phillip. Then again, he just might like it and maybe I would too."

"I think you need to talk to him as soon as possible; hopefully, he'll come home sober tonight. It won't do any good to try if he's drinking, but you can't live like this."

"You're right; I'll take the first opportunity I get to have that talk. He'll probably feel guilty about last night and come home early. Now, what on earth are you and Doug thinking?"

"Dianne, like I told you yesterday, Doug and I are having an affair and things are complicated. We met at a motel yesterday afternoon; it was heaven, but now I feel like I'm living in hell. My feelings are all over the place, I'm crazy about him and can't wait to see him again; but, I care about Ted. My marriage has been in a rut; Ted works all the time and I sit here wondering, is this all there is? I am still young,

I want passion in my life; I can't imagine living the next forty years in this dull existence. I have loved Doug for years; I don't love Ted in the same way. I never have, but we have two daughters that deserve two parents. Obviously, I am screwed up and don't have any idea which way to go."

"Do you know what Doug wants out of this? Is he in it because he still loves you, is he bored and wanting a fling; what is he telling you?"

"He says he won't let me go this time; that he's been a fool, but it bothers me that he never mentions his new baby or Linda. That seems to be a taboo subject and they have a lot to do with this. "

"Sounds like I'm not the only one needing to have a talk. When are you seeing him again?"

"I have no idea, probably as soon as he has time. I just know this is eating away at me, not having the freedom to see him when I want. I have no patience."

"That I know for sure; but right now, I've got to get to work. I'll call you later."

CHAPTER 10

Janet enjoyed her job at the bank. She loved talking to her customers, some of whom she saw daily. Workers cashing their paychecks, customers making their car or mortgage payments, the elderly cashing their social security checks and businesses picking up change or depositing their daily receipts; a variety of transactions kept the job interesting. There wasn't much room for advancement at the bank if you were a woman. Both men and women started out as tellers; the men were, according to the women, "vice-presidents in training." While the women remained stuck at the teller stations, the men were promoted into the trust or loan departments. She would like to be a loan counselor, but that didn't look promising. Those jobs, with their private offices, had always been held by men.

The bank examiners had arrived this morning and it always made everyone nervous, especially Dave Powers. They would be auditing loans being granted, deposits and withdrawals made by customers, plus various other activities. Their plans were to be at the bank for a week or so. Several employees had been whispering in the break room, wondering what they were looking for and why they'd be here so long. Dave had been working long hours in preparation for this audit; consequently, she had seen little of him during her tutoring sessions with Dani. She hadn't seen much of Debbie either; apparently being a socialite was time consuming, especially in the evenings. Dani was not as guarded as she had been during their first few sessions; she was beginning to warm up to her, which made the lessons much easier.

After a few weeks of the valium tablets, Jill began to feel better, as though she was coming out from under a black cloud. Her energy was returning and she didn't feel as drained. How miraculous that one little yellow pill a day could make such a major difference in a person's life. Her sons were still as ornery as ever, but she was coping.

It was a crisp autumn morning, a little chill in the air, a hint of frost on the ground. The leaves on the maples were a brilliant orange with traces of yellow, like a landscape. Jill was thinking about how much she enjoyed this time of year, the pumpkins and gourds in the garden, the smell of leaves burning, the hint of winter not too far away. I should have been an artist, she thought, as much as I love nature. The kids loved jumping in the leaves, picking up walnuts and hitting them with a hammer, asking when they could carve a pumpkin. Even the baby, at ten months old, loved playing in the leaves. He had just taken his first steps and was still trying to get his footing.

A car pulled into the driveway; she recognized the guy behind the wheel as Mel Wilson, a neighbor of her parents. What does he want? Jill wondered.

"Jill, we took your Dad to the hospital, you probably need to get over there as soon as you can. We think he may have had a heart attack. He's been out in the fields for days, trying to get the beans harvested and he's worn himself out. If you want me to, I can take the kids over to my wife and she'll take care of them today. Do you know where Johnny's working? I could go by his job."

"Oh God, how bad do they think it is? Is Mom there?"

"She went to the hospital, the doctors are with him; they'll know something soon."

Jill ran to get a diaper bag for the baby; she kept it packed, so she just needed to add bottles of formula along with two jars of baby food for his dinner. She felt as though she was moving in slow motion. Johnny's mother would know where the guys were working and she took a minute to phone her. Thankfully, she answered on the first ring.

"Helen, do you know where Johnny and his dad are working today? Could you go by the job and tell him that my dad has been taken to the hospital. Also, the kids are with Mrs. Wilson for the day and could you please pick them up later?"

"Jill, please slow down and catch your breath. Of course I will. I'll phone Mrs. Wilson and let her know that I'll be out there sometime this afternoon to pick up the boys. I will also get in touch with Johnny and let him know what is happening. Call me as soon as you find out anything about your dad."

It seemed to take forever to drive the fifteen miles to the hospital. How did this happen; I just saw him the other day. Mel is right; he's been working too hard. Dad is almost sixty-five; he needs to slow down and take it easy. Jill had been a change-of-life baby, a real surprise to her parents, but always felt loved and cherished. Her sister was ten years older than she; therefore, the two girls weren't very close.

She parked in the Emergency Room parking lot, which was packed. I hope he got in right away; at times the wait took hours. But, surely under the circumstances, they would have rushed him in ahead of anyone else. She went straight to the desk and asked if Harold Mullins had been admitted. The receptionist asked if she was a family member. Jill answered her impatiently, "Yes, I need to get in to see my dad."

"Come with me, I'll take you back to his room." Jill followed her, dreading what she might find. Her mother was sitting beside his bed and the doctor was talking to her.

"Mrs. Mullins, we are going to admit your husband. We need to watch him for a day or two and see if there is any recurrence. He has suffered a mild stroke and needs to rest. We will be monitoring his condition on an hourly basis."

Her dad was awake, but seemed to be in a daze. His face was drawn on the left side and he couldn't lift his left arm. "Doctor, how long do these symptoms last?" Jill knew very little about strokes, but she did know her dad suffered from high blood pressure.

"His symptoms will fade in time, but there isn't much we can do for the results of a stroke. We will see that he's comfortable and gets a lot of rest. Right now, we will be transferring him to a room."

"Mom, why don't we get a cup of coffee while they get Dad settled in his room. There's nothing we can do and you need to eat something."

"Jill, I'll get coffee, but I can't eat; I'm too worried. If he doesn't come out of this, what happens to the farm? At the very least, he needs to sell or rent the land. I've had a feeling something like this might happen. He's been tired, grouchy, just not himself. I can't run that farm alone."

"Mom, hold on a minute, we don't know how this is going to turn out. Let's wait and see how he feels in a few days." Jill offered her mom a Winston; each sat with her coffee and cigarette, lost in her own thoughts, until it was time to go.

Her dad was still sleeping, so Jill decided to pick up her sons and go home for a while. Jill told her mother, "Mom, why don't you go home; get some rest and come back this evening." Her mother wouldn't hear of it. "Okay then, call me after bit and let me know the situation; then I'll know whether or not to come back out here."

As Jill left, she was thinking about her morning. It had been such a nice day with the kids, the weather had been perfect; what a dramatic change from then to now. My dad could die or be handicapped the rest of his life; how would Mom handle that? She knew of no other family in this situation for comparison; her sister wouldn't be any help, living in California; she hadn't been home in two years.

Walking to the bank, Janet was thinking about her upcoming tutoring session with Dani. The tutoring was going well, and since the bank audit had been completed, Dave would stop in after each session to check on their progress. Dani would say good night and Dave would hang around and talk. She was beginning to look forward to their daily conversations much more than she enjoyed the tutoring. She saw him on a daily basis at the bank, but that was a professional relationship. The evening interactions were personal, even touching on intimate. He had begun to confide details of his family life, frustrations with his wife, Debbie and her unforgiving attitude. She had blamed him for allowing Dani to go out on the evening of the accident, even though she had earlier forbidden it. The distance between them had grown immensely with Debbie burying herself in her many social obligations, thus avoiding further contact with him.

"I look forward to seeing you every evening, Janet. Our conversations are becoming the highlight of my day; I hope I'm not putting a further burden on your shoulders by sharing my problems. Confiding in you is so easy; I would hate to think you were merely indulging me."

"Dave, I don't feel that way at all, getting to know you has been good for me too. Up until I began tutoring Dani, I was spending every weekday evening alone, due to Robert's afternoon shift at the factory. It's been a trying time for me; I was sometimes lonely as a single person, but when I married, I wrongfully assumed that would be over. Both of us have been experiencing loneliness in our lives and now we've found a way to fulfill that need by spending a little time together. That's what I would call a friend."

"Friendships are a rarity in my life. My position in town prevents me from developing close personal relationships with town folks; consequently, I spend a lot of time with my dad at the club. It's ironic that it took my daughter being involved in a life-threatening accident to find a close friendship."

They both heard the front door open; Janet stood up quickly to leave and Dave walked into the hall. "Debbie, I was just telling Janet how proud we are of Dani's progress. She seems to be flowering under Janet's capable skills."

"That's good, Dave" she said curtly. "I certainly wouldn't have the patience to deal with her and she would never accept my help under any circumstances. Congratulations, Janet."

"I appreciate the confidence you both have in me. I'll say good night and be on my way." Being with them made her feel very uncomfortable, even though there was nothing going on between her and Dave. There was such tension between the two and it infiltrated the room. She imagined it seeped into the lives of their children as well. Debbie's icy attitude toward Dave was very apparent. He hadn't shared events that led up to this situation; rumors over the years of infidelity on both sides were wide-spread, especially of Debbie with the tennis pro. She was a very attractive woman with lots of opportunities. Could this be the straw for the marriage?

Teresa and Doug were meeting weekly at the motel; at first, it had been difficult for her to get away; but since she had received her realtors' license and joined the George Ross Agency; she had found it easy to be out of the office for extended periods of time.

"Doug, do you think it's wise to continue meeting here; should we change our routine?" Teresa wondered as they snuggled together in the warm aftermath of their lovemaking. "It would be wonderful if we could have a weekend out of town. Would that be possible?"

He shrugged, "I'll have to give that some thought; perhaps we could go to either Fort Wayne or Indianapolis; they're both big cities, we could get lost in either one. I'd love it if we could just take off; I know that sounds silly, but I think about it a lot." He kissed her softly and held her close. "You feel so good to me."

"Doug, I hate to interject pressure into our situation; but I need to know where we're going from here? I've been doing a lot of thinking and I want to spend more time with you, one way or the other. Are the weekly meetings enough for you? I'm afraid we might get into a rut of our own, meeting the same place, same time, every week. Have you considered a future with me?"

"Yes, but due to my current circumstances, I prefer to stay the course. I want to wait until the baby is a little older and Linda can stand on her own. It wouldn't be fair to leave her right now; she would be at a real disadvantage in the work force."

"Oh, let me get this straight; you're considering leaving her, just not right now, am I correct?"

"Yes, that's what I'm thinking. She's been talking about going back to work at the bank; she worked for Dave Powers as his personal secretary before we got married. One problem is a baby sitter during the day. Her mother might do it, but she would spoil her." He glanced at his watch, "Honey, right now, we've got to get out of here; I have a four o'clock appointment with a new client."

She sighed, very disappointed, "I miss you terribly after our afternoons together; I wish I could see you every day."

"Teresa, you're so busy; you probably never think about me unless I call", he teased. "It won't be long before we can be together all the time." He kissed her lightly, checked the parking lot and told her to scoot.

Driving home, she was trying to imagine what life would be like with Doug. She would still have her kids, but he would only have visiting rights with his daughter, most likely on weekends. She wondered if this would work for him. Her girls would only see their dad on weekends also; she hated the thoughts of that; they loved their daddy. Do I have the right to wrench them away from him? Can Doug and I build a solid marriage on the ashes of two broken homes? Is he worth it?

Doug was thinking along the same lines on his way back to his office. I shouldn't have told her we'd eventually be together. I don't know that for sure. I'd rather keep things just the way they are; but she may get tired of waiting on me to make a move. Maybe it was a big mistake to get involved; I don't want out of it, but I can't see a solution at this point. He had lied to her about the appointment; Linda wanted him to be home early for a dinner with her parents and knowing he was doing something Linda wanted might upset her. He felt like a juggler.

Teresa had a few stops to make on her way home, the bank, the grocery store for the usual milk and bread and the dime store to buy a birthday gift for Rose's little friend. She decided to walk while she was in town and as she entered the dime store; she saw Doug leaving his office before his scheduled appointment. Was it cancelled? Or was something else going on with him? He was his usual affectionate self today; but she had sensed a bit of withdrawal as they were leaving. She remembered how hurt she was when he broke up with her before; was it going to happen again? I don't want to mistrust him; am I being paranoid? She finished up her errands and tried to put Doug out of her mind.

CHAPTER 11

Mrs. Morrow had invited Dianne to accompany her to the Apparel Market in Chicago the third week of October. They would drive to Chicago, attend the market for three days and return home. She was excited beyond words, but concerned as to how Mike would react to this trip. Mrs. Morrow was bringing in a past employee to run the store while they were away; she was taking care of Dianne's expenses, her mother would tend to Phillip; how could he possibly have any objections? Based on their recent history of fights, she dreaded telling him.

She fixed his favorite dinner: chicken and noodles, mashed potatoes, green beans and hot rolls, hoping to put him in a receptive mood.

"Hi Mike, I'm glad to see you home early; I've got your favorites coming up tonight." Phillip ran to see him, excited to tell him about the upcoming Halloween Party at school. How can he be so callous, she wondered; we both try so hard to please him.

"So, Phillip, what do you want to be this year? Last year, you wore a skeleton costume and scared us to death. Maybe you can be Superman, what do you think about that?" She was so happy to see him relating to their son; Phillip was beaming as a result of his dad's attention.

"Dinner's ready, you two. Come and get it." She poured

Phillip's milk, got their water and sat down to eat. "How was your day, Mike? Is there anything interesting happening on the new house?"

"We're ready to enclose the house this week; we have to get that done so we can work inside this winter. I've got a new dry wall guy starting in a few days; he should be coming on at about the right time."

"Well, I have some news of my own from work today. My boss has invited me to attend the apparel market with her next weekend in Chicago. We'll leave Friday morning and come home Sunday night. I've already checked with Mother and she can help out with Phillip, while you're working on Friday and Saturday. Mrs. Morrow is paying all the expenses; this will be like a free trip for me, plus a great learning experience. Do you think you and Phillip could manage a couple of days without me?"

Mike put his hand on the boy's shoulder, "Phillip, what do you think, can we be a couple of bachelors, fix our own meals and do some guy things?"

"Dad, that'd be so much fun, can we get my costume while Mom's gone. Do you think we could? Can we, can we?"

"I think so, Phillip. Actually, Dianne, maybe it would be good for us to have a separate weekend, a little time to sit back and take a hard look at things. You'll be busy, but there should still be some quiet time at night. Am I right?"

She couldn't believe what she was hearing. He was actually being agreeable. "Yes, Mike, you're right, of course. There will be down-time during the weekend."

They finished their meal; Mike went to his recliner and turned on the evening news, Phillip went to his room to finish homework, while she cleaned up the kitchen. This is what family life should be, normal, she thought.

Later that night, she put on her sheerest negligee and waited for him to come to bed. She wanted her loving marriage back: things had been going wrong for months. Mike got in bed and she snuggled up to him. "Dianne, I'm just way too tired; this job is sapping all my energy." Sorely disappointed, she turned off the bedside lamp and that wasn't all she turned off; his attitude had completely turned her off. What red-blooded man turns down sex? He's either got a problem with me or himself; apparently my needs are not important. We've had a fantastic sex life all throughout our marriage, up until about a year ago; now it seems to be a chore to him. Why did he want her to take a hard look at things; was it because he wanted out?

CHAPTER 12

After the initial stroke, Jill's dad, Harold, had seemed to rally, then a massive stroke hit him. Jill and her mother both knew he was near the end. Everything the doctors ordered was simply to make him comfortable. They had told the family members it would only be a matter of days. Marie, Jill's mother, was maintaining a daily vigil at his bedside, hoping for a miracle. Jill's sister, Carol, had come home from Los Angeles. Other family members and friends had stopped by to see him.

A few days later, during the early hours of the morning, Harold passed away. Marie had been sleeping in a bedside chair and awoke to find him gone. She notified the nurse and called her daughters. Jill came to the hospital to take her mother home. When they got to the house, Carol met them at the door and they all cried together.

"Mother, do you need something to help with your anxiety? I can call the doctor and get something for you" asked Jill. She felt like her mother was in shock, unable to comprehend what was happening to her family.

"Jill, I'll be fine; I just need some rest. We'll have to go to the funeral home tomorrow and make arrangements. Why don't you go home; Carol is here with me; you can come back in the morning and we'll go see the funeral director."

As Jill drove toward home, she was thinking about her dad. It wouldn't be the same at the farm without him. He was the life of it. Once the funeral was over, she and her sister would have to approach their mother as to her plans, that's assuming she had any. Jill had never heard her mention a plan in case her dad died first; she had no idea what her mother might have in mind.

She walked in the house, told her mother-in-law what had happened and asked if she'd be available to help out with the boys for a few days. Johnny came in just then, and asked her, "What's wrong, you're so pale?"

"Daddy died this morning, Johnny," she cried and he took her in his arms. She sobbed for a few minutes and then composed herself; she didn't want the boys to see her crying. Helen, her mother-in-law, went into the kitchen to find something to cook for their dinner. She is a jewel, thought Jill.

"When is your mother making the arrangements, or has she already?" asked Johnny.

"We're doing that first thing in the morning, going to the funeral home. I suppose the calling hours will be Thursday night with the funeral on Friday. Johnny, we should take the two older boys to the funeral; they really adored their grandpa. It will be hard for them, but they need to say goodbye." Johnny agreed.

CHAPTER 13

Janet's after-work plans were to visit her parents, George and Kate Hawkins, for dinner, then onto the Browns' to tutor Dani. She hadn't spent much time with her mom and dad lately and was anxious to see them. Sitting on the screened-in porch overlooking the river was a favorite place for the family to have cocktails. She felt like she could completely unwind there, cocooned with her parents, like she was as a child.

"Dad, how are things at the plant?" she asked, knowing that tomatoes were being processed around the clock this time of year. She sipped her old-fashioned, thoroughly enjoying it.

"Busy, which you would expect, Janet, I want to bring up the possibility of you taking on some responsibility at the factory. We've touched on this before, but you weren't ready. Now that you're older, I think it's time. You're going to have to learn the business operation in preparation for my retirement; since it will belong to you eventually. What do you think?"

"When would you want me to start? I love the numbers side of the business; would there be a position in that area?"

"I think that would be the perfect place to begin; you'd

get a feel for the income and expenses, payroll, the yield per acre, cost of our equipment, inventory on hand, the whole operation. I just want you to get your feet wet." He was pleased at her positive response and so was her mother. "Do you have a date in mind?"

"Gee, Dad, I'd have to put in my notice at the bank; I'd want to give them time to replace me. Could I have a month or so to wrap things up with the bank and my tutoring?"

"Absolutely, honey, I want your mind to be free and clear of any other obligations before you sign on."

They sat down to a scrumptious dinner of salad, crown roast of pork, new potatoes, asparagus and fresh-baked yeast rolls. "Mom, Mabel has outdone herself tonight, this is delicious, after all these years of working for you, her meals are still fabulous."

"Jannie, wait till dessert. She's fixed your favorite, Banana Pudding. When she found out you would be here for dinner; she wanted to surprise you."

"Mom, that is so sweet" she said as she went to the kitchen to thank Mabel for her kindness.

After dinner, she told her dad that she'd give him a date as soon as possible. Leaving the bank would be hard; she had developed a lot of friendships there and loved the customers, but eventually running the operation at the canning plant was an amazing opportunity, one she knew was handed to her only because she was family. Proving she deserved it would be her true challenge.

When Janet arrived at the Browns', Dani was already studying. Her schoolwork was progressing very well; in a matter of weeks, she should be able to go back to school, but the crutches could still be a problem; the school had no elevator and the stairs were old and steep. She might have to sit out the entire first semester and go back after Christmas. They immediately started working on the current Bookkeeping lesson; a complete set of ledgers and journals for a small business. There were invoices, accounts to bill, labor to figure, supplies to buy. Dani was enjoying this phase of the class and would probably earn an A. English was the tough subject for her; literature was not her favorite, neither were the book reports. Janet was making progress with her though and she wasn't as resistant as she had been at first.

Dave stopped in to say hello and ask if they needed something to drink. "Yes, Daddy, we'd like lemonade, but only if you'll have some with us, please." She was so sweet with her Dad and just the opposite with her mother. Dave got the drinks and looked over her work. "Very good, Dani, you'll be caught up in no time. Now, after you're finished with your lemonade, you can be excused. I want to talk to Mrs. Steele for a few minutes." Shortly, Dani said good night to both of them.

"Janet, I can't tell you how much I appreciate this. Spending four nights a week with a teenager is a real sacrifice. I hope it is turning out to be a rewarding experience for you; Debbie could never have handled this."

"It's fine, Dave. My nights are free; besides, I've enjoyed our little evening conversations. But, there's something I need to mention. I had dinner with my parents tonight and Dad thinks it's time for me to learn the operation of the plant. I told him I would need a month or so to train my replacement at the bank. Of course, I would continue to tutor Dani until she's back at school."

"I hate to think of you leaving the bank. After you're done tutoring Dani, when will I see you, unless you continue coming to the bank as a part of the canning plant's business. I know that sounds selfish on my part, but your friendship means a great deal to me. Debbie is never home, always involved with her friends and organizations and I'm just not interested in all that. Consequently, we have little to discuss, much different than you and I."

"Yes, I've noticed she's not around a lot, and our time together has meant a lot to me too; spending every evening alone is not fun; I know that from personal experience. But even with me leaving the bank, I see no reason why we can't meet for business lunches occasionally or for morning coffee. After all, I will need to maintain a relationship with my banker" she said.

He laughed heartily. "That's exactly what I mean, you make me laugh, I do that so seldom lately."

She glanced at her watch, "Darn, it's time for me to go; I'll see you in the break room tomorrow. Should I give my notice to Mr. Donahue or will you take care of that?"

"You'd better tell him, stay in the proper channels; it looks better that way." He gave her a quick hug and pulled away. "Good night, Janet."

He started upstairs, but thought he heard Janet having problems starting her car; the engine would try to turn over and then quit. She tried it several more times without any luck. He went outside to see if he could help. "Dave, I don't think it's going to start; I've had some problems with it lately. I'll have to call someone to pick me up."

"That's not necessary. I can run you home; it'll only take a few minutes. Then, in the morning, you can call Gary at the station and have him come out and take a look at it." He went to tell Dani and Dotti that he was leaving, but they were sleeping. He didn't know when Debbie would be home. "Well, let's go, there's no one here to wonder where I've gone. Are you hungry, Janet, maybe we could stop for a bite to eat?"

"That sounds good, maybe a piece of coconut pie at Millie's along with a cup of her good coffee, and no, it doesn't keep me awake."

There were no cars at Millie's. "The place looks empty tonight, maybe everyone's home in bed." They went in, decided on a back booth and ordered their pie. "There's lots of good music on the jukebox, what do you like? There are some Englebert songs, Supremes, Aretha, Platters, Elvis."

"Play something by the Supremes and Englebert. Any of the ones you mentioned; I still like rock and roll, even if I'm a lot older than you."

She punched in "Release Me", by Englebert, "Can't Take My Eyes Off You", by Frankie Valli, "Love Is Here And Now You're Gone" by the Supremes, "The Letter" by the Boxtops, "Light My Fire" by the Doors, and "Stardust" by the Platters. "Six songs for a quarter is a real bargain. Now, we can't leave till all my songs have played; I want to get my money's worth. Does our age difference bother you, Dave? I know you're older than me, but so what? We still have fun."

He was mesmerized by her. She was the most beautiful woman he'd ever seen and she made him feel young again. When he was with her, all his worries disappeared. He looked up and she smiled, "A penny for your thoughts."

"I was thinking about you, how much I enjoy being with you. This is the most fun I've had in ages, and all because your car wouldn't start. Fate must be intervening in our lives; do you believe in that?'

"My mother always said that everything happens for a reason and I suppose I subscribe to that belief. But, speaking of fate, I don't want to tempt it; I need to get home before Robert does."

"Yes, that's a good idea. Are you going to tell him about your car?"

"I'll tell him what happened to it and that you gave me a lift home; however, I won't mention coming here. That wouldn't set well."

He walked around to open her door. He looked down at her and murmured, "I'd love to kiss you, Janet; do you think I've lost my mind?"

She looked up at him, stood on her tiptoes and touched her lips to his. He pulled her close and she melted into him. A lot of pent-up emotion went into that kiss; they had both thought of this happening many times. He released her and she sat down in the car. Driving away, he was apologizing profusely. "Don't," she said, "it's what we both wanted; we've known this was coming and neither of us did anything to stop it."

He looked at her like a love-sick puppy, "This kiss has to be a one-time thing with us. I love your friendship, but I don't trust myself when I'm with you." They drove to her house in silence and said an awkward good night.

Robert got home a few minutes behind Janet. That was a

close call, she thought. He asked, "How did the tutoring go tonight?" He wasn't crazy about her doing this job, but he did like the fact that it gave her something to do while he worked; and as a plus for him, he wasn't worrying about her being with another man.

"It went real well, I feel like I'm getting through to this girl; she has been very reluctant to form any kind of relationship with me, but I'm beginning to see her softening up. She has improved immensely on her grades and was even studying when I got there tonight."

"That sounds good. Now, come here. I haven't had any loving for a while and I need it." Reluctantly, she sat down beside him on the sofa and immediately, he grabbed her and started groping. Why couldn't he be romantic like Dave?

"Robert, I'm really tired tonight, can we wait until the weekend? It would be so much better for me and maybe for you too," she said softly.

"Damn it, you're never in the mood lately, what the hell is wrong with you? Excuse after excuse, it's getting old. Don't you know that a man gets horny?" He stormed out of the room, heading for bed.

That didn't go well, she thought. I'm just not able to respond to him right now; he's so demanding and not the least bit loving toward me; he's definitely not like Dave. He acts as though I can turn it on anytime. Suddenly, she realized she had not mentioned the talk with her Dad; obviously; she wasn't ready to discuss this with Robert. How would he take it, his wife heading up a company, while he was still a production worker at the local factory? There was quite a dramatic difference. She knew he would not have a positive reaction to this. What was the best approach? It didn't make any difference; he wouldn't be pleased under any circumstances.

CHAPTER 13

Harold's funeral was held on Friday afternoon. There was only one funeral home in Creviston; Clarks', a red brick, ranch-style building on a large, well-manicured piece of property in the middle of town. Dark blue and cream floral carpet covered the floors, damask draperies in light blue with white sheers enhanced the floor-to-ceiling windows, all against an off-white background. Mortuary music played softly in the background and the sickening, sweet smell of funeral flowers permeated the air. All of this was virtually invisible to the widow Marieas she sat in the front pew greeting the arriving mourners. A lot of the town folks had shown up; Harold was a well-known farmer with lots of friends and business associates. He had grown up in the area and he and Marie were active in the church; therefore, the Methodist ladies had prepared a large dinner to take place in the church basement. Anyone attending the funeral was invited; large funerals were peculiarly becoming social events in the town.

Jill and Johnny, along with their two older sons, sat with her mother and sister, Carol, in the front pew. Their minister would be conducting the service. Jill's friends, Teresa, Janet and Dianne, along with their husbands, had attended the viewing the previous evening. The three women would be at the funeral; however, their husbands would be working.

Doug and Linda Jones stopped to pay their respects to Marie. Harold and his wife had been clients of Doug's for several years. Doug's secretary Joanne Howard, her brother Kris, along with his girlfriend Toni, were right behind them. Several others were waiting; the funeral was going to start later than expected.

Eventually, all the mourners were seated and the service began with the standard hymn, "Amazing Grace". The minister delivered his message, spoke glowingly of Harold's accomplishments in life, his devotion to his church and family and what a great friend he had been to many. The service completed with the singing of "The Old Rugged Cross". The pallbearers appeared at the front of the church. As they carried the casket out of the church to the awaiting hearse, the family followed and took their seats in the funeral home's limousine. The remainder of the attendees lined up their cars according to a plan devised by the funeral director. The town marshal led the procession out to the cemetery, where a short, graveside service was performed and the casket was lowered into the earth. Marie, Jill and Carol sobbed quietly during the proceedings, each taking a rose from atop the casket. People began to disburse and return to the church to partake of the meal.

The church basement was lined with cloth-covered tables and metal folding chairs. The food was being served buffet style with a dessert table along the side wall. Coffee, tea and soft drinks were available. Doug and Linda got their plates and sat down with Joanne, Kris and Toni. Doug had been wondering all day where he'd seen Toni; then he heard her mention something about her job at Millie's and it dawned on him. He hoped she hadn't seen him with Teresa; but even if she had, it didn't prove anything. Speaking of

Teresa, she had just arrived with Dianne and Janet. They all came over to say hello, and while they were there visiting, Linda got up to go to the ladies room. As she passed by Teresa, she got a whiff of her perfume. Damn, I knew it, Chanel No. 5, the same perfume I smelled on Doug a couple of months ago. Did this mean anything or was it just coincidence? I'm sure lots of women wear that scent. Am I a fool, in denial or what?

When Linda came back to the table, she told Doug she didn't feel well and needed to go home. He hadn't finished his dinner, but reluctantly got up to go. As they walked toward the door, he glanced at Teresa and she was watching them, trying to understand why they were leaving. He didn't understand it either.

They got in the car and driving home, she couldn't help herself. "Okay, out with it, are you having an affair with Teresa?"

"Why in the hell would you ask me a question like that? Linda, I don't know where you come up with this crap. Hell, No."

"You'd better not be lying to me, Doug Jones, I'll find out, one way or the other. You know I will."

Doug blew up, "I don't want to hear any more of this shit. I think you're nuts." He was dumbfounded. What had happened back there at the church that set her off? He had hardly looked at Teresa; they were very careful. Sometimes he thought his wife was physic. How am I ever going to get out of this, which woman do I want? I love my wife, but Teresa is so exciting to me, so witty and good in bed. I'm crazy about her; I just don't know how to deal with Linda.

Back at the church, Melanie, Linda's sister, had sat down with Toni; it had been a few months since the two friends had seen one another and this was a good time to catch up. Melanie asked her, "Toni, what have you been doing lately, besides dating this hunk, Kris?"

"I've been working at Millie's, six days a week; business is good, as are the tips. It's a really fun place to work, lots of people and great home-cooked food. Almost everyone in town comes through there at some point during the week. I even saw your brother-in-law there a couple of months ago. He was sitting with that girl over there."

"Oh, really? That's Teresa Farris, his old girlfriend. Could you hear what they were saying? What was their body language? My God, if Linda knew this, she'd have a hissy fit."

"Melanie, I don't want to cause any trouble for your sister. It was probably nothing. I couldn't tell what was being said; but I do remember thinking they looked pretty chummy. She wasn't there more than fifteen minutes after he sat down with her. There had been another girl sitting with her earlier."

"Do you think it might have been a chance meeting?"

"Exactly, I think she and the other girl had plans to meet; she left and he came in unexpectedly."

"That makes me feel better."

The crowd was dispersing, so they got up and left too. It had begun to rain, bringing with it that blustery, bone-chilling autumn air. The wind was picking up, a storm was definitely moving in; the gray skies looked like snow.

Carol was flying back to California on Saturday, so Marie and her two daughters needed to have a serious talk. She had carefully considered what she was going to tell them; she could only hope they would be receptive to her ideas.

"Okay, girls; here's what I plan to do. The harvest is in for this year; your dad made sure of that. I'm going to put the farm land up for sale, not the house and the five acres that surround it, but the farm ground itself. Then, I'm going to do some repairs around here that need to be done, plus a little restoration. It will be mostly cosmetic, but I may add another upstairs bathroom and enlarge the downstairs bath. The kitchen needs some work, maybe new appliances and the cabinets stripped and painted. Your dad never wanted to spend the money, but with the sale of the acreage, it will be a good investment. My thinking has been that I might rent the upstairs bedrooms and serve breakfast. What do the two of you think?"

They both sat there astonished. They had never seen this side of their mother, an entrepreneur. It sounded like a workable plan; she would get a good price for the land. Lots of farmers in the area would love to own it, plus she could sell the farm machinery as well. She would be a wealthy woman.

"Mom, what about renting for a weekend or to people here on business? It could be a bed & breakfast inn; there's none in the area and it could be a great getaway during the warmer months" said Jill as she hugged her mom. "We are so proud, can you believe it, our mom is a woman of the future." Marie laughed, it felt good.

CHAPTER 14

It was Friday night; Robert was leaving work, hurrying to make the poker game at Sam's, a tavern near the factory. He had already cashed his check, having been paid the night before. He had given Janet $30 for groceries and household expenses and he thought he could win enough to pay the mortgage which was due next week. He was feeling lucky. He had promised her he would quit playing poker when they got married, but he couldn't give it up. He suspected that she knew, just not to what extent; he didn't figure she needed to know any more of his secrets; she already nagged him about his hunting weekends and fishing jaunts. What the hell, I work, why shouldn't I enjoy myself?

He walked into Sam's, which was little more than a hole-in-the-wall, but suitable for a bunch of rowdy men. The smoke was thick, men stood around the bar drinking beer and trying to make time with the few women who inhabited the place; while some of the guys he worked with were shooting a game of pool. The place smelled like a mixture of beer, sweat, and cigarette smoke, with an occasional whiff of cheap perfume. The jukebox was blasting out an old Hank Williams song, "Jambalaya". The mood was upbeat. He sat down at the bar and ordered a PBR and a hamburger with fries.

"Hey, Steele, you ready to get your clock cleaned?"

hollered Leonard, one of his poker buddies. The guys stood up and headed for the back room. Gambling was illegal in Indiana, but, in the overall scheme of things, wasn't a high priority for the police. The only time it drew attention from the officers was if a wife complained about her husband losing his entire paycheck at a local establishment. Then, they would have to shut down the game for a few weeks.

Six of them sat down at the table and anted up their dollar to get in the game. Table stakes were set at a $5 limit. Sam had his own house dealer, Gene, who took a cut of each pot for the bar. As the hands were played, Robert kept betting on hands that turned out to be losers. After a few of those, he took a break to speak to Gene, who was known for under-the-table loans. He was already into Gene for almost $500, but his luck had to change eventually. Three hours later, the game ended. Robert had finally won a few hands; he pocketed his winnings and left the bar. He shivered as he stepped outside, winter was coming. Pleased with the final few hands, but concerned with his growing debt to Gene; he knew he'd have to come up with some cash to pay him before he could sit down at the table again.

Janet arrived at the Browns' for the nightly tutoring. Dave had not been stopping in for their nightly conversations since the night of their kiss. She was very disappointed, but didn't push it. As she pulled into the drive, she didn't see Debbie's car and assumed she was out for the evening. Dave opened the door for her and smiled. This is a start, she thought.

"Janet, could we talk?" He seemed quite nervous.

"Of course, Dave, what's on your mind?"

"Actually, Janet, you're on my mind; I've missed our nightly chats and hope we can get back on track. I felt we were good for each other and surely, I can control my emotions. I know I'll certainly try; I would never want to offend you."

"Dave, first of all, you didn't offend me; we were both responsible for what happened. I've missed our time together too, much more than I can say. Why don't we try it again and see what happens."

"I was hoping you'd feel that way. I'll see you after the lessons are over."

Dani was doing extremely well in her studies; she had taken a liking to Janet and strived to please her. She wished her mother was more like Janet; she never seemed to have time for her any more. Her dad was very pleased with her grades and told her so frequently. He came in just then to see how she was doing and she saw Janet's eyes light up. Hmmm, she thought, I may be a kid, but I can see what's going on here.

"Dani, Mrs. Steele and I have some things to discuss; you may be excused. Dani nodded, picked up her books, said good night and left the room. Dave sat down beside Janet and took her hand, "How have you been; I've not talked to you in months."

Janet laughed, "Yes, it does seem like months; I've just been lonely, as usual. I should be used to it by now, but I'm not. I will be starting at the canning plant on Monday; I'm excited about that, I know my heritage is the main reason I'm there; obviously, I will need to prove my worth; I want to make my dad proud. Robert has been staying out after work until all hours; he gets off at 11:30 PM and doesn't get in until two or three in the morning. I don't sleep well because of that; I'm always on edge late at night. I think he's playing a lot of poker, he comes home at night smelling like an ashtray; I have no idea how much money he's losing or winning. He doesn't contribute much to the household expenses; I pay most of those with my paycheck. I'm gaining access to my trust fund in about a month and he's not getting his hands on any of that money. Neither am I going to take responsibility for all our debt so he can play poker. Dave, I am sorry; I don't mean to dump all my problems on you." She began to cry, overwhelmed by the difficulties in her marriage. He pulled her to him and let her cry on his shoulder. A few minutes later, she whispered, "Dave, I'd better go, I don't want to cause trouble for you."

"Janet, let me decide that. We certainly seem to be kindred souls, don't we? Just being around you takes my breath away. Our feelings for one another are not to be denied; I can see that now." He kissed her gently, then deeply, as their passion mounted.

"Dave, how would you feel about going to my place; we can be alone there and Robert won't be home for hours, or am I being too forward?"

"Please, be as forward as you want, but I don't want to put you in a compromising situation. I'm not sure how comfortable I'd be in Robert's home, but it is your home too, and if you're sure, we'll go. I'll park down the street and walk to your back door; I'll be about five minutes behind you."

When she arrived home, she put on soft music and lit

candles. It was only nine, so Robert was, at the soonest, three hours away. She felt no remorse about this situation; it could not break her marriage, it was already broken. She hated to admit it, but her parents had been right in the assessment of their union. There was a light tap at the back door and she hurried to welcome her soul mate.

He kissed her again; she took his hand and led him into her guest room. She was not about to sully this relationship by spending any time with Dave in her marriage bed. They undressed each other slowly, relishing the pleasure of their first time together. Their lovemaking was sensational. He was so patient with her, taking her to the edge and bringing her back. His hands, his mouth, explored her completely. She had experienced sex, but nothing to compare to this. Her climax brought such a feeling of joy and ecstasy, she thought she would burst.

"Janet, you are so beautiful; I love being with you. Does that mean I'm falling for you? If it does, I don't care, it will just have to happen."

She sighed deeply. "I know; we are truly on the same wave length. I've never felt like this, ever. You make me so happy; you take all my cares away. I'm at such peace with you; I feel such a sense of security."

"Janet, I don't want the night to end, but my sweet, I must go. Isn't that what Cinderella did? She had to leave before midnight? I don't want to turn into a rat, or whatever it was."

"You're so funny" she laughed. "I think I'll have sweet dreams tonight." He dressed quickly, leaned over, kissed her goodbye and left out the back door. She eventually got up and took a leisurely bath. Maybe he is my destiny. She thought of her mother's words, "marry in haste, repent at leisure" or something like that; obviously a cliché from years ago, but the meaning was deep; however, she wanted her penance to be short. Tomorrow was Saturday; she wouldn't be seeing Dave until Monday night; it would be a long weekend. She wondered what he and his wife would be doing, probably attending one of her many charity function dinners. She didn't want to think about them being together; she only wanted to think about tonight. It had been heavenly. She went to bed, fell sound asleep and didn't hear Robert get in bed at 4:00 AM.

Dave was thinking about Janet on his way home, how different she was from Debbie. He knew he was falling in love with her and knew equally well that he wasn't going to fight it any more. Debbie had no interest in him; she hadn't for years. He had dallied in other love interests, maybe sexual interests would be a better definition, over the duration of their marriage, but this was different. He was fairly sure Debbie was up to something with all her evenings out, probably Jake, the tennis pro. Even she didn't have that many functions to attend. He had been checking the mileage on her car and she was racking up a lot of miles on a daily basis. The only stumbling blocks in their situation would be money and custody of the girls. David, Jr. was already away at college and would not be moving back home. He had considered divorce many times in the past, but had no good reason to pursue it; tonight that had changed.

CHAPTER 15

Mike Powers couldn't believe his luck. Dianne was leaving for the weekend; to him that was as good as a weekend pass. His mother-in-law would love to have Phillip for the two days and he could spend some time with his new interest. She was a real looker, Vicki Grey, the new girl behind the counter at the local lumber yard. She thought he was single; because of his job, he never wore his wedding ring. He had invited her to have a drink with him at the tavern a few nights ago and man, was she sexy. Now, with Dianne out of town, he could take her out, the old 'wine and dine' thing and maybe get her in bed. It was worth a try. He was planning on stopping by the lumber yard this morning; he could ask her then.

Vicki said yes, she'd love to go to dinner with him. He made plans to pick her up at her place at six on Saturday. He couldn't wait.

On Saturday, he took Phillip to get his Halloween costume; the little guy was so excited about being Superman. They stopped off at the new McDonalds and got a quick hamburger and fries. This was a treat for both of them. The restaurant was new to the town and was gaining in popularity, especially among kids and teenagers.

He dropped Phillip off to spend the night with his

grandmother. He told her he was going out to the basketball game with some of his buddies and he'd pick Phillip up the next day. He hurried home, put away Dianne's jewelry box, took her toiletries out of the bathroom and put family pictures in drawers.   He didn't want Vicki to see any evidence of Dianne. The sheets had just been changed, so that wasn't a problem. He checked the liquor supply; he knew she liked Manhattans; what a woman!   His only real concern was the neighbors; it would be dark when they got back here, but what if she spent the night? He'd just have to pull his car in the garage and hope no one was out when they left the next morning.

He showered, shaved, donned his nicest shirt and jacket and took off. He had made a dinner reservation at the Holiday Inn in Anderson, a nearby city. The restaurant had nightly dinner music, tablecloths and candlelight; the perfect venue for a romantic evening. Vicki was a brunette with deep brown eyes, looks inspired by Spanish ancestry. She had an ample bust line and liked to show it off. Tonight was no exception. Her red dress was clingy and low cut. He whistled when she opened the door.

"Are you ever looking good, I don't know if I'll be able to eat my dinner tonight; you may have taken my appetite."

"Oh, Mike, you're so sweet, I wanted to look my best for you; after all, this is our first real date, unless you count our drinks at the tavern, besides, you look pretty good yourself."

He held the car door for her; hopped in and sped away. They talked a bit during the drive to the restaurant; she was twenty-one, just old enough for a drink and had recently broken off an engagement, three months before. She was just getting back into dating. Her boyfriend had cheated on her and she had caught him in the act, which had been a very unpleasant scene. It was not one she would easily forget. Mike didn't have much to say in response. He just grunted.

Their table was in a good location, especially for him, out of the way and somewhat dim, plus, he had his back to the main part of the restaurant. He ordered cocktails, to be followed by chateaubriand with salads and a bottle of good cabernet for their dinner. They topped it off with coffee and cherries jubilee.

"Mike, this is the nicest dinner I've ever experienced. No one else has ever taken me to such a nice place."

"Vicki, you were cut out for this kind of an evening. You've got class, you're gorgeous; didn't you see all the guys looking at you when we arrived? It made me proud; you're on my arm, not theirs. Let's get out of here."

She had drunk more than her share of wine and was feeling the effects, giggling at everything he said, holding his hand and stroking his cheek. They pulled in the driveway of his home, got out and she commented, "Mike, this place is beautiful, I can't wait to see inside." They walked in and she was in awe. "It looks like something out of a magazine. Did you have a decorator?"

"Yes, I did, it's been a long time though, I can't even remember her name. Can I get you a Manhattan?"

"That would be wonderful," she said as she followed him into the kitchen. "You are good at making those; it looks like you've had lots of practice." He handed a drink to her, took her hand and went into the living room. He put a new log on the fire and they sat down on the sofa. After their drinks were gone, he took their glasses and sat them both on the coffee table. She slid easily into his arms and that first kiss was breathtaking. They continued to kiss and his hand moved up under her dress. She moved away slightly, he slowed down and caressed her leg. "I want you, Vicki; I've not been able to keep my eyes off you all night. Please don't make me wait." She hesitated, but with the wine and the Manhattan, her resistance was nil. He picked her up in his arms and carried her to the bedroom, unzipping her dress and removing her bra and panties. He quickly slipped out of his clothes and joined her in bed. She was so hot for him; her breasts were beautiful, so supple with those huge nipples. He could hardly contain himself. He moved her legs apart with his own and she groaned as he entered her. Their rhythm was perfect, moving together in unison toward their peak. Afterwards, they snuggled and he told her he wanted to see her again and again. She agreed. They fell asleep for a short time; he woke her up later and they made love again. He knew he had to get her home; he hated the thought. He couldn't get enough of her. They dressed and he slowly drove her home. He walked her to the door, kissed her and squeezed her rear, pressing her to him, feeling the urge to have her once again. "You could come in, you know, I wouldn't mind." He ended up staying the night, having sex with her the next morning; after which she fixed breakfast for him and then he had to say goodbye. "I'll call you next week" he said, slipping out the door.

Later, while she was in the shower washing her hair, Vicki realized one of the little jade earrings she was wearing the night before was missing. She looked around the bedroom and it was nowhere to be found. Maybe she lost it at Mike's; they had been rather rambunctious. He was quite the guy. Hopefully, he'll run across it. The pair had been a gift from her dad, one of the few gifts he had ever given her and now he is gone. She didn't call Mike about the earring though; it wasn't appropriate for a girl to call a man, no matter what the circumstances.

Mike looked around as he got out of his car; thankfully, the neighborhood was still quiet this Sunday morning. He hurried in the house, retrieved Dianne's things from their hiding places and threw the sheets, along with his shirt, into the washer. Emptying ashtrays, especially the butts with lipstick, was a must and washing the Manhattan glasses cleared the scene of any incriminating evidence. He felt like a criminal covering his tracks. Now, get the sheets dry, make the bed and pick up Phillip. Maybe I'll have dinner with her mother; Dianne would like that. He thought back over the prior evening, Vicki is something special; I can't wait to get my hands on her again.

CHAPTER 16

Dianne was stunned at the enormity of the market. The Merchandise Mart was a grand old structure, the second largest building in the world until 1943, when the Pentagon was built. This was her first trip to Chicago and she felt like a country bumpkin. Molly, (Mrs. Morrow) had insisted that Dianne address her by her first name, especially since they would be sharing a room later. She had scheduled appointments in advance, systematically seeing dresses on Friday, sportswear on Saturday and accessories on Sunday with a couple of hours each day for browsing new lines. There would be a fashion show on Sunday morning with a continental breakfast before the market opened. There were displays everywhere, with booth numbers where they could view the merchandise. Urns of coffee and trays of sweet rolls, bagels and fruit were set up in the lobby for the buyers. They were treated like royalty. After registration, where they received their name badges and market catalogues, they grabbed a cup of coffee and a bagel. Riding up in the ornate elevator was even a treat to Dianne.

Their first appointment was with Leslie Fay Dresses. In 1942, during World War II, John Pomerantz had been commissioned by the army to make dresses for the female soldier. The army had done a study of the most common female measurements and he had designed and made the dresses according to their scale. After the war, he decided to manufacture dresses with those same measurements and named the company Leslie Fay after his daughter. They made dresses for daytime, luncheons, church, business attire and evening. Ten styles were required per order with three of a style, thereby insuring the label had a good representation in the store. That was an easy requirement; staying at that number was not quite that easy. The dresses would sell for $15-$32 retail. Molly was looking at the spring line, which would start arriving in February. She sailed through the next four dress appointments, anxious to maintain her schedule.

Lunch was a quick sandwich and soda at a nearby cafe. The first afternoon appointment was with Vicki Vaughn, whose key dress for spring was a sleeveless, embroidered floral in a simple A-line. Other lines she chose were Roberta Lee, Gay Gibson and Patty O'Neill. Button-down collars, shirtwaists, mini tents, rolled collars, bright florals, hem lengths above the knee, mini to modest, Dianne's head was spinning with all the details. Molly only took notes at some vendor booths, planning to write orders that evening and turn them in the next day. She decided they would buy evening dresses on Sunday. Her total dress order for spring came to slightly over a hundred dresses. They would order summer styles at the next market. Spring was the biggest dress season of the year, mostly due to Easter and Mother's Day events.

That evening, they ordered room service so they could work on the remaining dress orders. On Saturday, they began early, at 8:30 A.M. with Bobbie Brooks, followed by Robbie Bee, Joyce and Devon separates. Johnathan Logan had a good selection of upscale knits geared toward the more fashion-conscious customers and the line had sold very well in the store the past season. Koret was another sportswear line the ladies liked, reasonably priced, with a well-fitting mainstream design. The rest of the day was spent browsing, picking up item separates from various vendors. That evening, Molly treated Dianne to a formal dinner at the Palmer House, one of the most prestigious hotels in Chicago. Dianne had been very impressed with the Conrad Hilton Hotel where they were staying, but she thought the Palmer House, though smaller in scale than the Hilton, was far more grandiose. The lobby ceiling was magnificent. She had to laugh, she who had never visited the city, what could her opinion matter? She loved the majestic buildings, the horns, the quirky people, even the noise. She had fallen in love with Chicago.

They wrapped up business late the next afternoon and headed home. She offered to drive and surprisingly, Molly allowed her. She assumed Molly was exhausted after the busy weekend; she knew she was. She couldn't wait to get home and put her feet up. The drive took a little over four hours; they arrived back in town around eight, just in time to say good night to Phillip, she thought.

Mike was lounging in the recliner, as usual, watching the Ed Sullivan Show. Phillip was lying on the sofa asleep. Mike said he had already taken a bath and was ready for bed, but wanted to wait up for her. She roused him, gave him a hug and kiss and sent him off to bed.

"How was your weekend, Mike, did you and Phillip spend much time together?" She had thought about the two of them frequently over the weekend, wondering what they were doing, if they were having a good time together.

"Yeah, we did, we got his Superman costume and had lunch at McDonald's. Your mother wanted him to spend the night on Saturday. We had Sunday dinner over there today. It was delicious, baked ham, sweet potatoes and green beans. She topped it off with apple pie and ice cream."

"So, what did you do Saturday night?

"I went to a game with some guys from work; then we stopped for a beer. That's about it." She thought he sounded evasive, but maybe that was her imagination, working overtime.

"Well, I just wondered, you wanted some time to think. So did you come up with anything and if you did, what's your solution to our problems?"

"I don't know, Dianne, it just seems like we don't have a connection lately; we're like roommates instead of husband and wife and that's no way to live."

"Well, gee, whose fault is that? You don't want anything to do with me; for example, you've not shown any interest in my market trip."

"Good Lord, you just walked in ten minutes ago, cut me some slack. I've had a lot on my mind with work these past few months; anyway, did you enjoy your weekend?"

"It was wonderful, Mike, I had no idea there was so much to the business; the ordering, ship dates, fabrics, cost, it's mind boggling. I did learn a lot though, and even helped Molly write some orders."

"Oh, it's Molly now. How did that come about?"

"She has asked me since I began working for her to call her Molly, but I wasn't comfortable with it until this trip. I admire Molly; she is so intelligent and savvy with the vendors. She doesn't let anyone get anything over on her."

"I'm glad you had a good time; will you be going again?" He was hoping so, he enjoyed these free weekends.

"I'd like that, the next market isn't until January, but the weather will dictate whether we go. Don't you remember this past January; Chicago had their worst blizzard in years, something like thirty-five inches of snow."

She thought he seemed different tonight, perhaps not as up tight as he had been lately. Maybe things would get better. She took her suitcase to the bedroom and started unpacking. That's strange, she thought, my jewelry box is on the other end of the dresser. She didn't remember moving it there. She threw her clothes in the hamper and got ready for her bath. She took off her panty hose, glad to get out of them and the painful high heels. It's unbelievable the pain women go through for the sake of fashion. The carpet felt good under her bare feet until she stepped on something. Ouch, what the heck is that? She leaned down to look and saw something small and green, imbedded in the shag carpet. She pulled it out and realized it was an earring. This isn't mine; I don't own a pair of jade earrings. For a moment, she was dumbfounded. Who does this belong to? Did he have a woman in here this weekend? If Phillip was gone Saturday night, maybe! Damn him to hell, I need to investigate, but I can't very well do it with him in the next room. It will just have to wait until tomorrow; he'll go to work early in the morning and I can do it then. In the meantime, I'm keeping my mouth shut. I wonder if anything else is out of line? She looked around the bathroom, checked the trap in the sink and there was a couple of long, dark hairs in the trap. Is this proof? I have dark hair, but I distinctly remember cleaning this sink before I left. She started her bath and returned to the bedroom to check the sheets. She had laundered them a few days ago; did he wash them again? They smelled fresh, like Tide and bleach, but she couldn't be sure. The bed wasn't the way she usually made it, but there again; that didn't prove anything either. She'd have to keep her eyes and ears open where he was concerned. It was making her physically sick to think he may have had another woman in their bed. Was he truly that low? She soaked in the tub, not wanting to look at him any more tonight. She was afraid of his temper, so she wasn't planning any confrontations; but she did need a game plan. Maybe her friends could give her some direction.

The next morning, she called Teresa, Janet and Jill and asked if they would be free for lunch. She had two days off because of the market and she wanted to meet them at Millie's. They were all anxious to see her and hear about the market. They planned on meeting at 11:30 before the lunch crowd arrived.

She went over the house thoroughly and found nothing else out of place. She placed the earring in a plastic bag and put it in her purse. He never looked in there, so she considered it safe. She brushed her hair, put on lipstick and rouge and went out the door. Dianne arrived at Millie's first and chose a back booth for privacy. She didn't want anyone else hearing their conversation. The other three girls came in almost at the same time, greetings were dispensed with quickly and coffee was ordered.

"Okay, let's hear all about market, we are all so jealous of you" said Jill.

"I'll tell you about that in a minute. But first, I have a big problem, or at least I think I do. I left Friday morning and got back Sunday night. Phillip stayed with Mom on Saturday night and Mike picked him up yesterday afternoon. They ate dinner there. When I went into the bedroom last night, I stepped on this and she showed them the earring. It's not mine and it shouldn't have been there. Damn, I just remembered, I ran the sweeper in there on Thursday, the day I changed the sheets and surely the sweeper would have picked it up. Also, my jewelry box was on the other end of the dresser from where I keep it and I know I didn't move it. Plus, I found two long dark hairs in the sink trap. What do you think?

"Was there anything else incriminating, like a used condom or lipstick-covered cigarette butts? He couldn't have cleaned up all the evidence, surely." Janet was being both sarcastic and brutally honest. The other girls agreed, indicating they believed he'd had another woman in her bed.

"Sometimes our husbands screw up, but at least they're not doing that" said Teresa. She didn't think Ted was cheating, but who knew? Were they all out running around with other women? "I wouldn't put it past Mike to have done this. He's always been arrogant; he probably thinks he deserves a fling."

"So many questions; he ignores me for the most part and never wants sex. I don't know how I'd find out what he's doing, unless someone sees him and tells me, or I go to the tavern and check up on him, which would cause a major fight. I could follow him when he leaves the tavern."

"Dianne, that's a good idea. I could take you; Robert is always working and Mike wouldn't notice my car. You could take Phillip to your mom's; it would have to be spur of the moment, a night when he was late getting home. But, we might have to follow him more than once to catch him."

"That wouldn't be hard. He's always there on Wednesday and Thursday nights; he tries to come home earlier the other nights. I've been expecting something like this; he's been mean and restless for months. I'd just like to know what's going on; then I can make a decision about my future. Do you still want to hear about the market?"

They sat there eager to hear all the details. She gave them a description of events from beginning to end. They teased her about being a woman of the world and it took her mind off the problems at hand for the moment. She felt better being around her friends. They were completely supportive and understanding.

Jill told them the news about the bed & breakfast her mother was planning. Janet shared the news about her new position at the canning plant and Teresa was flying high with the pending sale of her first house. Neither Janet nor Teresa mentioned anything about their extra-curricular activities. Janet had not wanted to betray Dave by telling her friends about their relationship, so she was keeping it to herself.

Janet made plans with Dianne to come by on Wednesday night for their surveillance activity. She told her to bring spy glasses. It wasn't a bit funny, but a little dark humor didn't hurt.

The girls talked about the upcoming Halloween party at the country club and what they planned to wear. It was a masked ball and costumes were mandatory. Jill was considering Little Bo Peep, with Johnny going dressed as Jack and the Beanstalk. Someone suggested, "You two could go as Jack and Jill, with your pail of water." They all laughed. Dianne hadn't decided, Teresa and Ted were going as a Fifties' couple at a sock hop, and Janet and Robert as Cinderella and the prince. Dianne suggested that her husband should dress as Snow White and she as the wicked old witch with the vat of boiling water. They all roared with laughter at that.

CHAPTER 17

Jill was meeting Marie, her mother, at Sears this afternoon. They were looking at new appliances for the kitchen. Her mother wanted a built-in oven and range, a new refrigerator and dishwasher. Jill was so envious of the dishwasher; she didn't know many women who had one; she had only seen them in new homes. They decided on white; they looked at the new chocolate brown, but it wouldn't work with the cabinets. Marie had decided to paint her cabinets light blue with white trim, add white eyelet cafe curtains and have the hardwood floors refinished. She would put down a few throw rugs for color and make blue and white buffalo-plaid cushions for the white kitchen chairs. Dillon's was sending a crew to the house next week to start on the bathrooms and install the new kitchen appliances. Johnny could plumb the new dishwasher and the bathrooms, once Dillon's finished the framework. They would come back later in the month to finish the job.

    Jill and Marie were planning to complete all the upgrades this winter and be ready for guests when spring arrived. They made plans to wallpaper the bedrooms in subtle floral prints and had narrowed the choices down to six. Selecting wallpaper was akin to a root canal, thought Jill. A color scheme for the new upstairs bath was still up in the air. They were trying to choose between black and white or navy and white. Marie had planted lots of tulip and daffodil bulbs, which would give the place a lot of color come next April. She already had loads of perennials which would bloom when the temperatures got warmer and the color from the bulbs had faded. Jill had been working with a graphic designer to come up with a logo for the inn. They had considered a few names: The Creviston Cottage, Marie's Bed & Breakfast, The Colonial Inn, The Hoosier Hospitality Inn, but were still undecided on a name.

Immersing herself in this project had gone a long way toward Jill's healing. She was still taking the prescribed dosage of Valium and the doctor wanted her to remain on it indefinitely. She didn't like the idea of not being able to have a drink; what could one or two possibly hurt? She'd have to give that some thought.

CHAPTER 18

Wednesday night came and like clockwork, Mike wasn't home. Janet knocked at the door and asked Dianne if she was ready. "Ready as I'll ever be. How do you psych yourself up to spy on your husband? Anyway, Mom picked Phillip up, so we could sit and have a drink before we leave. What's your preference?"

"Well, if I have to drink one, make it a sweet old-fashioned. I love those things, almost too much. Has anything new happened since Monday? It's incredible how you've been able to keep quiet and not say anything to him. How do you do it?'

"It's easy, I don't want to get his temper riled, who knows what he'd do, that's why. If I catch him red handed, he'll not be able to deny it. I wonder what she's like."

"Who? Oh, you mean the little tramp he's sleeping with. Or, have you considered it could be some nice girl who got taken in by a smooth talker. I suppose I have no right to make judgment, based on my life at the moment."

"Okay, that was a cryptic statement, what's going on with you? Come on, talk to me. I know you too well; you don't say things like that without a reason."

"Oh, it's probably just me. My marriage has not turned

out like I hoped. We just don't click; we never spend time together, he doesn't get home until the wee hours of the morning. He isn't interested in the same things I am; we're living separate lives. Plus, my parents don't approve of him and that hurts me. Maybe we're just going through a slump. "Hey, look at the time, we'd better go."

They parked on a dimly-lit street near the tavern. From this vantage point, they could see people coming and going through the front door as well as a good view of the parking lot and Mike's truck. He usually came home around nine, so eight was a good time to start their surveillance. They could hear the music coming from the bar and could see a few people milling around inside.

It wasn't too long before Mike ambled out, got in his truck and drove away. "Let's follow him, Janet; I want to know where he's going."

"Well, it looks like he's headed home. I think our little plan fizzled tonight. We might have to repeat this tactic or just wait and see what happens."

"Can you take me by to pick up Phillip? Thanks so much for your time. I know you had to cancel your tutoring tonight. Can you make it up tomorrow night?'

"She had assignments to finish tonight, so it's just as well. This gives her the opportunity to work on her own, but I'll miss seeing Dave tonight."

"Dave? What's that about?"

"Oh, we spend a little time together after the tutoring most nights, just friendly conversation. We're both lonely and it's nice; Debbie never seems to have time for him."

Janet was reluctant to share any further details of her affair with Dave. It wasn't that her friends wouldn't understand; she felt like Dave wouldn't approve.

"Hmm, are you sure that's all it is? He's a good-looking guy. I've heard a lot of things about him over the years."

"Yes, I've heard the same things, but it's hard to match the rumors to the man."

"Be careful, Janet. You know how jealous Robert is, you might find yourself in a bad situation."

Timing was everything and this time it saved her. "Well, here we are, run in and get your son, I'll wait out here."

Dianne and Phillip got into the car and they drove silently back to her house. The girls knew better than to talk in front of a child. Janet dropped them off and headed home. There were lights on at her house, did Robert get off early? She walked in and there he was; dinner was on the table and he had even bought a bottle of wine. She was shocked; first off, she wasn't aware he knew a thing about wine, she thought, what's going on here?

"What are you doing home, Robert? This is a surprise. Did you take the night off for some reason?"

"No, they gave me the night off, so I can work the day shift tomorrow. I got a promotion to Shift Supervisor and now I'll be working days. I'll go in at seven and get off at four. Isn't that about the best news we've had lately?"

"Wow, that's wonderful, Robert." She was so stunned she could hardly speak; she felt like her life was being turned upside down. Dani's tutoring, Dave, their evenings together, the freedom she had enjoyed. Was it all about to end? Robert always insisted on knowing her whereabouts every minute of every day when he was home on weekends; she shuddered to think she would now have to cope with that every night. A horrific thought entered her head, what if this had happened the night Dave was here?

"Come here and give me a kiss to celebrate and we'll sit down for dinner. I stopped and picked up steaks at the grocery, I'm about to get them off the grill right now. By the way, where've you been tonight?"

She sidestepped his request for a kiss, saying "Oh, I had the night off, so I stopped by to see Dianne. She fixed me a drink and we started talking. You know how that goes. Mike wasn't home yet, so we had a nice chat."

"What's going on with her? Is she still working? Mike wasn't crazy about that idea, but I guess he's adjusted to it."

"She was just telling me about the market she attended last weekend. She went with Mrs. Morrow and had a fantastic time. She loves her job. Speaking of jobs, has this been in the works, your promotion, you haven't said a word about it?"

"Yes and no. I knew the job was opening up, but I didn't know if I'd get it, so I didn't want to get your hopes up. I know how you've hated spending every night by yourself."

"This will be great, but it will be an adjustment for both of us. I have a couple of months left on my tutoring and sometimes I work late at the plant, usually at month end."

"Can't they get someone else to do that tutoring? I'd rather you were home than out there every night."

"Robert," she said curtly, "I've made a commitment and I'm going to keep it. She is a difficult teenager and I've been able to get through to her. Changing tutors now could be a real setback for her, besides, I enjoy it. It's very rewarding and it will only be for a couple more months, probably shortly after Christmas, after this semester is over."

"Well, I can live with that if I have to; but it doesn't mean I have to like it. I suppose the money is good, not that you need it, what with your big job at the plant, Chief Accountant, whatever the hell that means."

She could hear the sarcasm in his voice and she didn't like it, at all. Her job stuck in his craw. But now that he had gotten a promotion, maybe he wouldn't be so jealous. In the meantime, this was going to be such a dramatic change for her; she wondered how she would cope with being on a leash. For so long, she had wanted him to have a day job so they could be a normal couple, and then, she had gotten to know Dave. The irony of the situation was unsettling; she could only hope it didn't blow up in her face.

CHAPTER 19

There were almost two hundred people at the country club for the Halloween party. The ballroom was decorated with cobwebs, ghosts, black spiders, pumpkins and black and orange streamers everywhere. Teresa thought it looked corny, especially for a high-class social event. Hors d'oeuvres covered three buffet tables and waiters circulated the room with trays of champagne-filled glasses. There was also a cash bar, popular with the men. This party was a three-step affair: first, the cocktails and snacks, second, dinner and third, the dance.

As Teresa walked around, she noticed most of the guests weren't wearing masks. Most costumes were appropriate, with only a few on the outlandish side; a tiger and a bear, Daniel Boone, Elvis, Snow White, lots of fairy tale figures, plus traditional Halloween characters. She and Ted had dressed up as Fifties' teenagers at a sock hop. Having short hair, she'd bought a fall and concocted a pony tail. Her saddle oxfords and bobby socks were far from comfortable. Ted looked cute in his black pants, pink shirt with black trim and saddle oxfords. He had a pack of cigarettes rolled up in his sleeve and his hair was slicked back in ducks. Jill and Johnny stood out; she looked precious in her blue and white pinafore with matching bonnet, carrying a cane along with a stuffed toy lamb. Johnny wore bib overalls, a tee shirt and a straw hat, "Farmer John" she concluded. Janet was wearing her Cinderella dress and Robert had on a military uniform befitting a prince; they did made a stunning couple, too bad they had problems. Dianne and Mike arrived as Anthony and Cleopatra; with her dark hair, she carried it off well; Teresa could hardly stand to look at him. I'm being a real hypocrite, she thought. What would Ted think of me if he knew about Doug?

Janet was talking to some of her old bank customers when Dave came up and joined the conversation. They hadn't been alone together for a few days and she realized how much she missed him. The other couple walked away and he smiled and raised his glass of champagne.

"Here's to you, the most gorgeous woman in the room. You look incredible tonight and I only wish I had accompanied you."

"That's sweet, Dave, but I hope no one heard that; we do have to be discreet, not raise any suspicions. Do you suppose it would be appropriate if we danced together later?"

"I'll ask Robert if he minds, maybe he won't; then we can at least have a few minutes together tonight."

"I have something else to tell you; the factory gave Robert a promotion to Shift Supervisor and moved him to days."

"Oh, that certainly puts a different spin on things; will that interfere with your tutoring?"

"No, of course not, I told him that was a commitment I'd made and it wasn't up for discussion. He backed off."

"We'll just have to become more creative, Janet. You know the old adage: "Where there's a will, there's a way" and I don't think either of us is lacking in will."

Robert walked up and Dave congratulated him on his promotion. He told Robert his wife had been bragging, which made him puff up with pride. Dave is a real diplomat, thought Janet; he should have gone into politics.

The cocktail hour was over and the guests filed in to locate their place cards. Not everyone was thrilled with the arrangement; couples would not be seated at the same table. Supposedly, this practice promoted lively conversations and the networking was always good for the small business members of the club.

Of all people, Teresa found herself seated next to Linda, Doug's wife, a situation she didn't relish. She wondered if the person in charge of the seating had a bizarre sense of humor. A welcome addition to the table was Marie, Jill's mother. Teresa was anxious to hear all about the new bed & breakfast she and Jill were planning. There were a few guests at the table that were new to her, so perhaps she might pick up leads for her real estate agency.

Janet hoped Robert would be okay with this unique table configuration. He wasn't adept at social skills and had no concept of small talk. He'll have to flounder through it. Everyone has to learn the social graces at some point, but she feared he would embarrass her. He was sitting with the town marshal and a local grocery store owner. Luckily, she was seated at a table across from Dave. Ted Farris was to her right and to the left was the owner of the Five & Dime, a nice guy, but a bit boring. Doug was the last one to take his seat. Great, she thought, Doug and Ted both at my table.

Mike Powers and Debbie Brown ended up at a table seated next to each other. Jill was also at that table as well as Toni, Kris Howard's girlfriend. This should be an interesting evening, thought Jill. I will definitely need to watch what I say. She really wanted a drink, just one, maybe a glass of champagne. The waiter came by and she discreetly grabbed one; she didn't want Johnny to see her having a drink. Mike was busy trying to impress Debbie; who thought he was cute in a rugged sort of way and was flirting shamelessly with him. Mike was eating it up, one of the "in" women coming onto him.

Johnny and Dianne were two of the last guests to locate their seats. They were together at a table along with the high school principal and the florist, plus a new girl in town, Vicki Grey. Everyone introduced themselves, and soon lively conversations were under way. Dianne asked Vicki how long she'd been in town and Vickie replied "Only for about two months, I started working at the lumber yard behind the counter; my parents knew the owner and recommended me. I like the town."

"It's a great place to live; I work at the dress shop, Molly's, down on Elm. You'll have to come by; we have lots of things that'd be cute on you. By the way, my husband is in the lumber yard all the time; I'll bet you've met him, Mike Powers?"

"Vicki turned white as a sheet and said shakily, "Yes, I think I might have met him; I meet so many construction workers on a daily basis."

"Oh, I didn't say he worked construction; but I suppose that was a logical assumption. He works at Dillon's; he's their superintendent."

Vicki couldn't believe what she was hearing. She had thought Mike was such a great guy; when in truth, he was a two-timing jerk. "Sounds like you both have good jobs; do you have children?"

"Yes, a son, Phillip, he's in third grade." Vicki wished the floor would open up and swallow her; she was mortified.

Meanwhile, at Teresa's table, Linda was talking about Beth, her daughter and how much she and Doug adored her. She also mentioned a trip they were planning; Teresa thought Linda was really trying to needle her. Marie noticed the tension building between the two women and tried changing the subject to her new project. Unfortunately, it didn't work; those two were more interested in upstaging each other.

"Oh, by the way, Teresa," Linda asked, "what scent are you wearing? It smells familiar, but I can't place it."

"Chanel No. 5, why do you ask?"

"I've noticed someone else wearing that scent lately. I'm not sure who."

Why would she care what perfume I wear? Oh my God, I bet she has smelled that perfume on Doug recently. I always wear it when I'm with him. She is definitely a smart cookie. I'll either have to switch scents or just not wear any.

At her table, Janet was having the same problem as Marie, trying to steer the conversation in another direction. Doug and Ted didn't have a lot to say to each other. For Doug, the salesman, this was completely out of character. Someone asked him about the insurance business and he replied that things were good these days. Janet asked Ted about the new construction and when the house might be finished. He told her now that the weather was getting cold; they would be working on the interior. When spring arrives, they'd finish the exterior. Doug asked who was writing the insurance for the spec homes and Ted didn't know. Doug said he'd be interested in getting that business. Janet thought, yeah, fat chance of Ted helping you, Doug, like the proverbial snowball in hell.

Salads and small loaves of bread were served. Someone noted, "How interesting, everyone has quit talking now that the food has arrived." Next, the waiters served the entree, prime rib au jus, small red potatoes and asparagus. The meal was wonderful, but it was all Vicki could do to choke it down. Why had she ever come here tonight? Her boss at the lumber yard had given her his extra ticket, thinking she could meet some of the locals. Well, she certainly had. What a way to start off in a new community.

The dessert, Bananas Foster, was the highlight of the meal. First, trays laden with dishes of ice cream were brought out. Then, the waiters took center stage with their hot plates on wheels, quickly preparing the syrup with brown sugar, butter, lemon and cinnamon. Next, they topped the ice cream with sliced bananas, poured the syrup over the bananas, drizzled the rum over the syrup, lit a match and flambee'd the dessert. It was a spectacular sight and quite delicious. The kitchen had scored a home run on this dish.

Soon, tables were cleared, coffee was served and the band began playing the first set, which was always soft and easy. Dancers took to the floor. Mike showed up to ask Dianne for a dance and when he saw Vicki, his jaw dropped. She stared daggers at him and he knew he was busted. He took Dianne's hand and they joined the others dancers. He asked her if she was enjoying the people at her table.

"Mike, everyone's nice, especially Vicki, I may ask her over for a dinner party soon. She's new in town and doesn't know anyone, except her co-workers." Mike was getting visibly nervous. "What's the matter with you? Are you feeling alright?"

"Actually, Dianne, I'm not; I may have to go home. Maybe it was something I ate. You can stay if you like."

"Oh, are you sure you're going to be okay? I can get a ride home with someone. I'm just not ready to leave yet; the party just started." He assured her he would be fine and made his escape.

When Mike and Dianne started dancing, Vicki excused herself and went to the ladies room. She wasn't feeling too well herself, hurt, angry, disappointed, embarrassed, a litany of emotions. As she exited the restroom, she saw Mike leaving the building. She followed and quickly caught up with him.

"Hey" she called. He turned around and saw her. "You lying son-of-a-bitch, playing Mr. Nice Guy, taking me to an elaborate dinner, acting like you were falling for me. I think you're a total creep and for two cents, I'd tell your wife. She's nice; she sure deserves better than you. If I ever see your face again, it will be too soon."

"Vicki, please let me explain. Give me a chance, please. I didn't set out to hurt you, just the opposite. My marriage is on the rocks and has been for a long time; I saw you and couldn't help myself. I knew if I told you the truth, you wouldn't go out with me, not in a million years, so I lied to you. I needed an incentive to end my marriage and I put you in that role. I am so sorry. Please, Vicki, try to understand."

"I can't deal with this right now. I am too confused to think straight. What you say makes sense, but I hate the cheating and the lying; that's why I'm no longer engaged. It's not fair to your wife; she's sweet and I feel like a home wrecker. Just leave me alone." She turned and hurried back inside, not wanting to spend another minute of her time with him.

Dianne was talking to one of her customers when she saw Vicki coming back to the table. "Vicki, I want to introduce you to some of my friends. Come with me." She located Janet and Teresa, saying "I want you both to meet a new girl in town, Vicki Grey; she just moved here recently and we need to make her feel welcome. We're supposed to get together at my place a week from Monday night for drinks and I want Vicki to come." She looked at Vicki and said, "Does that work for you?"

Vicki felt like she was being railroaded. "Sure, Dianne, thanks for asking me. I'll give you my number and you can call me with the details."

Dave smiled at Janet as he walked toward her. "Hey, I got your husband's permission to have this dance. Will you kindly do me the honor?" Janet laughed as they joined the other dancers.

"You are such a gentleman" she said, mocking him. "One of my friends has already warned me against you; I told her you were harmless."

"Oh, harmless is it, well, we'll just have to see about that." The band broke into "Sweet Soul Music", an Arthur Conley tune and he twirled her around the floor like a pro.

"I take back whatever I said, you are a fabulous dancer. I continue to learn such wonderful things about you; I'm very impressed." He escorted her back to her seat, whispering to her on the way, "I can't wait to see you on Monday night." Janet had butterflies in her stomach; she felt like a teenager with her first crush.

Teresa had been unable to speak to Doug all evening, due to the close proximity of Linda. He and Ted stopped by at almost the same time to lead their wives in a slow dance. Doug winked at her as they took the floor. She thought back over some of the other parties and in comparison, at least for them, this one was a flop. To her surprise, Robert cut in on Doug and Linda; then a domino effect took place. She ended up dancing with Doug, while Ted ended up dancing with Dianne, whose husband seemed to be missing.

"Linda, you look good enough to eat" gushed Robert as he spun her around the floor. "I've been watching you all evening, sitting next to Teresa; I'll bet that's an interesting conversation. You know I could make you a lot happier than that half-ass husband of yours; if you'd only give me a chance."

"Robert, between you and me, that opportunity may come along sooner than we both expect. Who knows?" She was teasing and flirting with him, enjoying every minute of it because she knew he wanted her, bad.

"I've been waiting all evening to put my arms around you" Doug whispered to Teresa as he held her a little too close.

"Watch it, big boy; I'm sure Linda is watching. She asked about my perfume. Has she smelled it on your shirt?"

"Oh, I suppose, but right now, who cares. I want to enjoy the moment. Are we still on for this week, usual time and place?"

"Yes, of course, have you worked out anything on an overnight trip? It would be wonderful to wake up next to you."

"I'm looking at an insurance convention in a couple of weeks; you need to come up with a reason to be away for the night."

"I think I can manage that; there are always two-day realtor classes which require an overnight stay."

The song ended and he said "See you" and she floated back to her chair, still next to Linda, who was none too happy.

"Why is it you always end up dancing with my husband, Teresa? I know the two of you have a history; after all, he's your old flame; are you trying to rekindle it?"

"Linda, I'm going to pretend that you didn't ask me those questions. Now, can we be civil to one another for the remainder of the evening?"

Linda took her clutch bag and headed for the ladies room. Teresa began talking to Marie about her bed and breakfast, wondering what they were planning to call it. Marie asked her if a situation arose, such as new clients coming to town needing an overnight room; would she be so kind as to recommend the inn? Teresa assured her she would do so, gladly. Apparently, they planned on being open to book guests by the first of April.

The band was playing its' encore song and she noticed people saying good night and preparing to leave; she knew Ted would be ready to go. The evening had been a big success for the club; they were bound to sign up new members as a result. For the town to prosper, this club had to become an important asset to the community.

On the way out, Teresa saw Dianne and asked her what had happened to Mike. "Oh, I think he had a tummy ache, something like that" she said in a facetious tone. Jill and Johnny were giving her a lift home; it seemed they were the only couple amongst her friends who seemed happy. Jill was feeling very dizzy; she had indulged in too many glasses of champagne and didn't want to tell Johnny, but she had to hang onto him or lose her footing. They finally made it home; she told Johnny she felt nauseous and went straight to the bathroom. Trying to throw up in the stool, she was reeling and went backwards, falling into the tub and hitting her head. She was out cold.

Johnny came running into the bathroom, "What the hell happened, Jill?" She didn't answer; he picked her up and carried her to the sofa. Calling Dr. Nelson this late was not what he wanted to do, but he had no choice. Once he got the doctor on the phone, he explained how he'd found her, that she was knocked out and that she might have had a few drinks.

"Okay, Johnny, I'm just getting home from the club too, so I'll run over and check on her." About fifteen minutes later, Dr. Nelson was at the door. Jill was beginning to come around; he checked her heartbeat and blood pressure, and looked at her eyes.

"Jill, it's obvious to me you've been drinking tonight. Your heart is racing, your pupils are dilated and your blood pressure is up. You need to rest; I'm giving you something to counteract the effect of the alcohol. This could have been a very serious episode. I don't know if you have a concussion from your fall; Johnny says it was so loud he could hear it from upstairs, but just to be on the safe side, I want you to rest for two or three days. A concussion is a bruise on the brain and it needs rest to heal. Young lady, you are very lucky."

Jill and Johnny thanked him for coming. He helped her to the bedroom and got her pajamas out of the drawer. "Can you get undressed, or do you need me to help you?"

"Johnny, you're so wonderful, I can do it myself. I'm going to be okay; I just need to get to bed. Are the kids asleep?"

"Yes, they're in bed, the sitter went home and I'll be here tomorrow, so you're going to stay in bed for the day. I'll take care of the boys. Then on Monday, your Mom can come over while I go to work. Maybe by Tuesday, you'll be good as new."

Jill turned over and fell asleep. Johnny was really worried about her; she needed to kick this depression, but he wasn't sure Valium was the solution. Maybe this project with her mother would be the answer, keeping her busy with something more to do than dealing with the kids.

CHAPTER 20

When Jill awoke on Sunday morning, she didn't recall the events of the night before. She was shocked to hear that Dr. Nelson had made a house call. Apparently, she had suffered a black-out; this scenario frightened her. She didn't like not being in control of herself and especially not remembering. Had she blacked out like alcoholics do or was it the fall in the tub? At any rate, she had a very large lump on the back of her head and apparently, she was supposed to rest for a couple of days. That's a joke, she thought, there is never a minutes' peace around here with three boys. She loved them dearly, but at times, they simply drove her crazy. Am I crazy, she pondered; no, I'm just a mom. Johnny was taking them to his parents today so they'd be out of her hair. Then, tomorrow her mother was coming over to help out. Poor Mom; what would I do without her? I wonder if my sister and I got on her nerves when we were little; well, of course we did. We still do at times; it's just part of being a parent.

She got out of bed, poured a cup of coffee and sat down to read the paper. The print was blurry. This isn't right, my eyesight is perfect. She picked up a book, same result. She turned on the television and sat down. The local news was on and snow was forecast, early November, not unusual, but she hated it. Bad roads, ice, freezing rain, cars that won't start, all the fun things of winter. She couldn't wait.

Jill started feeling sleepy again. She was hungry, but didn't feel like fixing anything. The phone rung and as she got up to answer it, she began to feel dizzy again. It was Dianne, asking how she was doing. She did remember them taking Dianne home last night, but that was before her fall. She related the events of the prior evening to Dianne and told her how she was currently feeling. Dianne insisted on coming right over.

She walked in without knocking and was shocked to see how pale Jill looked. "Can I get you anything?" Dianne asked. "Yes, if you could please fix me a couple slices of toast and a cup of coffee, and get yourself a cup while you're at it. Have you eaten breakfast yet?" Dianne wasn't interested in food, just coffee; she buttered the toast, asked Jill if she wanted jelly, which she did not, and poured their coffee.

"Jill, do you think you still need the Valium? Maybe you could begin to taper off, or at least, don't drink alcohol of any kind as long as you're on it. I know it's hard, everyone else is having a drink; you want one too. But this you don't need. Have you told Johnny your sight is blurry?"

"No, not yet. Hopefully, it will improve as the swelling goes down. If it's still this way in a couple of days, I'll go in to see Dr. Nelson. Can you believe he actually made a house call last night? That is incredible. Doctors have hardly done that since the fifties."

Dianne looked around. The sink was full of dirty dishes, every toy was out of the toy box, empty coke cans and potato chip bags were strewn around the living room. "Okay, what can I do around here to help you? Maybe I can gather up the laundry and catch it up? Then, I'll do the breakfast dishes and pick up the clutter. I'll have this place spiffy in no time."

"Dianne, please sit down. You don't have to do any of that. Johnny will take care of things; Mom is coming tomorrow and I'll be back in business in a couple of days."

"Okay, but I am going to do the dishes. Men hate that job. What did you think of Vicki last night? Mike didn't seem to remember her from the lumber yard, which is strange, as pretty as she is. I don't know what his problem was last night; he was fine this morning. Anyway, she is coming to lunch with us tomorrow. I hope you'll feel like going, but don't push it. It's not that important."

"I thought she was very nice, actually a knockout. She looks like the girl on "Peyton Place", Barbara Parkins. Did you notice that?"

"I hadn't thought about it, but now that you mention it, she does. Anyway, she is a beautiful girl; I can't believe she doesn't have a boyfriend, but as pretty as she is, that won't last long. Hey, I'm keeping you from resting. Go back to sleep and I'll clean up the kitchen."

As Jill dozed off, she was thinking how lucky she was to have such a wonderful friend. Two hours later she woke up and saw that Dianne had picked up the clutter in the living room, ran the sweeper, emptied ashtrays, washed and folded towels and some of the boy's clothes. Jill chastised her, "Dianne, sit down with me for a cigarette. You've done enough, thank you so much. Please don't think you have to spend the entire day here; when you have two days off a week, I'm sure you have things of your own you'd like to be doing. I'll be fine, Johnny should be home soon."

"I do need to leave soon, I have some errands to run; after that, I'm going home and put my feet up for an hour or so. Mike was taking Phillip to a movie this afternoon and I'll have the house to myself. Hallelujah! Let me know if you feel like going to lunch tomorrow and I'll pick you up."

Jill doubted she'd feel like lunch tomorrow. It took all her energy to make a cup of coffee. She had no interest or motivation to do much of anything. She felt like she was slogging through a sea of mud. I don't even feel anything when I hug my kids. What kind of person am I becoming? Maybe counseling is the answer. I still have those phone numbers Dr. Nelson gave me. The first thing I need to do tomorrow is make an appointment with one of them. I can't stand this numbness.

The next morning, Jill opened her eyes and things didn't seem as blurry. She sat up and the dizziness washed over her, so she laid back down. She could hear Johnny coming up the stairs with her coffee and she sat up slowly this time.

"Good morning sunshine. Your mother is here with the kids and I'm off to work. How are you feeling; you have a little more color today. Is there anything else I can get for you before I go?"

"I was dizzy when I sat up the first time, but I'm okay now. My plan today is to make an appointment with one of the counselors and take it easy. My eyes seem better today too. Will you try to be home early so Mom can leave?"

"Sure, I'll be back here by four this afternoon. If you need anything, call my mother and she'll know where to find us." He leaned over and kissed her goodbye and left the room whistling.

Jill could never understand how anyone could be so chipper in the morning. Did he ever have a negative thought? Comparing her husband to those of her friends, Johnny was by far the best. She sighed, lit a cigarette and leaned back on the pillow. The noise coming from downstairs was deafening, but the smell of bacon was tantalizing and she suddenly realized she was very hungry; perhaps breakfast with her family would get this day off to a good start.

Everyone showed up for lunch at Millie's, except Jill. Dianne commented that she wasn't surprised and related to them the events of the prior weekend. Janet was upset over Robert's shift change and the effect it would have on her life. Dianne was sure Mike was seeing another woman; Vicki sat there wishing she could disappear. Teresa didn't have much to say; after her confrontation with Linda, she didn't even want to think about it. Each girl seemed to have her own agenda today; consequently, it wasn't the usual harmonious setting. Vicki said she needed to get back to the lumber yard and bypassed lunch. The checks came and soon everyone was gone except Teresa and Janet.

Teresa said glumly, "I'm almost sure Linda knows; she recognized my perfume; I'm sure she's smelled it on Doug after one of our afternoons. We're planning a night out of town, the week after Thanksgiving. Something to look forward to, isn't that a large part of happiness?"

"Yes, along with someone to love and something to do. That is overly simplified, but there's a lot of truth to it.

Teresa, I don't think I'm going to stay married to Robert much longer; I'm not happy with him and I don't see much of a future for us. Our lives are moving in two different directions. His shift change jolted me into reality. I have become used to having my nights free and it's going to be a tremendous adjustment."

"Does this have anything to do with Dave Brown? I noticed the two of you together Saturday night and I know there's something happening there. Others might not notice, but I've known you too many years."

"Yes, you do know me too well; it has everything to do with Dave. He makes me happy; Teresa, we have so much in common and he's a wonderful lover. I can't find any redeeming qualities in Robert lately; he suffers by comparison. Truly, there is no comparison. But now, with his different hours, I won't have the freedom or the opportunity to see Dave once the tutoring is over. At least, we have that right now."

"You'd better be careful. I think Robert could be mean if he's crossed. The last thing you need is for him to find out about Dave. You'd have hell to pay and Dave would too."

Janet crushed her cigarette in the ashtray. "How well I know. I've got to plan this very carefully. It would be easier if I just got out of the marriage. That's the direction I'm leaning. Damn, look at the time; I've got to get back for a meeting."

"Okay, see you later; things have got to get better, for both of us. Call me when you have a minute."

CHAPTER 21

Melanie was planning to stop by Linda's after lunch today. She was still in a quandary over telling her about Teresa and her husband having coffee at Millie's. I would want to know, she thought, but what will she do with the information?

When she walked in, Linda was feeding the baby, "As the World Turns" was blaring from the television and her hair looked like it had never seen a comb. My God; is this what having a baby does to a woman? Maybe I won't have one, but, in any case; finding a husband first might be the best. Wow, the way she looks, this story will send her one of two ways, either into a bad case of the blues or she'll be hell on wheels. Knowing her sister, Melanie was betting on the latter.

"Hi Mel, get yourself a cup of coffee and turn the TV down so we can visit. It's been a while since you've been here. Hasn't Beth grown? She takes so much time; it seems like I never get anything done. I'm just not very organized. "

"That will come with time, I suppose. How are you and Doug getting along? Any more arguments over Teresa?"

"Oh, you haven't heard the latest. I had to sit right next to her at dinner Saturday night at the club. I smelled her perfume and I'm sure it's the same scent I noticed on Doug a couple of months ago, Chanel No. Five. Then, of course, she ended up dancing with him toward the end of the evening. For days before one of these parties, I feel this terrible dread of going, knowing what is going to happen. It's driving me nuts. I know something is going on, but what am I supposed to do?"

"I can tell you one thing I know. Do you remember Toni, Kris Howard's girlfriend? Well, she works at Millie's and a while back, Teresa was in the restaurant and Doug came in and sat down with her. Toni said they were real chummy. She couldn't hear their conversation, but as Teresa was leaving, he was holding her hand. They were there for about fifteen minutes. Teresa had been sitting with another girl, who left before Doug got there. So, I think it was a chance meeting."

Linda's heart sunk. "Possibly; unless he saw her car and went in to see her. He rarely goes to Millie's; he doesn't like it that much, so there had to be a reason for him to stop. That bastard, I know he's screwing around on me."

"I thought that would be your reaction. Maybe it hasn't gone that far yet; it could just be a flirtation. Has he had any unexplained absences?"

"No, but that doesn't mean anything. Who knows where he goes during the day? He could be most anywhere. Plus, she's selling real estate now, so she'd have a lot of flexible time to see him. How do I find out?"

"We're going to have to give that some thought. Nothing ever happens in this town that doesn't eventually hit the rumor mill, but you'd think we'd have heard something by now, especially if it's been going on for a while."

"Somehow, I'm going to find out, one way or the other and when I do; he is going to wish he'd never seen the likes of Teresa Farris. I'm wondering if Ted suspects anything."

"Probably not, men tend to be oblivious. They talk about the wife always being the last to know; I think it's the husband. It would have to smack him in the face and I imagine she's pretty careful."

"You know, one thing I need to do, is make myself a little more presentable. I try to fix myself up before he gets home, but occasionally, he stops in during the day and this is what I look like."

"Linda, don't make excuses for him, whether or not you put lipstick on shouldn't make a damn bit of difference. The only thing I can say about that is fixing yourself up would give you a better outlook; if you look good, you feel good. But, he needs to grow up and quit being so selfish. I'm going to have to go; I have a few more stops to make, but let me know if I can do anything to help you in this situation."

Doug had made reservations for the week after Thanksgiving at a new hotel in Indy. That was almost three weeks away, but he needed time to lay the groundwork for this trip. Even getting away overnight was a major undertaking. Maybe it wasn't a good idea; it might be too risky. Teresa was hell bent on doing this though and she wasn't a person who took "No" easily. On the other hand, it would be fun, a night away, just the two of them and in spite of everything, he found himself looking forward to it. He phoned Teresa at her office, told her the schedule and she agreed it would be fine.

Teresa looked at her calendar; a Wednesday night might work, Ted doesn't have any obligations on Wednesday, so he'd be here with the girls. I feel so guilty; what would Ted do if he found out? Would he divorce me, or forgive me and want to stay married? As well as she knew him, she wasn't sure of the answer. She had found a two-day realty course she could sign up to attend that week. This should be simple for me, maybe not so much so for Doug.

Doug called Linda before heading home to see if she needed anything. "Yes, I could use a pack of Winston's and a jar of Vaseline. I think Beth is getting a diaper rash and I don't want it to get any worse."

Doug was not anxious to get home; Linda didn't seem to care how she looked since the baby came; she had always kept herself up before. There was no romance in their married life; it had become drudgery to him. He didn't know if being with Teresa had caused him to become dissatisfied with his marriage, or vice versa. She never talked about her marriage, so he could only surmise it wasn't that good; otherwise, why would she be with me?

CHAPTER 22

Janet ran home before going out to see Dani. Robert was already there; she told him supper was in the electric skillet, a pot roast with potatoes and carrots, one of his favorites. She changed into jeans and a sweater, reassuring him she'd be home as soon as possible. As she walked to her car, she was thinking that was too easy. I wonder if he's up to something. She hated not completely trusting Robert, but he didn't share any of his thoughts with her and she felt he was much too secretive.

When she walked in at the Browns', Dani and Dave were both waiting for her. They were excited to tell her that Dani would be able to get rid of her crutches in two weeks and possibly return to school.

"That's wonderful, Dani. That means you'd be going back right after Thanksgiving. Isn't that what the doctors said originally; that the best possible outcome would be late November?"

"Yes, Mrs. Steele, I'm so excited to be going back to school, to see my friends and have my life back, but I am going to miss you so much. You've been like a second mom to me. Will you keep coming over to see me?"

"Dani, I'm going to miss you too, and I'd love to come

back to see you, but you're going to be so busy with your friends and activities, you won't have time for anything else." Dave was standing in the background, looking crestfallen, mirroring her feelings. Oh boy, what else could go awry?

"We should get started on your lessons; we want to be sure to keep caught up in the next few weeks. Dave, I'll see you later?" He nodded and left the room.

An hour later, Dani was finished with her bookkeeping; she needed to read three chapters of "Grapes of Wrath" for English, after which she and Janet would discuss it. She took the book and headed to her room. She ran into her dad as she was going upstairs and said to him: "She's all yours, Dad." Little did she know she had just uttered a prophetic statement.

Dave came in and sat down beside Janet. They looked into one another's eyes, holding hands, each trying to comprehend the events of the past few days, what was happening? Will it be over between them? She waited for him to take the lead, something she had never learned with Robert.

"Janet, we have three weeks left of tutoring, time for us to figure out how to go on from here. It's something we both need to think about, how we'll be able to see each other; I can get away most any evening, but now it's going to be tough for you. Do you ever go out with your friends for the evening? What about meetings, or time during the day? That might be the answer. We could work around Robert and Debbie's schedules. We could meet here; we're a bit more secluded, but would you feel comfortable?

"Dave, I'd feel comfortable with you anywhere. I just want to be with you, as much as possible." He took her in his arms and kissed her lovingly. He whispered to her, "We've got the downstairs to ourselves until at least eleven. Debbie went to Fort Wayne tonight, so she'll be late. Dani never leaves her room once she gets there, what with the crutches." He stood up and went to close the door to the den. They made love in desperation, as though this could be the last time, holding on as tightly as possible to the joy they were feeling. Afterwards, as she lay in his arms, he kissed her tenderly and rubbed her back. "Janet, I've fallen in love with you. I don't want to scare you away, but I want to spend the rest of my life loving you."

"My darling Dave, I love you too, more than you'll ever know. This is the happiest I've ever been; I too want it to last forever. And you can't scare me away; you couldn't run me off if you tried."

"Since we both feel this way, don't you think we should start making plans for the future? We're both in dead-end marriages; should we consider separating so we can be together? Or do you think we'd be rushing it?"

"No, I don't, but you'd be giving up a lot more than I would. You wouldn't see your kids as often and you'd probably have to give up this house."

"Janet, I don't see the kids now; they're out and gone all the time; you know how teenagers are. As for this house, Debbie can have it; we can build our own place. Of course, I'll pay child support and maybe even alimony."

"Okay, then what is our time frame? My house belongs solely to me; Robert would have to find another place to live. Of course, I would never mention you; he is going to be very angry and hurt, but he's a strong guy. He'll make it. I will skip tutoring tomorrow night and talk to him. Then, I'll see you on Wednesday night. How does that sound?"

"That's great. Now, are you afraid of him? Has he ever hit you or threatened you?"

"No, he hasn't, but he does have a jealous streak and a temper; that's why I'm not mentioning you. I don't think he'd ever hurt you or me, but he might threaten."

"I'll be home tomorrow evening, call if you need me. Meanwhile, until the dust settles with him, we'll keep our meetings brief. I will tell Debbie this weekend, best we don't do it the very same day; you know the gossip mill."

"Absolutely, now I do have to go; I love you and I'll call you tomorrow."

"I love you too, Janet; I love saying those words and hearing you say them. You make me the happiest man on earth, corny as that sounds."

"It's not corny when it's true." She kissed him good night and hurried to the car. This was a sudden turn of events; circumstances beyond their control were dictating their future. First, Robert changing shifts and then, Dani not needing her any more. Fate does intervene. She dreaded going home, how was she going to act normal when she was planning on ending their marriage the very next day?

CHAPTER 23

That evening at dinner, Teresa told Ted about the real estate seminar in Indianapolis the week after Thanksgiving.

"The seminar is a four-day event, Monday through Thursday, but looking at the schedule; I am only interested in the seminars on Wednesday and Thursday, which means I will stay over on Wednesday night. There are special rates at the hotel for those attending the seminar. Rita, my friend who took the course with me, wants to share a room. Will that work for you, being here with the girls for the night?"

"Do I have a choice; it seems like you have everything covered. Apparently, you feel okay in making these decisions, instead of the two of us discussing them. Your career has sure changed you and I don't think it's for the better. In the past, we have always talked about things; what's happened to that?"

"So, are you saying you don't want me to go? I don't object to your weekend fishing trips, which you never discuss first with me. Someone wants to go fishing; you guys decide what weekend and then you tell the wives. What's different about this? Oh, I know, it's because I'm the wife, not the husband."

"Women's Lib, is that what you're touting now? That's all

over the news, Gloria, what's her name and her cronies. Is that where this is coming from? And, no, I don't care if you go, but I don't like the way you approached it. Just let me know a couple of days in advance, so I'll be sure to be home early to be with the kids."

Ted got up from the table without finishing his dinner and went to the living room to pout. He lit a cigarette, picked up the newspaper and said nothing the remainder of the evening. It was indeed a very chilly night in the Farris household.

Teresa was surprised at his reaction. Obviously, her job bothered him far more than he'd ever indicated. She was earning nice commissions, but it was nowhere near what he made for a living. Was he afraid she'd eventually surpass him in earnings? She knew this was a possibility, if she excelled in her job, which she had every intention of doing. At least, she hadn't been forbidden to go, which would have caused a huge blowup. He didn't dare do that. Now, she was free to see Doug that night and oh, what a night it would be. She felt giddy just thinking about it.

Doug walked in the house with the Vaseline and Winston's. Linda was in the kitchen, trying to put together grilled cheese sandwiches, a pitiful excuse for an evening meal. She looked like crap. He kissed her and asked about her day.

"How in the hell do you think it was? I've been cooped up in this house for days; I never get out of here, you're never home and I have no help. So how do you think it's going?"

"Sorry I asked. I didn't realize you were so overwhelmed. Do you need household help?"

"There's no way I'm going to have anyone come in here to help. How would that look to everyone? Especially your mother! She would never let me forget it. No, I have to learn how to cope and you need to help out once in a while."

"What do you want me to do? I have to work to keep a roof over our heads; let me have the baby and you go take a hot bath and relax. I'll fix us a sandwich and feed Beth. Your stress is probably rubbing off on her, making her cranky. It's a vicious cycle."

Linda gladly left Beth with Doug and went upstairs to bathe. She had been doing a lot of thinking about him and Teresa and it was killing her, making her crazy with jealousy. How could she find out; certainly not by asking him. He became irate when Teresa's name was even mentioned. Denial, denial, denial. She definitely needed her sister's help; Melanie would know what to do. She sat down in the tub and wondered if things would ever be right in their marriage again. Maybe if she initiated sex tonight, that would help. That was one place where they had never had an issue. After her bath, she applied lotion to her freshly shaven legs and the rest of her body. Brushing her hair, she was anxious to get him in bed. I'll show him a real woman!

After putting the baby down for the night, Doug came into the bedroom. "Are you feeling any better?" She came out of the bathroom wearing a filmy piece of lingerie.

"Do you think I look like I feel better? Why don't you find out for yourself." She walked over to him and started unbuttoning his shirt and kissing him. He found himself responding; they hadn't had sex since Beth had been born. Even though that had only been a couple of months, it seemed like an eternity. Being with his wife was easy, she was warm and loving; definitely not as exciting as Teresa, but comforting. He felt like he was home.

Afterwards, Linda fell asleep immediately. He laid there for what seemed like hours thinking about his situation. Could he be satisfied long term with his marriage or did he want Teresa to be his wife? Then, if Teresa was his wife, would it result in the same situation, a boring rut? That was the question and he didn't have an answer. Plus, he hadn't mentioned going to Indianapolis either. Tonight just wasn't the right time; he wondered, would there ever be a right time?

CHAPTER 24

Tuesday morning Janet was conducting a staff meeting when she received an urgent call from the bank. According to her instructions, the head teller was to call her with any unusual transactions on her accounts. Apparently, a check for a thousand dollars, with her signature, had cleared her personal account and the banker had deemed it suspicious. The check was made out to Arnold Epperson, the owner of a bar located near the factory. Janet surmised Robert had forged her signature. That's why he was acting so nice last night, I should have known. That low-life snake, this has to be a gambling debt; he gave me his word that his poker days were over. Obviously, I cannot believe anything that man says. I wonder how long this has been going on; he must have been really desperate to write a check out of my account. There was nothing she could do about the check, but at lunch she was drawing everything out of that account. This would not happen again.

When Dianne reached the store, the doors were still locked and it was dark. Molly isn't here for some reason, she thought, as she unlocked the door. She turned on the lights and got out the cash drawer. Was she taking the day off and

I forgot about it? She looked at the calendar and nothing was scheduled. Maybe she's just late.

Dianne busied herself steaming and tagging the new inventory. It was always fun to see the new things coming in; opening the boxes was like having Christmas every day. The bell on the door rang; it was her first customer of the day, who brought in a skirt to be matched up. She found her a coordinating jacket, shell and scarf to complete the outfit. The customer was very excited about her purchase.

Molly had still not shown up or called. Dianne was beginning to get worried, so she decided to call her. There was no answer. She had a bad feeling about this. Locating the local phone book on the back room shelf, she called Molly's neighbor, Sally Connor.

"Mrs. Connor, this is Dianne Powers and I work for your neighbor Molly. She hasn't arrived at the store yet and I'm getting concerned. This isn't like her at all. Would you mind checking on her and getting back to me? I'm at the store right now."

"Of course, Dianne, I'll go over there right now and then I'll call you back."

What seemed like hours, but in reality only fifteen minutes, the phone finally rang. It was Mrs. Connor and she told Dianne that Molly wasn't well and she and Mr. Connor would be taking her to the hospital. Dianne wasn't surprised; Molly had been unusually tired lately and not her usual energetic self. She made plans to finish up at the store and visit her at the hospital.

Lunch came and went with no customers. Dianne was beginning to think this would be a dismal sales day. Then, in walked Debbie Brown. This was her first time in the store and Dianne wanted to make sure it was worthwhile.

"Hello, Debbie, I'm glad to see you. I'd like to show you some of our new items if you have the time. Most are just out of the box. Look at this darling suit from Junior House. The jacket has the new bell sleeves and rolled collar that's so stylish in the marketplace. The mini skirt has the narrow pleats and the bright blue would look wonderful on you. And the newest look in fashion is this hounds-tooth checked dress in navy and red, a mod A-line with navy piping. Also, we just received our new shipment of fake furs; look at this: a shaded beige in a three-quarter coat with rolled cuffs, gorgeous and warm for winter. Could I find your sizes and start a dressing room?"

"These are good, Dianne, I don't need to try anything on; I'll take the suit, dress and coat, all in a size four. I also need some basic, black-wool pants and a crisp, white shirt. Plus, what do you have in turtlenecks?"

"Over here are my cashmere turtlenecks, which work well as layering pieces. They'll go nicely under jackets, or wear them alone for a more casual look. They're in the new, bright tones of hot pink, orange and turquoise. By the way, how is your daughter doing?"

"She's doing great; she'll be able to go back to school soon. I can't wait to get the tutors out of my house, especially Janet Steele. I will take those three colors, plus white and black, if you have them."

"Oh, yes, I do have the extra colors you need. Has Janet not been a good tutor?"

"She's been fine, but I think she'd rather spend time with

my husband. I've probably said too much; you're her friend, aren't you? Is she happy in her marriage or do you know?"

"Debbie, as far as I know, everything is fine with her. Maybe she and your husband were discussing Dani."

"I doubt if that's all there is to it; I will definitely be glad to see her go. Why don't you write up my things and I'll be on my way. I assume if something doesn't fit, I can return it for a refund."

"Of course, Debbie, but if something doesn't work, call me and perhaps I can put back another size for you."

"That will be $162.49, including sales tax." Debbie wrote out her check, gathered up her bags and thanked Dianne for her help.

Dianne was thrilled by the big sale, but wondered whether Debbie had been on a shopping expedition or a fishing expedition. She certainly was curious about Janet and it was probably justified. Janet had told her that she and Dave were spending time together every evening; apparently, Debbie had noticed this and didn't like it.

Janet's desk phone was ringing and her secretary picked it up. "Yes, Mrs. Steele is in, she's just away from her desk; oh, hold on, here she comes now. May I ask who is calling?" Her secretary put the phone on hold, told her it was Dianne calling and closed her door for privacy.

"Hi, Dianne, what's up?" She related the context of her conversation with Debbie and Janet was stunned. "My God, I can't believe she would be asking my friends for information. She must be desperate. I had no idea she was suspicious of us, maybe I should have known. At any rate, Dianne, it's all going to be out in the open soon. You have probably figured out by now that Dave and I are seeing one another, so I doubt Debbie will be shopping with you again."

"What do you mean, Janet? Are they separating? What about you and Robert? I'm not surprised, but are you sure this is what you want? You surely haven't been seeing him for that long."

"Long enough to know he's what I want, Dianne, we have it all. Great sex, love, conversation, humor, same interests, you name it, we've got it. It's nothing like what I've had with Robert."

"But, what about the age difference? Doesn't that bother you? Sixteen years isn't bad right now, but what about when you're fifty and he's sixty-six?"

"I'm not worried about that, Dianne; I'll think about that when the time comes. Right now, I need to call him and let him know what Debbie is doing. Thanks for calling."

Dave was in a meeting and couldn't be disturbed. With Debbie resorting to grilling my friends, what else might she do? Would she talk to Robert? That would be catastrophic. With his temper, he would be capable of anything.

Janet closed the door to her office and sat gazing out the window. The leaves were off the trees, the skies were wintry gray and it looked like it could snow. Suits my mood exactly, she thought. Maybe the best thing for me to do is file for divorce and let the dust settle before I move ahead. I know I want to spend my life with Dave, but I want it to be completely his decision. I would have gotten divorced with or without Dave, especially since this gambling debt has come up. How dare he forge a check from my account! She looked at her watch; Robert should be home by now; I need to settle this once and for all.

CHAPTER 25

Dianne closed up the store and headed for the hospital. She wanted to see for herself how Molly was doing. What if she had to close the store? Molly was sitting up in bed, but looked very pale. Apparently, she had suffered a heart attack and the doctors wanted to keep her for a few days. Her prognosis was good, if she quit working and got plenty of rest. Dianne wasn't sure how that would play out.

"My dear Dianne, I didn't want to worry you, but I am glad you had Sally check on me. I might not be here if you hadn't done that and I thank you so much. I'm sure you're wondering what happens to the store now. I've been thinking about this possibility for a while now and I've reached some conclusions. I want to sell the business and I'd like for you to be the one to buy it. If necessary, we could do it on a contract basis and I would consult with you for as long as you need."

"Oh, my, that's a lot to absorb, Molly. I will have to do some thinking and planning, perhaps talk to my parents. They would be instrumental in my making the purchase, cosigning a loan or backing me in some manner. This has been a dream to me, to have my own store, but I didn't want it to happen under these circumstances."

"Nonsense, I'm going to be fine. I just have to reduce my

work load and take it easy. I've been expecting something like this to happen; heart disease runs in my family. So, please don't feel like you're taking advantage of an old lady, because you're not. You'd actually be doing me a huge favor; it would take a big load off my mind."

Dianne left the hospital, unsure of what her next step should be. She hadn't even asked the purchase price or the terms. What kind of businesswoman would she make? Would her parents be willing to cosign on a business loan? Obviously, she needed to get more information from Molly. Her Dad was an accountant, so he would know what questions to ask. He would have to know the monthly utilities, whether Molly owned the building, the worth of her inventory, insurance, advertising, freight. A list of items required was the first priority. As soon as Molly was released from the hospital, they would sit down and discuss the details. In the interim, she would continue to run the store as usual. When she got home, she called her dad and asked if she could stop by the next evening. Of course, he agreed.

CHAPTER 26

Dave arrived home early, surprised to find Debbie there. Usually, she was off with her friends somewhere; he had hardly seen her lately. Dani was busy studying; she had lessons to prepare for tomorrow's tutoring. Debbie asked if she could fix him a drink. Now he was shocked. Something is on her mind; she wants me to mellow out before she brings it up. He'd been down this road before and wasn't looking forward to it.

"I stopped at Molly's in town today to do some shopping. Did you know that one of Janet's good friends is running the store? At any rate, we had an interesting talk, just girl talk, if you know what I mean."

Dave shrugged, "I'm not sure what you mean, Debbie. Please clarify yourself. I don't like conversing in riddles."

Debbie paid no attention to his obvious irritation. "Well, she insinuated that Janet might be having marital problems. She has certainly taken a liking to you. Is that affection reciprocated?"

"Debbie, I have no idea what you're talking about. She is a nice person and we've done some talking after Dani's tutoring, but that's it."

She took a long time to answer, taking a drag off a

cigarette and exhaling slowly, "Oh really, Dave, do you seriously think I'll believe that you aren't interested in her? How long have I been your wife? I've endured so many affairs and flings, I've lost count."

"Debbie, it's as simple as this: I've been doing a lot of thinking about our marriage. I'm not happy and I think it's time we went our separate ways. Actually, we've already done that, or at least you have. You're never home; you have your own set of friends apart from me and I'm never included, not that I care. You can have the house; I will continue to take care of the family and you, after a fashion. I'm sure there will be alimony involved and a division of assets and I can deal with that. I'd like to see an attorney this week and I only hope we can do this in an amicable manner."

"So, you want a divorce, do you? What are your grounds? I was right; Janet is at the center of all this. She must be something special; you've never wanted to leave for any of the others. You do realize, at your age, you're having a mid-life crisis. Why don't you just go get yourself a red sports car and forget about her?"

"Debbie, I'm not having a mid-life crisis; that is ridiculous. For your information, I don't need grounds, this is now a no-fault divorce state or didn't you know that? I can file with "irretrievable breakdown" as my grounds. It can be final within sixty days, if both parties agree to the terms. We could start off the brand new year as single."

She started to cry. "I can't believe after all these years, you want to leave me. What can I do to change your mind? Maybe we could take a trip, go to Hawaii; you've always wanted to go there. We could get to know one another again. Dave, please, I don't want a divorce; I want my life to stay the same."

Dave sighed and shrugged his shoulders. "I'm sorry, Debbie, I know I loved you once, but I'm not willing at this stage of my life to continue beating my head against the same brick wall. It wouldn't make any difference if we took off somewhere; it would be merely a diversion and once we got back home, life would resume as usual, no change."

"What will happen with the kids? Are you going to take them too? I suppose you don't think I measure up as a parent either?"

"Debbie, they're old enough now to decide for themselves, but I'm not sure I want to inflict that decision upon them; it would be tough trying to choose between your parents. If you want them to stay with you, I will have visiting privileges or they can split their time between the two of us. I won't be that far away."

"What do you mean, you won't be far away? Do you have a place in mind already?"

"No, not really, but I'll stay here in town, most likely with my dad for a time. That wouldn't be an ideal situation, but in the short term, it would work. In fact, I'll plan on getting out of here this week, no reason to put it off."

"Are we going to break the news to the kids together, or do you want to do it? I don't want to have to do that by myself. Dave, are you sure there's no chance for us?"

"I'm sorry, Debbie, I've felt this way for years, I've just never had the courage to leave."

"Why now, then? What's different? There has to be a reason and I think it has a lot to do with Janet. She's your incentive."

"Debbie, I'm getting older and I want to be happy again. I don't know if Janet is the answer or not, but she's absolutely not the entire reason. This is for me and me alone and now that I've made the decision, I won't reconsider. Too much time has gone by already."

"Well, it's obvious you've made up your mind; I won't fight you on it. The kids will be hurt, but maybe not surprised. When do you want to tell them the bad news?"

"There's no time like the present. Dani is in the den studying. Call Dottie to come downstairs. We'll wait to tell David when he comes home in a few weeks."

Both girls broke into sobs when they were told. They had lots of questions, mostly about what would happen to them; where would they live; did they have to change schools? Dave and Debbie did their best to reassure them, telling them they could split their time between parents or stay in their own home with Dave having visitation rights. Each girl was unsure what she wanted and hugged both parents, telling them "I love you". Dani asked her dad when he'd be moving out and would Mrs. Steele be coming to tutor any more. He told her he'd be leaving in a few days, and yes, she would be tutored as usual. The girls asked if they could be excused and went back up to their rooms; it was a very gloomy time in their lives.

Dave told his wife he'd sleep in the spare room until he moved out. She agreed and went on to bed. He sat there in the den, going over the events of the last few days. He had planned to wait until the weekend to talk to Debbie; tonight was unexpected, but he was glad to have it behind him. He wondered how Janet was doing. Was she confronting Robert at this very moment? He was sure he was doing the right thing, at least for himself and probably Debbie as well, she deserved to be happy and now; she'd be free to pursue a new life. The kids were, for the most part, raised and they would adjust as soon as they realized they weren't losing either of them. The financial end of the equation would be the sticky part; their assets were many and how to divide them might cause a royal battle.

Janet had been home for over an hour when Robert finally showed up. He smelled strongly of smoke and had been drinking. This did not bode well for a conversation about their future.

"Where've you been? I've been waiting dinner for over an hour. Did you forget how to dial a phone? I got a call from the bank today about your payoff to the bar owner, a Mr. Epperson, of $1,000. Did you think I wouldn't miss it, or did you care what I thought? I'm really tired of this whole situation. What happens to your paycheck each week? I sure haven't been seeing any of it for household expenses. You do realize we have to pay a mortgage and utilities here? Plus, buy groceries? You make your truck payment and that's all I know that you do with your money. How much are you into with this guy?"

"Slow down, Janet, you're hitting me with too many questions. I know I was wrong about the check, but there just hasn't been a good time to tell you. I've been gambling and don't contribute much, but you've got plenty of money."

"Robert, I want you out of here tonight. I am done with this so-called marriage, you look at me as a money tree and I've had it. You're disrespectful; you show up whenever it suits you and have no regard for my feelings. I should have never married you."

"Aw, c'mon Janet, you don't mean that," and he took hold of her arm and pulled her toward him. She shoved him away and he fell over the coffee table. "You're a real bitch, you know that? I just ought to beat the hell out of you."

"Get away from me; if you so much as touch me, I'll have you arrested for assault. You've gone too far this time, it's over. Get out!"

He grabbed his truck keys and shouted at her "You've not seen the last of me, bitch. I'll be back." He shook his fist at her and slammed the door so hard the glass broke.

She ran to lock the storm door and pick up the glass. He is such a bastard, how could I have ever thought this would work? Her hands shook as she picked up the shattered pieces of glass. Maybe I need to let someone know what's happened. If he comes back, it's hard to know what he'd do. She called her parents and they insisted she pack a bag and stay with them until he cooled off. They saw no reason for her to stay in harm's way. She quickly gathered up a few things and left, not noticing his truck parked in the shadows at the end of the road.

Robert slowly pulled away from the curb, trying to stay as far behind Janet as he could without being noticed. His curiosity was getting the best of him; he wanted to know if she was up to something. Seeing her turn into her parents' drive satisfied him. Apparently, she was staying the night;

she wouldn't be going there this late to visit. He was still so angry; she had so much money, what was the problem with him writing that check? If he hadn't, those guys would have been after him for the money in other ways and he wasn't anxious to find out what methods they used to collect. Driving back to their house, he decided he'd just spend the night there, but walking into the house pissed him off all over again; the longer he thought about her high-and-mighty attitude, the more it burned his ass. He started pulling his clothes out of closets and drawers, collecting his guns and grabbing whatever he deemed his. Seeing all her expensive clothes in the closet set him off. He tore her fancy things from the hangers and threw them on the floor, turned her jewelry box upside down, dumping it all into a big heap and in one motion, swept everything off the dresser. Necklaces, earrings, bottles of perfume, powder, lamps all went flying across the room. It felt good to get even with her; let her come home and clean up this mess. Leaving the bedroom, he noticed the neatly made bed. He took out his pocket knife, ripped the sheets and spread from the bed and shredded them maliciously. This would teach miss uppity-up bitch to keep her mouth shut. He'd warned her! He started packing his truck, figuring he could spend a few days with his mother; staying here was not such a good idea after all. What the hell do I care; I'll never see this place again, he muttered to himself.

He called his mother before he left the house, telling her he needed a place to stay for a few days. She knew this was coming; Janet was riding too high to stay with her son. She'd always known this was a mismatch, a little rich girl with a factory worker? This town was too small for their marriage to ever have had a chance, too much talk, too much humiliation for her son. He's too proud.

"Hi, Mom, sorry to be coming in so late, but I had nowhere else to go. If I can stay for a few days; I'll get on my feet and get my own place."

Betty Steele loved her son, faults and all. "Nonsense, you can stay here as long as you want. This old house is too big for me anyway; it'll be nice to have the company." Robert's dad had left the family years ago, leaving his wife and two boys to fend for themselves. She had supported them by cleaning houses, taking in ironing and working part-time at the school cafeteria. Consequently, Robert had never seen a decent, male role model. His older brother, John, had married a nice girl, had three kids and seemed to be doing well. Betty couldn't understand how they could end up so different from each other; she'd raised them the same, probably spoiling Robert a little more, could that be the problem? She wasn't going to accept that responsibility though; he was a big boy and would have to suffer the consequences of whatever he'd done wrong.

CHAPTER 27

Dianne stopped by to see Molly before opening the store on Tuesday. She needed to nail down the terms of the sale before she could present it to her dad. Molly was sitting up in bed having her breakfast, feeling and looking much better.

"Molly, I did a lot of thinking last night and I'm very intrigued with your offer, but in order for my dad and me to make a decision, I need more details. What do you want for the business, do you own the building and how does it fit in, what is the current value of the inventory, will I receive it free of any residual debt, what is your monthly overhead? I plan to visit my dad tonight and we'll need those figures. I believe if he feels it's a good deal for me; he'll be happy to back it."

"You certainly have done your homework. I can give you most of that information because it's all in my head, but some of the figures will either have to wait until I'm released from here, or I can give you a very close estimate for starters with a true figure as soon as possible. "

"That will work, Molly. I'm really anxious to start working on it. I was so excited last night, I could hardly sleep."

"Well, dear, owning your own business will give you some sleepless nights, but the rewards are worth it overall. I'd like to have $30,000 for the business itself; that is approximately two and a half times my annual profit. I do own the building and you can either purchase it at appraised value or lease it at $300 a month. Utilities are electricity, water and gas and run around $125 in the winter, much less in the warmer months. Inventory cost is dependent upon your sales and how much money you have in your 'open to buy' account; do you remember how we figured that before we went to market? We will go through it again because it's extremely important and somewhat tedious to figure. I spend very little on advertising since I've been a fixture in town for so many years. Sale signs in the windows are usually sufficient. As you know, our monthly sales fluctuate during the seasons and fall is normally better than spring, in part due to fabrics costing more, upping the cost at retail. If I remember correctly, my sales last year were a little over $155,000. Does that give you enough information to help you and your Dad reach a decision?"

"Yes, this will get us started. I will add my payroll to the expenses and I'll need to get more detail on property and inventory taxes and insurance premiums, but I can get those figures later. Molly, I am so excited about this; you cannot imagine how I feel."

"Oh, yes, I certainly can, because I experienced some of the same emotions you're having now when I first opened the store. There is so much for you to learn, but you seem to have the key ingredients: a flair for fashion, a good business head and a superior sales ability. Those three things are what it takes to succeed in this business."

At that point, a nurse came in to take Molly for tests. Dianne said goodbye and they agreed to finish their talk later. Dianne drove to the store daydreaming about being the owner of her very own business. Imagine! This little girl who had to get married may become a business woman. What will Mike think of this?

Actually, Mike Powers wasn't thinking of Dianne at all, but of Vicki Grey. She wasn't at the lumber yard today; they said she wasn't feeling well, so he was on his way to her house, hoping she'd agree to talk to him. She'll probably throw me out, he thought as he pulled into her driveway. After ringing the doorbell, he thought he heard footsteps, but no one answered the door. He was walking down her steps when the door opened.

"Mike, what are you doing here? Did you not understand that I want nothing to do with you, ever again?" She couldn't believe he had the nerve to show up at her door.

"Please, Vicki, will you just hear me out? I tried talking to you Saturday night, but you were in no mood for conversation. At least, please let me have my say."

"I don't know, Mike; it's not going to make any difference, you lied to me and that's unforgiveable. Since you're here, you can come in, but only for a few minutes."

Mike went in and Vicki motioned for him to sit down. She must not be feeling well, he thought, she looks sick. "Vicki, I've been such a heel; you have reason to despise me, but the truth is when I saw you that first time, I really fell hard and just couldn't help myself. My marriage has not been good for a few years, but I've not had any reason until you to stray. That is the God's truth and I'm not proud of it, but I wanted you to know. I loved the time we spent together and I thought you did too. I can't blame you for being mad at me; you're a decent person and don't like that crap. Is there any chance you'd continue to see me; I am going to leave my wife, that's for sure. But without you as an incentive, I may never do it. I really need you, baby."

"Mike, I loved being with you and I fell for you too; that's why it hurt and made me so angry when I found out you were married. Do you really think that's what I want: to be someone on the side, sneaking around and playing house when your wife is out of town?"

"No, Vicki, that's not what I want for us either. But, it would only be for a few months until I can get some money together. That's my plan."

"This is something I need to think over. I care for you and enjoy your company; but could I ever trust you after this?"

"Yes, a million times yes, I won't be hiding anything from you, ever again. Come here, baby, let me hold you and tell you how much I want you." He reached for her but she stood up and walked away.

"I told you Mike; I need time to think; don't push me. I'm not going to be swayed by a litany of sweet words. You need to leave now; I'm not feeling well and there's nothing more to say." She walked over and opened the front door, indicating to him that he was going, whether he wanted to or not.

Reluctantly, he left, telling her on the way out "I'll give you some time, but I'll be back, that's a promise." When he walked out the door, Vicki reprimanded herself; why would I even consider seeing him again; he's married, he's in it for one thing. Maybe he really does want to leave his wife, but what are the chances that would happen? Do I want to be some man's "other woman"? No way!

CHAPTER 28

Janet had an early-morning meeting scheduled, so she left her parents' home before they had a chance to talk about things. She needed time to think. What was the best way to go about this: Should she see an attorney right away, or wait? She decided to attend her meeting, make an appointment with her lawyer and stop at the house during her lunch break to retrieve a few clothes to tide her over until the weekend. She hated being away from her little house; she missed it already.

The meeting was geared toward the forecast of the company for the upcoming year. Did they plan to expand, add employees, venture into other markets, or stay the course? She listened to the various scenarios, took notes and set up a meeting for the following week with all the participants.

She stopped by the attorney's office on her way home at lunch. As it happened, he had a cancellation later in the day and would be able to see her that afternoon.

When she pulled into her driveway, she noticed the front door ajar. That's funny, she thought, I know I closed that door when I left. She wondered if Robert had been back and was he still there? Janet wasn't feeling very brave, but she knew she had to go in and see for herself. As she entered the house, she felt a chill. Walking back to her bedroom, she stopped, horrified. The whole room had been turned upside down; the bed linens were torn off the bed, things had been thrown on the floor, including her clothes from the closet. Lamps were broken, her jewelry was in a tangled heap on the bed, and he had taken one of her lipsticks and written the words "rich bitch" on the mirror. She felt like she'd been violated; she collapsed on a chair and sat there crying, unable to move for a few minutes. Finally, she got up and went to the phone.

"Marshal Bates, this is Janet Steele. My home has been vandalized and I need you to come and have a look." He told her he was on his way. She couldn't believe Robert would be so cruel; had she ever known this man?

"Hi Janet" Ed Bates said as he walked in and surveyed the damage. He took photos, asked her when she'd left the night before and what time she came back, what the situation was between her and Robert and had he been angry or threatening when he left?

She relayed all the information, told him a divorce would be forthcoming and that Robert had been very mean, shaking his fist at her, telling her he'd be back and breaking the front-door glass.

The marshal advised her to leave the house for a few days for her own safety; file a restraining order with the court against him and change her locks. He also said he'd go have a talk with him; he should be responsible for the damages.

"That's not going to happen, Ed, he doesn't have any money and he'll just deny it, even though it's obvious who committed this act. I'd like it if you could put a little fear in him as to what could happen if he comes back here."

"I can do that; I might even do a little better. We have our ways." He grinned at her and asked if she wanted him to stay around while she got the rest of her things.

"That would make me feel better, Ed. I will have to get someone in here to help me clean up this place too. Do I need to call my insurance agent?'

"That's a good idea. If nothing else, you can file a claim and recoup some of the damage. The insurance company will have someone in here right away to clean up the mess. That's why we pay our premiums."

She packed a suitcase, got her book of phone numbers, her jewelry and left the house. It was already time to meet with her attorney and did she ever have a lot to tell him.

"Janet, how've you been?" said Mr. Perkins, her family attorney.

"I've been better, John, my house was vandalized last night, probably by my husband, and I'm ready to begin divorce proceedings against him, using whatever grounds are necessary. He's been gambling with my money and I need a restraining order to be filed against him as well."

"It sounds like you've made up your mind. Irretrievable Breakdown is the grounds used most commonly for divorce in Indiana; it covers a wide berth of complaints. A restraining order is drawn up as part of a normal proceeding. It sounds like it has teeth, but in my opinion, it isn't worth the paper it's printed on, but the general public isn't aware of that. Do you have an address where he can be served?"

"I imagine he's staying with his mother, Betty Steele. I had Ed Bates come out to the house and look at the damage; he was going to go have a talk with him, maybe they'll know where to serve him."

"One other question, Janet, how about distribution of assets? I know you've not been married long, but is there anything that will need to be divided?"

"He has fishing and hunting equipment; he can take all that. There's nothing major; he has his truck, of which he makes the payments. There's nothing else. The bank accounts are in my name and so is the house."

"This should be simple; I'll draw up the papers and have them served tomorrow. I'll also get that restraining order filed right away. No reason to delay."

"Thanks, John. You've made me feel a bit easier. I just wish it was all over."

"Sixty days, Janet, maybe a bit longer with the holidays thrown in there; it shouldn't be more than ninety at any rate.

Janet was relieved; one major step had been taken. She called Doug Jones, her insurance agent and informed him of the potential liability. They made plans to meet on Wednesday to file a claim.

That evening, Marshal Bates was patrolling the area when he saw Robert pulling into his mother's driveway. He pulled in after him and stepped out of his car. "Hey, Steele, I need to have words with you."

"Sure, Ed, what can I do for you?"

"First off, I've been to your house today and I saw the damage you did. Don't think for one minute that you're going to get by with it. If anything like this happens again, or if you threaten her in any way; I will throw you in jail so fast your head will be swimming. Second, I'll look the other way when my deputies kick the hell out of you. Do I make myself clear?"

"You sure do, Marshal, is that all?"

"Yes, for now. Just keep it in mind; you don't want to cross me again." Ed got back in his patrol car and pulled out of the driveway, leaving Robert somewhat unsure as to what his rights were. Did Ed have the authority to threaten him like that? He hadn't planned on bothering Janet again; so, better leave well enough alone, he thought.

Dave Brown was trying to maintain his composure waiting for Janet to show up on Tuesday night. Dani was impatiently waiting for Janet too, suspecting that she was the reason for her parent's pending separation. She liked Mrs. Steele, but did she want her around all the time? She had noticed the way they looked at each other; maybe she was only seventeen, but she was already familiar with that look. Surprisingly, she felt sorry for her mother and knowing she was hurting made her sad. So much of the time she was angry with her; she was never available and when she was there, it was constant harping, but she still loved her. Her mom had left immediately after dinner, saying she'd be back around ten.

Dave heard the knock and when he opened the door, he could tell something had happened. "Are you okay?"

"Yes and no, we'll have to talk later. Let me get through the lessons first; then I'll tell you all about it."

Dave went back to the kitchen and Janet proceeded to the den to work with Dani. She seemed shaken, feeling insecure, he thought, has she changed her mind about us?

"Hi Dani, how are you doing tonight? I'm sorry I couldn't make it last night, but I had things that couldn't wait."

Dani shrugged, "That's okay, Mrs. Steele, we had a bad night around here too. My parents are splitting up and Dad is moving out to who knows where."

Janet gasped. "Oh, Dani, I'm so sorry to hear that. Do you want to talk about it or do your lessons? I can be a good listener."

"No, I'll do my lessons; my dad said you'd still be coming to tutor me until I return to school, is that right?"

"Of course, Dani, but what would my tutoring have to do with anything?"

"Well, my mom thinks he wants to be with you. Is that true?" Janet was stunned, but suspected Dani was trying to get a rise out of her. They had been so careful, why did Debbie suspect her? Had Dave let something slip?

"Dani, we're friends and we've been coworkers. What did your dad say about it?"

"Well, he said the two of you were friends; that's all."

"That's right, let's just leave it at that and get busy on your homework."

Janet was struggling to keep her focus. Ever since Robert had come home last night, she had felt like she was on a roller coaster and now, she'd just gone over the top and was headed down. Her stomach ached and her head hurt; she hoped this didn't take long tonight. After the lessons were over, she packed up, getting ready to leave.

Dave came in, asking "Do you have to leave; I was hoping we would have a few minutes to talk; I've been anxious to see you all day."

Janet couldn't seem to stop shaking. "Dave, I really have to get out of here; if there's somewhere we can talk; okay, but I don't feel comfortable talking here."

"Okay, I think I understand that, let's go to Millie's. I'll meet you there in about fifteen minutes." She nodded and hurried out to her car. It was getting very cold and she was still shivering; was it her nerves or a chill? She felt like she was having a panic attack; so much had happened in the past twenty-four hours, maybe she just needed to get away for a few days to clear her head. Staying at her parent's home was only a temporary solution; she wanted to be in her own home.

Janet and Dave weren't the only ones on their way to Millie's. Robert had been waiting for her to leave the Browns' and was following a block behind her. She pulled in the lot and went inside, taking a seat in the back booth. Robert could see her from the street, so he decided to check back on her in ten minutes or so. Meanwhile, Dave arrived at the restaurant and joined her.

They both started to talk at once. Dave smiled at her and relinquished the floor. "I filed divorce papers today and a restraining order. He left last night; I was scared and went to my parents for the night; he apparently returned later and tore up my house, did a lot of damage. He had written a check from my account for $1,000, payable to a bar owner who runs a poker game. I've had it with him; he sure made it easy for me to carry out my plans."

Dave was frowning. "Are you afraid of him, Janet, do you think he would hurt you?

"I don't think he'd hurt me, but I wouldn't have believed he could devastate my home, either; so I'm at a loss. He may be capable of anything; he actually shredded my sheets with a knife. And, by the way, Dani told me what happened last night and that Debbie thinks I'm responsible for it."

"Yes, she does think that; I told her she's being paranoid, but let her think what she wants. We can't change her mind about things. I am moving out tomorrow; I'll be staying with my dad for a few weeks and I'll also be filing papers. Debbie seems to be in agreement; her real concern is maintaining her life style."

Janet excused herself to visit the ladies room; on her way back to the booth she noticed a truck driving slowly past Millie's; she couldn't be sure, but she thought it was Robert. We've got to get out of here, she thought. I don't want him to see me with Dave. The truck was now out of sight and she grabbed her purse, told Dave what she'd seen and to wait a while before leaving. He moved quickly to the bar. She hurried out to her car and drove away. When Robert circled back around, she was gone.

What can I do about him? I can't go home, he might come by. I can't meet someone for coffee; he's following me. He must have been waiting for me to leave the Browns' tonight; otherwise, he wouldn't have known I was at Millie's. Shortly after she got to her mom's, Dave called to see if she was okay and Janet asked him if they could meet for lunch tomorrow. At least, during the day, Robert wouldn't be a problem; he'd be at work. Exhausted, she poured Southern Comfort over ice, settled herself in front of the fire and took a deep breath. Her mother was concerned; it was rare to see Janet so upset, usually her demeanor was calm and controlled. Janet informed her of the day's events, the damage to her house, the meeting with Perkins, the attorney and Robert following her tonight. Now, her mother was really concerned. "Do you think we should contact the marshal, dear?"

"Mom, I don't know what he could do. My understanding is that until Robert does something threatening; he's not breaking the law. In other words, he can follow me all he wants and nothing can be done. That is a law that needs some attention."

CHAPTER 29

Ted had taken all the measurements needed to outfit the kitchen in their home. He had already ordered the cabinets and countertops; now, he needed to pick up the appliances he had purchased. He had heard Teresa mention that she loved the chocolate brown appliances shown in one of her "Good Housekeeping" magazines. Finally, locating that particular magazine in her mile-high stack, he had used those pictures as an example of what to buy. He was trying to surprise her by having a new kitchen installed before Thanksgiving. She loved having her huge family over for the holiday, but she'd always been hampered by lack of space, countertops and the monumental clean-up task. A new dishwasher should simplify that. Now, the problem was to get her out of the house for a day or two; it was too bad the real estate seminar was scheduled for the week after the holiday. Her sister lived in Ohio and had been bugging her to visit; so he contacted Sandy and suggested she invite her and the two girls over for the upcoming weekend. Sandy excitedly agreed, thrilled to be in on the surprise. When she called Teresa, she immediately accepted the invitation; they would be there as soon as possible and that she couldn't wait. She needed a break from her routine. The kitchen plan was coming together; a lot of work had to take place in two days, but with a little help from his crew; he should be able to get it done. Ted couldn't wait to see her face when she walked in Sunday night. He felt like she was withdrawing more and more from him; this was an effort of love that he hoped would bring her back.

Dianne laid out all the figures for her Dad to scrutinize. He had lots of questions and fortunately, most of the answers were evident. He was happy, but guarded, in his enthusiasm for Dianne. He didn't want her taking on more than she could handle. This was a big step for his daughter; he and her mother wanted her to be successful and they had a lot of confidence in her intelligence and ability, but were somewhat hesitant to invest in this business.

"Dad, what do you think?" She felt like he was a bit reluctant and she didn't want to put undue pressure on him.

"Dianne, this looks like a sound investment to me. Mrs. Morrow has been bringing in a decent income of around $12,000/year for the last four years. Her overhead is less than yours would be because she owns the building; that would reduce your estimated income by $3,600/year, but $9,400/year is still a very respectable income in today's economy. My advice is not to buy the building at this point; wait a year or two and then decide. The building will still be there; you could be financially stronger, plus be in a better position to negotiate. I think she will reduce her price; this was her start; we need to make a counter-offer to her, perhaps $22,000. What I would want from you is a ten-year note for the amount of the loan, at 3% interest. That would not cut into your profit a great deal and would give you opportunity to grow. How does that sound to you?"

"Oh, my God, Dad, I'm practically speechless. Thank you so

much; you won't regret this decision; this store is going to be even better than it is now. I have so many fresh ideas, new things I want to try; but I plan on continuing down Molly's path, because she has been extremely successful. Changing things too much could drive people away."

"That's absolutely right and you're a smart girl to recognize that. What you need to do now is meet with her again. Type up an offer and present it to her. Don't be surprised if she comes back with her own counter. We'll just have to look at it. That is called negotiation. You mentioned she would consult with you for as long as needed; get that in writing as part of your final agreement. You don't want any surprises later."

"Okay, Dad, I'll go home, type it up and go see her tomorrow. I need to tell Mike what I'm doing also; he's not been home long enough during the past few days for us to have a lengthy conversation. I'm not sure what his reaction will be; but I am going through with this, no matter what he says."

"Dear, Mike is your husband; show him the respect he deserves. I'm sure when he considers the situation; he'll be very proud. Plus, this will be quite a nice annual income boost for your family. He can't be displeased with that."

Dianne was excited beyond words. She couldn't believe what was happening; a few months ago, she had been sitting home bored to death and now she could become the owner of her own business. What a difference in her life, in her attitude, in the way she felt about herself. She hoped Mike would be happy for her and not fight her on this. It is just too important to me; I will not give it up.

Mike had gotten home early for once; of course, it was a night she was not there and he was annoyed. She explained to him that she and Phillip had gone over to visit her parents as she had a matter to discuss with her dad.

"What did you need to talk over with your Dad?" He was very curious; usually she would talk to him, then her father. He was a bit put out.

"Mike, as you know, Molly is in the hospital with a mild heart attack and the doctors have advised her to take it easy, to cut back on her activities. She has given me the opportunity to buy her store. I would be buying the current inventory, fixtures and an ongoing business. Her income from the store is around $12,000/year, which Dad says is very good. I would have to rent the building from her, but that is also negotiable. Dad has offered me a ten-year loan at 3% interest to buy the business. I am offering her $22,000 total. She originally asked $30,000, but that was merely a start; now, we begin our negotiating. Plus, she has agreed to consult with me for however long I need. I discussed this with my dad first, mainly because I needed him to back my loan. There would have been no need to even bring it up to you if he had turned me down or thought it was not a sound investment. I hope you're not upset that I didn't come to you first, but it's happened so fast and you haven't been home at all the past few nights."

"Well, it sure sounds like a lock. Do you think she'll accept your counter-offer?"

"I don't know; she may or she may make another counter. I'm taking it over to her tomorrow. Isn't it exciting?"

"Yes, it is. I haven't seen you this happy since Phillip was born. It suits you. I think you'll make a go of it." It bothered him that she had shut him out on this decision. She had changed so much from the young girl he'd married. She had been so anxious to please him; now, he was not even close to the top on her list of priorities. Maybe I deserve it; he thought, I've not exactly been the model husband. She has tried and I've just thought she'd always be here. Maybe she won't. He suddenly felt very insecure, which for Mike, was a completely foreign concept.

CHAPTER 30

Jill apprehensively stepped into the counselor's office, thankful she had gotten such a speedy appointment, but anxious as to what lay ahead. The lady's name was Mrs. Elizabeth Garr and she was a psychologist, an older woman, perhaps in her fifties.

"Good morning, Jill, please sit down and tell me what's on your mind."

"My doctor has diagnosed me with postpartum psychosis. I have been depressed since the birth of my last child, eleven months ago. The valium Dr. Nelson prescribed for me has helped somewhat, but I am still struggling with it. He thought you might be able to help me."

"We are going to do everything possible to help you; Jill, but ultimately, it will be up to you to accept that help and move forward with your therapy. Now, tell me about yourself."

"I am married, have three sons, all preschool and do not work outside the home. My husband and I have a good relationship; I love him, he's fun and very good to me. I know I should be happy, but I'm not. I feel numb most of the time; my emotions seem to have vanished, I feel nothing, not even when I hug my children. My dad died recently and

I have not cried a tear over that, even though I loved him very much. My mother and I are working on her house, preparing to open it in the spring as a bed and breakfast inn. That has taken my mind off my other problems, but not entirely. What is wrong with me?"

"Basically, Jill, you have all the classic symptoms of depression. Your file that Dr. Nelson sent over says you have problems sleeping and consequently, you're tired all the time. Our first step will be to straighten out your sleep schedule so that you're sleeping at least eight hours every night. This will not only solve some of the tiredness issue, but will help in any weight gain you've experienced. I am going to prescribe a mild sedative for you to take each evening. The next thing I want you to do is to keep a diary. In that journal, I want you to write down what you ate each day, what your accomplishments were and what your plan is for the next day. I am going to give you a chart of exercises that I want you to do three to four times a week. I'd also like for you to walk outside at least a half an hour a day. The last thing is no alcohol beverage of any kind. Alcohol is a depressant and should not be combined with either the Valium or the sleep medication. Apparently, you did suffer some consequences recently after having a few drinks; am I correct in assuming that?"

"Yes, Dr. Garner. I've learned my lesson there. I will not be imbibing during my therapy. It's not something I need."

"Good. Jill, start your diary today and my secretary will give you a list of exercises. Use a couple of soup cans for weights. They work very well. I'd like to see you back here in two weeks; hopefully, we will see some improvement."

"Thank you, Doctor. I will do my best."

Jill left the counselor's office feeling encouraged; she had not experienced much hope of late. The doctor had given her several things to accomplish; now, all I have to do is summon the energy to complete them, she thought, feeling as though she'd been handed a herculean task. I'll take one day at a time and manage somehow.

CHAPTER 31

Janet and Dave were meeting for lunch at The Heritage House, the only other dining establishment in town besides Millie's. The restaurant was quieter and pricier than the diner, therefore, not as popular for lunch. The knotty pine paneling and large windows overlooking a small lake gave the place a log-cabin atmosphere. The tables were oak as were the wide plank floors. There were a few other patrons when Janet walked in and she knew most of them. She wondered what they'd think, seeing her here with Dave; but for all they knew, it was merely a business lunch.

She sat down at a corner table, ordered coffee and waited for him. He arrived shortly thereafter, greeting townsfolk as he made his way to her table.

"Have you been waiting long?" he asked. She shook her head no and they opened their menus. This was the first time they'd been together in a public place and it was disconcerting to both of them.

"Do you feel strange sitting here with me? I feel a bit self-conscious; this is a first for us." Janet felt as though everyone in the restaurant was watching them.

"I understand what you're saying, but just relax and everything will be fine. What have you been doing since I saw you last?"

"I am still staying with my parents until I'm able to file an insurance claim, which should be tomorrow. I thought I'd get together with Doug today, but he got called out of the office for some reason. I did file the divorce papers and a restraining order. I don't know if Robert has been served or not. I really need to call Ed and find out, but, what about you?"

"I'm staying at my Dad's temporarily; I have seen my attorney and I need to get a listing of all our assets and turn it over to him. He did file the papers and Debbie is aware of that; she knew this was my plan."

"Do you think she is hurting? I would hate to think I had any part in that. With Robert it's hard to tell. He has so much anger toward me and it's scary."

"Janet, Debbie and I have discussed divorce a number of times over the years; we both knew it was only a matter of time until we went our separate ways. I think she is somewhat relieved; now she can live her life without any encumbrances and not feel guilty about me."

"Do you think she had guilt feelings toward you? Were the rumors about her and Jake, the tennis pro, true?"

"Yes and yes. The guilt was due to her long-term affair with Jake; as far as I know, they're still an item. I was in denial for a long time, but I finally had to come to terms with it."

"Well, I'm relieved to know that she's okay. Now, if only Robert would be. Once I meet with Doug, I'll be able to go back home. I've had my locks changed and I'll take other precautions. I can't see him coming back there if I'm home. I think he vented his anger and hopefully; that part is over.

As soon as I get moved back to the house, you can come there to see me. We won't have to sneak around."

CHAPTER 32

Teresa was excited about visiting her sister. She hadn't seen her for three months and it would be fun to have the kids together for a weekend. Ted had really encouraged her to go and that was unusual for him; he normally didn't like her being away overnight. He had been very loving lately and she was actually enjoying the attention. She still wanted to be with Doug, but this was nice too. Sometimes she felt really sad about Ted; she knew this affair was the ultimate betrayal. She hoped he never had to find out. But, if she and Doug were ever going to be together permanently; Ted would have to know. Will he hate me, she wondered. I would probably hate him if the roles were reversed. Wasn't my life a lot easier before this affair, boring, but much simpler? Meeting Doug this afternoon is just what I need, she thought. I need to feel his arms around me, his body close to mine. How are we ever going to work this out? Linda is no closer to getting a job now than she was two months ago, is he putting me off, stalling for time or seriously being careful? She pulled into the motel parking lot and drove around to the back. Doug was already there, waiting for her. Another afternoon in heaven with my lover; too bad this motel is so trashy.

Vicki was back to work at the lumber yard, answering the phone, taking orders, working with contractors on deliveries and doing the billing. She wasn't excited about her job; there was no possibility of advancement and the pay was barely over minimum wage. Consequently, she had decided to look for something else. The women at the beauty shop were saying the secretary/bookkeeper at Dillon's was retiring after the holidays and they'd be looking for a replacement. Vicki knew her shorthand and bookkeeping skills were good, even though she was not using them in her current position. Earlier in the week, she had gone into their office and filled out an application; subsequently, she had been called in for an interview with Roger Dillon to take place later today.

Their office was small, but seemed efficient. The walls were knotty pine, the floors were tiled, nothing fancy. Two chairs with green vinyl upholstery and a small lamp table sat in the reception area near the front door. The lady whose job she was seeking also acted as the receptionist. She must do everything around here, thought Vicki; I'm sure she makes the coffee; hopefully, she doesn't have to clean the bathrooms.

Roger appeared at the doorway and invited her into his office. They discussed the job, her experience, when she could start, her marital situation, confidentiality, and the pay.

"Vicki, you come highly recommended by your previous employers and your boss at the lumber yard said he would be sorry to lose you. However, his loss would be our gain. Why don't you plan on starting in two weeks, before Mrs. Wolfe retires; she can break you in on all the things she does, especially the payroll. That's a very important part of her job. The men like to get paid on a timely basis."

"I will give my notice tomorrow, Mr. Dillon. I appreciate you giving me this opportunity. It's a chance for me to use my office skills, especially the accounting. The pay is much better too."

"Okay, we'll see you two weeks from tomorrow. That will be a good day to start; that's when Mrs. Wolfe figures the payroll. We look forward to having you aboard."

Vicki was thrilled. She wished she had a girlfriend she could call to share the good news. She thought of Dianne. I could go by the dress shop; she's probably there. As she walked downtown, Mike came to her mind. I've got to put a stop to that, especially now, with me working at Dillon's. He could cost me my job and he's just not that important to me.

"Hi Vicki, I wondered when you'd be coming into the shop. How've you been? I haven't seen you since lunch the other day."

"Dianne, I've been sick; actually, I just went back to work today and then had to take the afternoon off for personal time. I have some very good news; in two weeks, I'll be the new secretary at Dillon's, isn't that terrific?"

"That's fantastic, Vicki, I heard Mrs. Wolfe was going to retire. That will end up being a good job for you; the pay should be good too. The Dillon's treat their employees like family. You'll love it. Of course, you'll be working around a bunch of ornery men, but I'd bet you can handle it."

"I hope so, Dianne. It's the same way at the lumber yard. This will just be the other end of the business."

"Now that you're finally here, we need to look at some clothes. You'll want some new things for your job, won't you? Slacks are probably the best choice to wear in their office with maybe a few cute jackets or sweaters. If I remember correctly, that place is cold in the winter and unfortunately, cold weather is on the way."'

"That sounds great; show me what you've got and I'll get busy in the dressing room. I love buying new things, don't you?"

Vicki ended up leaving with three new outfits, a couple of scarves and jewelry. She still wished she could find her jade earring, but it was probably long gone. When she was looking at the earrings, she mentioned to Dianne that her jade earrings would have been perfect with the green jacket, but she had lost one recently. Dianne made no comment; actually, now that she thought about it, she hardly had anything else to say during the remainder of her visit. Did I say something to upset her? She was troubled by this; she liked Dianne and would much rather have her as a friend than her husband as a lover.

Dianne was floored. Could Vicki be the one Mike is seeing? Or is it just a strange coincidence? She needed to find out where Vicki lived; oh, the check she wrote, of course. She opened the cash drawer and wrote down the address from her check. Okay, the next time he's out late; I'm going to drive by her house. Damn, I really liked this girl; I introduced her to my friends, even invited her to lunch and was planning to invite her to my next dinner party. That's probably not going to happen now. But, what if it is just a coincidence? Great, she's going to be working at the same place as Mike now. Not knowing is hell. But, when I find out for sure; it's going to be hell for him, not me.

Doug was meeting Janet at her home after lunch.

Apparently, her husband Robert had done a lot of damage or at least, that's who the marshal thought did it. Is this what happens when couples split? Would Linda behave like this? He thought she might; she could be very spiteful at times, here lately, more than usual. Janet pulled into the drive; they exchanged hellos and went inside.

"Doug, all the damage is in the bedroom. I'd like to get it cleaned up as soon as possible; I'm anxious to move back home. Staying with my parents is comfortable, but it's not like being in my own place."

He looked around, took several pictures and said "Janet, we'll get someone out here tomorrow to clean up the place. In the meantime, you need to make a list of everything that's been damaged and its' value. The insurance will pay for the cleanup and will replace the items lost, less your deductible, of course. I looked before I came out and your deductible is fifty dollars. Some of the items may only need cleaned. Obviously, the lamps are broken, some of the jewelry and perfume bottles also. It adds up quickly. I'm sorry this happened to you; is Robert usually an angry guy?"

"I didn't think so, but he does like being in control of things. That's what's bothering him now; he's not in control."

"I'll let you know about the cleanup procedure this afternoon. Get me that list and I'll forward it on to the adjuster. It shouldn't take long to get this resolved. I hope he doesn't give you any more trouble."

"Yes, me too, Doug; thanks for coming out." Janet was thinking about Doug's last comment. Would Robert be back to cause her more anguish? Should she be afraid of him?

She wondered if the marshal had served the papers yet. That might set him off again; she shivered just thinking about it.

Robert pulled into his mom's driveway and the police car pulled in right behind him. What the hell did I do now, he muttered to himself. He recognized the deputy, having seen him around town, but didn't know his name.

"Robert Steele?" said the deputy.

"Yes, sir, that's me."

The deputy handed him a packet of papers and said, "Mr. Steele, you've now been served." He then returned to his squad car and drove away, leaving Robert staring after him.

Robert opened the papers and saw the word, DIVORCE, and knew immediately what they were. There was also a restraining order restricting him from getting within five hundred yards of Janet. "Well, I'll be a son-of-a-bitch," he said aloud. He couldn't believe she'd actually done it. I guess this says it all, he thought. It's over for sure. He felt empty; he wasn't in love with her, but she had been his wife. He got back into his truck and headed for the tavern; if ever I needed a drink, I need one now, he told himself.

CHAPTER 33

As soon as Rose got home from school on Friday, Teresa left with the two girls on her way to Ohio. Driving over there, she felt so free; this was going to be a great weekend. She was looking forward to spending time with her sis; but she wasn't sure about confiding her problems to Sandy; she'd decide that when the time came. Sandy was five years older, more settled, and had never worked outside the home. But, the two sisters were still very close, even with their differences.

By the time they got to Sandy's house, almost a three-hour drive, the girls were tired and hungry. Sandy had made a big pot of chili and there was plenty left for Teresa and her girls. They gathered around the oak pedestal table in the dining room, ate and reminisced about previous times spent around this same old table, which had belonged to their parents. Once the girls were finished with their supper, Sandy's daughter took them upstairs to play.

"So, Teresa, what's been happening with you? I haven't seen or heard much from you for over three months."

"I know; I'm sorry I've been so negligent. I did get my realtors' license and I'm now working for George Ross at his agency. I've sold two houses so far and I have several listings. Currently, it's slow with the holidays coming. No one wants to move this time of year. But come spring, everything will get busy again.'

"What's new in Creviston? Are you still friends with the same girls? What are they doing now?"

"Let's see; Dianne started working at Molly's this summer and loves it. Janet has gone to work for her dad at the canning plant and Jill and her mom are planning on opening a bed and breakfast at Marie's in the spring. I think Janet has filed for divorce from Robert; that's not any big surprise; she should have never married him in the first place. Dianne and Mike always seem to have problems; he spends a lot of time at the tavern and she hates it. Jill and Johnny are fine; her dad died in early October and she's been suffering from depression, not just from his death; her doctor says she has postpartum blues. He's treating her for it and she is seeing a counselor."

"Wow, there's been a lot happening since we last talked, now; how about you and Ted? Are you happy? I get the feeling all is not well."

"Oh, sis, there's a lot going on with us; then there's nothing going on with us. Do you understand what I mean? You remember Doug, my old high-school boyfriend? I have been spending some time with him and now, I'm really confused. I still love him, but I don't want to give up my marriage. Ted is so good to me and I suppose I love him too. Is that possible, to love two men?"

"Teresa, I would say you love one and are infatuated with the other. You were a lot younger when you were involved with Doug and you've romanticized that relationship. I can't say I'm surprised at this turn of events, but I am disappointed. Ted loves you and those girls love their Daddy. Do you want to split them up? Marriages go through good times and bad times. You and Ted may be having one of those bad times, but, it can get better. Affairs don't solve the problems; they magnify them. Do you think Ted knows or suspects anything? Bill and I have not always been happy together; we've had outside temptations, but you have to be strong and resist."

"Sis, I have struggled with this for years. At night, when Ted and I were making love, I would fantasize that it was Doug. Isn't that awful? I have kept track of where he was living, what he was doing; then, at the Fourth of July party, we danced together and shortly after that, we started seeing each other. They just had a little girl in August and I feel terrible for her. I ask myself how he must feel about her or about Linda. I do know she is suspicious; she actually confronted me about dancing with him at the club's Halloween party. But, he asked me to dance; I didn't ask him."

"Well, I know Ted wanted you to come over for the weekend; he felt like you needed some time away. He must know something is bothering you. The best thing you could do would be to knock it off with Doug and concentrate on your marriage."

"I know you mean well and that's good advice. That's what my head tells me too, but then I listen to my heart and it says Doug. I just don't know how to get out of this mess."

"I think you know what to do. As the old saying goes, "you can't have your cake and eat it too." You need to make a decision and stick by it, one or the other. You can't keep going back and forth between the two of them. It's not healthy. If Doug is what you want; you need to be honest with Ted and separate. If not, tell Doug you can't see him anymore. Where does he stand on this? Does he want a future with you?"

"He says he does; but can I believe that? When it comes right down to it; will he really leave his wife and daughter? Plus, what effect would it have on his business? I think I know the answer; now I just need to muster up the strength to act on it."

Shortly after four, Ted came pulling up to the house with the new cabinets. He and his crew unloaded them into the garage and headed to the kitchen to tear out the old ones. Ted hurriedly emptied the cabinets of dishes, cooking utensils and canned goods. Once they removed the cabinets, they'd start redoing the floor. Within a couple of hours, the cabinets were all out and they called it a night. Ted was going to work on removing the old tile so they'd be ready to go the next morning. He had selected a pale-yellow, marbleized tile that would go well with the off-white cabinets and dark brown appliances. He had considered walnut cabinets, but the entire look would have been too dark. These light cabinets would brighten up the entire room. He knew she would want to paint, so he'd let her do that. He hoped this would improve her mood; she had been so tense lately. Maybe being a realtor was more stressful than he had imagined. Business was slow right now, but that was something she had expected, so he doubted that was the reason for her stress. What else could it be?

CHAPTER 34

Janet went home after work on Friday. The cleaning business had done an excellent job of restitution. Some of her broken jewelry couldn't be repaired, but the new sheets and comforter looked nice and inviting. She was very relieved to be home and now with new locks on the doors, she felt safe again. Her plan this evening was to relax with a book. Dave was coming for dinner on Saturday; he had plans with the girls to take them to a school event tonight and then out for a late pizza.

It had been somewhat uncomfortable tutoring Dani this week; she had dreaded the possibility of running into Debbie while she was there. On Wednesday night, Debbie had stopped into the den to see how Dani was doing. She asked Janet, "Will she be entirely caught up by the end of next week?"

"Yes, I believe so; actually, she may be a little bit ahead. She is doing so well in her Bookkeeping packet; she may have it finished by then."

"That's good. Janet, you've done a superb job with Dani. I couldn't have accomplished what you've done. Mothers and daughters don't always mesh. I hear you and Robert are divorcing; I'm sorry about that. Of course, you know about Dave and me. I hope that has nothing to do with you."

"Debbie, I will leave my friendship with Dave for him to

explain to you. I have nothing to say about it; your separation is none of my business."

"Let's leave it at that then; once again, thanks for your work with Dani."

Debbie went back upstairs, thinking about Dave and Janet. She was sure Janet was the major reason for their break-up; but she knew it was inevitable, with or without Janet, and perhaps it would prove to be the best for both of them. Now, she could be with Jake and he was certainly happy about that, after all these years.

Janet felt like she had just been interrogated. She felt guilty about their marriage, even though Dave kept telling her the separation would have happened eventually, especially now that the kids were leaving the house. She was very anxious for the tutoring to be at an end. This episode between her and Debbie was not the least bit enjoyable. Maybe this was the only one; she could only wish.

Sitting in her cozy living room, the scene between her and Debbie seemed a distant memory. At least, she was home and could finally relax a little. She hadn't heard a thing from Robert, which, in itself, seemed odd. He was such a verbal person, always having something to say. She couldn't imagine not hearing from him again.

Friday nights usually found Robert at the local poker table; however, tonight he was driving around trying to sort things out in his head. He had driven past Janet's house, and she appeared to be home alone. The thought went through his mind to stop and see if she'd talk to him, but after that restraining order, he doubted it was a good idea. What would he say to her? That he was sorry he hadn't lived up to her expectations? Or that he'd ripped her sheets? Maybe she'd like to hear that he still loved her. Or had he ever loved her? Or was she just his wife, a possession? He'd heard that she and Dave Powers had something going on, that son-of-a-bitch, he has it all. Big job, big house, beautiful wife. "Now, Powers has apparently set his sights on my woman," he muttered to no one in particular. Who in hell does he think he is anyway? A big shot, I guess. Whatever he wants, he takes. She'd been fine until she started this tutoring deal; I figure that's how they got together. I'd sure like to take him down a notch or two. Maybe I'll just do that one of these days. Then she'll see I'm the better man!

CHAPTER 35

Dianne was getting more and more upset as she waited for Mike to come home on Friday night. Phillip had gone to a friend's house to spend the night and sitting there by herself, her imagination was working overtime. She decided to take a drive and go by Vicki's house; what could it possibly hurt, she thought, at least I might find out something. The first thing she did was drive by the tavern and she didn't see his truck. Turning around, she headed to the south side of town where Vicki lived in a small, nondescript house. As she approached Vicki's street, her heart started beating faster and there were butterflies in her stomach; what would she do if he was there? She slowed down and couldn't believe what she was seeing; there was his truck parked in the drive. Her heart sank; she felt crushed. How could he be doing this to her? Just when her life was taking a turn for the good; Molly had agreed to the terms of the sale and now, this. Fight or flight, what do I do? She parked her car down the street from the house and got out. Do I have the guts to knock on the door and confront them? She was shaking like a leaf; she wondered if she was going to pass out. Stopping for a minute to get her bearings; she then walked on down the sidewalk toward the front door.

Meanwhile, inside Vicki's house, she had just finished mixing a Manhattan for herself. She deliberately didn't offer

Mike anything to drink; he had shown up unannounced and she wasn't going to prolong his stay. Vicki sat down on the chair next to the sofa where Mike was sitting and asked him what he had to say that was so important. "I came by to see if you'd made a decision about us?"

"Mike, I've given this a lot of thought and I've decided that there's no future for us at this point. Actually, I'm going to be working at Dillon's now and I don't feel it would be appropriate. I wouldn't want to jeopardize my job. Please don't try to change my mind; it's made up and that's that!" The knock on the door startled both of them.

"Gee, this must be my night for unexpected visitors. I have no idea who that could be; but I guess there's only one way to find out." She opened the door and there stood Dianne. Vicki was so shocked to see Dianne; she couldn't get a word out.

"Vicki, is my husband here? I'm assuming he is, since his truck is in the driveway." She brushed past her and strode into the room where Mike sat, dumbfounded, on the sofa.

"Mike, I think you'd better get home. We, obviously, have a lot to discuss. As for you, Vicki, I certainly misjudged you. I thought you were a nice gal; but you're nothing but a tramp, sleeping with someone else's husband. Oh, and by the way, here's your earring; I found it imbedded in my bedroom carpet a month ago. Gee, now you'll have a pair of earrings to go with that green outfit; the last one you'll buy in my store. You're not welcome there anymore. Mike, get up and get out of here. I am not in the mood to take any more crap from you."

"Dianne, please let me explain. Vicki is just a friend."

"Stuff it, Mike, save your lies for someone who might believe them, like Miss Vicki here. She's swallowed all of them, hasn't she?"

"Dianne, I am so sorry, I didn't know he was married until the night at the club. I told him that night to stay away from me. I'm sorry you had to be hurt; almost the same thing happened to me. That's why I'm no longer engaged. There's nothing between Mike and I now; he just showed up here tonight, uninvited."

"Is that true Mike? Has she cooled it toward you? Did you just pop in here tonight?'

"Yes, she doesn't want to see me anymore. I thought I could talk her into it by coming over here tonight. Don't blame her; I had her fooled from the beginning."

"Mike, you are really an SOB; you need to leave right now. I don't want to see your face again, here or at work. I'm turning that job at Dillon's down; I don't want to have to see you on a daily basis."

"Vicki, don't do that. You're single and that's a good job. It doesn't matter at this point; he's probably going to be single before long anyway, after this." Mike got up to leave and Dianne followed him out the door. They stood on the sidewalk; he with his head down and her telling him what a worthless bastard he had turned out to be. She walked quickly to her car and drove away; he followed her home.

Getting out of their vehicles at home, she said "Mike, get your things. I don't want you here tonight. I don't care where you go; it doesn't sound like Vicki will welcome you with open arms; but I don't want you around for a while."

He knew there was no talking to her. He grabbed his shaving kit, a change of clothes and left the house. He'd have to see if he could bunk at his brother's house. He wouldn't be thrilled; nor would his wife, but he had nowhere else to go.

CHAPTER 36

As Robert was driving through town, he saw Linda coming out of the drug store. He pulled over to the curb and hollered, "Hey beautiful."

She turned around and smiled. "Hi Robert, how are you?"

"Not so good, why don't you get in and I'll take you home. Maybe I can tell you my sob story."

She walked around and climbed in the truck. "I heard you and Janet split up; is that what you're talking about?"

"Yeah, that's it. God, you look good, girl. You just get prettier every time I see you. Even with that new baby, you still have a dynamite figure."

"Oh, Robert, you're sure laying it on thick. You're just lonesome, no one to go home to tonight, is that right?"

"Yeah, it's rough being separated from Janet; you know she filed for divorce and wants nothing to do with me. She filed a restraining order against me; I would never hurt her in a million years, but I did do some damage to the bedroom. I guess I took it out on her jewelry and the bed sheets."

"Well, I guess that's better than taking it out on her. I am sorry; Robert, I know it's hard for you. I'm not sure how I'd react if it happened to me."

"From what I've heard about Doug and Teresa, you might be closer to finding out than you think."

"What have you heard, Robert? You've got to tell me!"

"You know I'm not a big fan of Doug, and I've always thought you were too good for him. The rumor around town is that they've been getting together once a week at a motel outside of town. I don't know which motel or even what day. But you could probably find out easy enough."

"How would I go about doing that? I have been suspecting this for a long time, but I was hoping against hope it wasn't true, that I was just being too suspicious. He has so much free time and I suppose she does too. I'm glad you told me, there's probably a lot of people who know, but just haven't wanted to say anything."

He could tell Linda was devastated by this news and he felt bad for being the one to tell her; but damn it, she needed to know what her husband was doing. Doug was being a real jerk and didn't deserve someone as sweet as Linda. "Is there anything I can do to help?" wishing there was something he could say to make her feel better.

Robert, the only thing you can do for me right now is to be my friend. I am going to need all the friends I can come up with in the next few weeks. I'm not sure how to handle this; should I just confront him or what?"

"Well, since you're asking me for advice, I think he'd just deny it. You need to get some concrete evidence before you say anything to him. If they're getting together during the day; is there any way you can follow him?"

"No, there really isn't. He is always out seeing clients,

business meetings, that sort of thing. I'm just going to have to start checking his pockets, looking in his wallet, his car. Do you have any ideas?"

"Receipts, things like that. Does he usually pay for most things with cash; or does he use a credit card? Would he try to write off any of the expenses?"

"Surely he wouldn't be that dumb or would he? God only knows, he's not being too smart if he's having an affair."

"Well, you're about a block from home, so I'll let you out here. Let me see what I can find out. I'm staying at my Mom's, so if you need to talk, get ahold of me. But for sure, give me the weekend to see if I can come up with something; then call me Monday night. Maybe I'll know something by then."

"Good night, Robert and thank you so much. You're a great friend."

"Good night, babe. Talk to you soon."

Robert felt sorry for her. She was a really nice gal and Doug had never treated her right. He'd never liked him; Doug was the typical high school jock, always looking for the applause. Too bad I didn't end up with Linda instead of Janet; at least she doesn't act like she's better than me.

Linda walked the rest of the way home, wondering if what Robert had told her was true and how could she find out? The first thing she planned on doing was getting out the telephone book and looking in the Yellow Pages under "Motels" to see what ones were nearby. She hated going in the house and seeing him; how can I look him in the eye, she thought. She felt like she had the weight of the world on her shoulders, a new baby, and now this.

"Where've you been; Beth is really fussy and wants her mommy. I was beginning to get worried about you."

"Sure, Doug, you were worried; Beth is fussy all the time, you're just never here to enjoy it" she said sarcastically, thinking to herself how selfish he was.

"Did you mistakenly take a bitter pill while you were at the drugstore? Your mood has sure changed since you left earlier. What's wrong with you?" He knew something was going on; she was obviously pissed. Because of his guilty conscience over Teresa, he felt panicky every time Linda was in a snit.

"Doug, there's nothing wrong with me that a little truth won't cure. Why don't you try it sometime? It might be your salvation, who knows?" She hadn't planned on saying anything, but she was so overwrought, she couldn't help herself.

"You're talking out of your head. I wish you'd just spit it out."

"Well, maybe I will one of these days. Right now, I've got to get Beth fed, changed and put to bed. I do have obligations to this family, whether you do or not."

Now, he was sure she'd heard something. Apparently, she only had suspicions, no concrete proof of anything; otherwise, why wouldn't she confront him? Maybe she didn't want to rock the boat. He tried to put himself in her place; would he want to have a confrontation; she had no job or security, it would be a tough decision.

Around eleven, Doug said good night. Linda told him she'd be up later. Once she heard him on the stairs, she got the phone book and started looking for motels. Creviston had none, but there were a few toward Anderson and Fort Wayne. She found several that might be a possibility, but she couldn't visit them all. This was an exercise in futility. She'd have to find out another way; maybe Robert would come up with new information.

After dropping Linda off, Robert drifted over to the tavern. While sitting at the bar, he struck up a conversation with Greg, one of Ted's workers, who had been helping out on the kitchen project. He was telling Robert how Ted wanted to get it finished in a hurry, so he could surprise his wife when she came home Sunday night. Ted told them he was trying to lift her spirits.

"Well, that's an interesting story. What's wrong with her, does he think she's got another guy or something like that?

"I never gave it any thought, Robert. He did say she was heading to Naptown for a seminar after Thanksgiving. She's quite the career woman and I'm not sure Ted likes that."

Robert was finishing up his beer when a commotion broke out over by the pool table. Some guy he'd never seen was threatening one of his buddies with a pool cue. Robert jumped off his stool to break up the fight, but the bartender already had it under control. The guy was told to leave and he snarled at the bartender, picked up his jacket and cap and sauntered out the door. "Who the hell is he?" asked Robert, "I've not seen him around." None of the guys seemed to know and they all went back to minding their own business. Later, when Robert left the tavern, he saw the guy sleeping in his truck, probably passed out, he thought.turday morning came and so did Ted's crew. By noon, the floor was done and the lower cabinets were in place. They would finish up this afternoon, giving Ted Saturday night and Sunday morning to put the kitchen back together. What a whirlwind job! The island was the gem of the kitchen; this was Ted's idea and would give the kids a place to eat their breakfast and afternoon snacks, plus give Teresa the much-needed counter space she'd been missing. They could finally get rid of that old formica table. For the time being, it would go to the garage. He couldn't wait for her to get home and see this incredible transformation. She would be speechless; and for Teresa, that was highly unusual.

CHAPTER 37

Janet had shopped for dinner. Having been indecisive about the menu, she finally opted for braised steak, mashed potatoes, and asparagus. She had put together a romaine salad with tomatoes, cucumbers and avocado. Dinner rolls would complete the meal with pumpkin pie for dessert. She was nervous; this would be the first meal she had cooked for Dave and even though he had told her anything she served would be fine, she still wanted to make a good impression. The table looked pretty; she had picked up a bouquet of autumn flowers this afternoon at the florist which complimented her pair of rust-colored candles. These touches, plus her dinnerware for company, cloth napkins and stemware created an attractive table. He was due to arrive at five for cocktails and she couldn't wait. A bright-blue sweater and ivory slacks was the outfit she selected for the evening, relaxed but dressy.

Promptly at five, Dave knocked on the door. He had brought a bottle of cabernet to open for dinner. He put his arms around her, told her how much he had missed her and gave her a lingering kiss. "Something smells good and you told me you didn't cook a lot".

"Well, I have a few special dishes I fall back on and this happens to be one of those. What would you like to drink?"

"If you have any scotch; I'll take that with water. If not, I'll take whiskey on ice."

"I do have the scotch; I remembered it's your favorite and I bought some today. I'll fix myself an old-fashioned and we'll go in and sit by the fire. It's a good night to snuggle up."

He followed her into the kitchen while she made the drinks. "You have one more week of tutoring with Dani. How's she doing? I saw her last night, of course; she says she's doing fine, but won't elaborate. She did mention that you and her mother had a conversation the other night."

"I'm assuming there were two questions there. In response to the first, Dani is making excellent progress and should have no problem transitioning back into school. As to the other subject, yes, I did have a conversation with Debbie. She thanked me for doing a great job with Dani and asked me about my split with Robert. She also mentioned your separation and made the comment that she hoped I wasn't the reason. I told her she would have to get an explanation of our friendship from you, not me. Therefore, she may be asking you about it."

"I am not surprised. I'm sorry you had to be subjected to that. Hopefully, once the holidays are over, both of our divorces will be final. Then, we can make some plans."

"What are you doing for Thanksgiving? I am planning on being at my parents for the day. I'd love to have you join us if you thought it would be appropriate."

"Thank you, Janet, that's sweet; however, I plan to spend the day with my dad. We need to keep a low profile until the divorces are final; I wouldn't want to make anyone uncomfortable, especially your parents."

"I suppose you're right. If you'd like to serve the wine; I'll put the salads on the table and we'll have dinner."

Her meal was delicious and she was so pleased. The remainder of the evening was perfect. They listened to music, finished the wine and made love in front of the fire. They agreed this was much more pleasant than the furtive relationship of the past few months. After he left, she blew out the candles, cleaned up the kitchen and went to bed. Lying there, she couldn't believe how happy she was. When would the other shoe drop?

CHAPTER 38

Teresa was coming home today and Ted was pumped up in anticipation of her seeing the kitchen. He wasn't going to say anything; he wanted her to walk in and be totally surprised. He heard the car pull into the drive and car doors slamming. The girls were running up the front steps, into the hallway and rushing at him for hugs. He had missed them and they must have missed him too, based on that greeting. Teresa was standing at the door and he opened his arms and hugged her too.

"I've really missed you, honey. It seems like you and the girls have been gone for a couple of weeks instead of a couple of days. How were your sister and her family?"

"They were fine, and I've missed you too, Ted, especially at night, sleeping by myself. That's hard to do when you're used to someone being by your side and all of a sudden, he's not there." That was a prophetic statement, she thought. "I think I need a cup of coffee to wake me up; I got real sleepy driving home."

"I just put some on right before you got here. It should be ready. Let's go get a cup."

They walked down the hall into the kitchen, Teresa ahead of Ted. "Oh, My God! What have you done with my old, ugly kitchen? This is absolutely gorgeous! Did you do all this, well; obviously you did, while I was gone?" She was stunned. "The countertops, the new cabinets, the island, this is amazing. Oh, Ted, you have no idea what this means to me." At times like this, she felt herself overwhelmed with guilt. Here he was, redoing her kitchen, while she was telling her sister how much she loved her old boyfriend. At least, he didn't know about that; he deserved so much better.

"Teresa, I didn't do it all; my crew came out both days and helped. I left the paint colors up to you; I didn't know what colors you'd want on the walls. You can pick it out and I'll get it painted for you." He was happy with her reaction; this was exactly what he had wanted, to please her and apparently, he had gotten the job done.

"Ted, this will be perfect for Thanksgiving. All the space I need, the new stove and oven, a big refrigerator, the double sink; a big meal will be a breeze. After seeing this, I don't even care if we ever build a new house; I wouldn't want to give this up."

"Well, we can talk about that later. But, for now, this will be a big boost to our home and up the resale value, as you know."

"Okay, now I need to fix the first meal in our new kitchen. What would you like for supper, sir? Perhaps pork chops, or fried chicken, what will it be?"

"I'd like pork chops with fried potatoes and some mustard greens with a pan of cornbread. Is that asking too much?"

"No. This will give me a chance to use my new oven. This is going to be so much fun. Ted, thank you. I can't believe you accomplished this in one weekend. How did you do it?"

"I special ordered the cabinets and they'd been in for a

week. The appliances were in stock at Sears and I had already purchased the flooring; all I needed to do was supply the man power. It was a couple of very long days."

"Tell your men they did a wonderful job and I appreciate it. But it was you who did the real work. How you managed it without me finding out is a mystery to me." Ted was eating up her praise.

"It's going to stay a mystery. By the way, woman, I'm a hungry man, where's supper?"

Teresa laughed and said "Coming right up". This is such a great feeling, she thought. A good marriage should be like this, having fun and sharing; I would miss him if we split up. That's for sure and what would I gain? Would Doug leave Linda? Possibly, but I don't know for sure. Sandy is right; I need to give my marriage a second look.

CHAPTER 39

After her session with the counselor, Jill found herself very busy. Journaling her diet and recording her thoughts took a lot of time; but she supposed it would become a habit and eventually, much easier to do. Walking each day was also a challenge; either she had to have her mother come stay with the boys during the day or wait until Johnny came home in the evening, but by that time, it was beginning to get cold outside. What I need is a dog, she thought. I would have to get up every morning and walk the dog, plus a few times during the day; however, I don't think I need another being looking to me for his welfare. The list of exercises was easy; in fact, they made her feel energized. Supposedly, they released some sort of hormone into the brain to make a person feel good. I can use that for sure, she thought.

Johnny didn't need to be at the job until later on Monday, so Jill decided to take an early morning walk. She was feeling a bit low and couldn't figure out why. Fretting about it, she thought, I had been feeling better; then today I feel like I'm in a fog trying to fight my way out. Nothing has happened specifically to cause this; why can't I relax and be happy like other women? I have everything I could possibly want, yet something doesn't seem quite right. Feeling frustrated, she started walking faster, swinging her arms to keep warm. She didn't notice the truck pulling up beside her until she heard a man yell. It was a guy she'd never seen before and she felt the hair stand up on her arms.

"Where ya goin in such a hurry, lil lady? I can take ya whereer ya wanna go, clumb in." Jill's instincts kicked in and she started to run, but he jumped out of his truck and came running after her. When he caught up, he grabbed her and threw her to the ground. She was flailing at him, but he managed to catch both her hands and hold them over her head. With his other hand, he started yanking at her pants, pulling them off and sliding between her legs. Jill was no match for his strength. He started laughing, "I'm gonna get me some this mornin, not had any fer a long time and girl, do I ever need it." She was screaming as loud as she could, but there was no one to hear her. He finally finished and stood up, adjusting his pants. He tipped his cap and said, "Thank ye, mam, sure was good," then ran to his truck and sped away. She noticed the truck was dark blue with rust around the fenders. She struggled to get up, vomited and eventually was able to pull up her pants. Shaking almost uncontrollably, she wasn't sure she could walk, but her instincts were telling her to get away from here before he decided to come back. She stumbled along the road until she saw a house and went up the walk. When the homeowner came to the door, she saw immediately that Jill was hurt. The woman asked for her phone number and called Johnny, telling him that his wife was at her house and had been injured. Johnny asked where she lived and said he'd be there within ten minutes. She gave Jill something to drink, suggested she lie down until her husband arrived and covered her with a blanket. Jill was shivering and sobbing so hard; she was almost incoherent. Johnny knocked on the door and when he saw her, he was shocked. He asked, "What the hell happened to you? Did you get hit by a car?"

"No, Johnny, I was raped by some awful man driving a dark blue truck. He grabbed me, held me down and I couldn't get away from him. I tried so hard and kept screaming, but there was no one around. He was filthy and smelled terrible." She was hysterical and shaking like a leaf; Johnny thought she had to be in shock.

"I'm taking you to the hospital. Thank you, mam, for helping my wife. I really appreciate it."

"Please, Johnny, don't tell anyone, I'm so ashamed. I don't want anyone to know what happened to me."

"People don't need to know anything; that's the last thing you should be worrying about right now; but I've got to get you checked out. We'll call Ed Bates too. Maybe he can catch the guy."

Johnny couldn't believe this. He had never heard of anything like this happening in Creviston. Why did it have to be Jill? For that matter, why did it have to be anyone? Jill was finally getting back to her old self and now what would this do to her? Who was this creep? They'd better find him before I do or he'll be a dead man. He was racking his brain trying to remember a dark blue pickup, but he wasn't coming up with anything. When they reached the hospital, the nurse immediately took her back to a room for an examination. Ed Bates, the Town Marshal, happened to be at the ER checking on another patient. Johnny motioned for Ed to come over and they sat down in a secluded area to talk.

Johnny told Ed what he knew. "Did Jill give you a description of the guy or what he was wearing?"

"Ed, what she told me is how he smelled and about the truck he was driving, an old, dark-blue pickup."

"Do you think she'll be able to answer any questions? I need to talk to her as soon as possible, while everything is still fresh in her mind."

"The only thing we can do is ask her. I'm worried; this could send her over the edge. She's being treated for depression and this could be a real setback."

"Yeah, it probably will be. That's just too damn bad. There haven't been any rapes in Creviston since I've been marshal; that's been over eight years and I don't know about before then. I can't remember any, can you?"

"No, none that were reported anyway, I suppose it happens, but not by a total stranger. She's going to be scared to leave the house now."

The nurse came out and asked for Johnny. "You can go back now to see her. The doctor will want to talk to you in a few minutes." Johnny looked over at Ed and told him he'd check to see if he could talk to Jill.

"Jill, honey, how are you feeling? The marshal would like to ask you some questions, but only if you're up to it."

"Tell him to come in. I might as well get this over with so I can rest." The doctor came in just then to talk to them.

"Mr. Hines, your wife has suffered a severe trauma, both physically and mentally. We administered a rape kit, so if the man is apprehended, the semen can be matched. Jill, you have had a considerable amount of bleeding, have several abrasions and need a few stitches, which I will be doing shortly. I understand Marshal Bates would like a few moments of your time; after which we will proceed with the stitches. I'd like to admit you for the remainder of the day;

then you may get to go home tomorrow. I will be giving you something for the pain, watching for any infection and also something to help you relax. Mr. Hines, do you have any questions?"

"No, Doctor Morgan, not at this time; can I go get the marshal and have him come in now?"

"Yes, that will be fine. Jill, I'll see you shortly."

Ed Bates stepped into the room, took Jill's hand and told her how sorry he was that she'd been a victim of this man. "Jill, I want you to know, we will do everything we can to find this creep. Now, what can you tell me that might help me run him down?"

"Ed, I've been laying here thinking back over it and there are a few other details that I remember. He talked like he didn't have much of an education and he is probably in his forties or maybe late thirties. He has sandy colored hair, at least what I could see of it, because he was wearing a black Cincinnati Reds cap. He was dressed in jeans, an old blue plaid flannel shirt and a black jacket. He smelled awful, like he hadn't bathed for a long time; he also smelled heavy of tobacco and alcohol. I wish I could have seen his license plate, but I didn't. He wasn't as tall as you, but taller than Johnny."

"That's real good information, Jill. Now, do you remember where the attack took place?"

"I was out taking my morning walk and decided to walk out past the cemetery; it happened somewhere past there. There were no houses close by, I do remember that, but I did manage to get myself up and walk down the road to the first house I saw. That took me over twenty minutes, so it had to be at least a mile away from that house. The lady was very kind and helpful to me."

"That's enough for now, Jill. If you think of anything else, have Johnny give me a call. We're going to start working on this right away. Once we find him, you may have to come down to the jail for a positive ID, but I'll keep you posted." Jill could hardly stand the thought of having to see this man again, but she didn't say that to Johnny or the marshal.

Ed Bates left the room and the nurse came back in to bathe Jill and prep her for the procedure. She took Jill's clothes for evidence and helped her into a hospital gown. She then inserted the IV and told her the doctor would be there in just a few minutes. You'll probably start to feel the anesthetic right away. After the doctor is finished, we'll be transferring you to a private room.

"Johnny, could you please call Mom and let her know what's happened. I really need her right now. I'd also like for you to call my therapist; her number is in the book on the desk. Ask her if she could come visit me sometime today. Johnny, I just don't know if I'll ever feel clean again." She started sobbing and asked him: "How will you ever want to have sex with me, after this?"

"Jill, I love you and what happened today doesn't change that. We are together no matter what and we'll get through this. You need to rest and not worry about those kinds of things right now. Here's the doctor, so I'll see you in just a little bit." Johnny took the doctor aside and asked him if she'd be okay if he left for an hour and came back. The doctor told him she'd be feeling the effects of the anesthetic and wouldn't even notice him being gone.

Johnny couldn't stop thinking about this man with his hands on Jill. I could kill that son-of-a-bitch in a heartbeat, he thought. I'm supposed to be her protector; why did I let her take these walks alone? Who would have ever thought this could happen in Creviston? Nothing bad ever happens here, until now. Was it some guy just passing through town or someone they knew? He couldn't remember ever seeing a dark blue truck in town. He drove out to Marie's, dreading telling her the bad news. She was busy with the workers when he got there and he had to wait for her to finish up.

"I'm sorry, Johnny, they needed to know where I wanted towel rods in the bathroom. Honestly, you'd think they'd never remodeled a bathroom. What's the matter, you look pale. Are you feeling alright?"

"Marie, there's no easy way to tell you this; Jill's in the hospital; she was out walking this morning and some guy stopped his truck, ran her down and raped her. She's had some injuries and really needs to see you."

"Oh, my God, Johnny, that poor girl, I'll get my coat and tell them I don't know when I'll be back." Marie bombarded Johnny with questions on the way to the hospital and he answered the best he could. She offered to come into the house and stay until Jill was feeling better. He thanked her and said they would really appreciate that; he knew Jill would be grateful to have her mother there. When they arrived, Jill had already been transferred to her room. They hurried up to the fourth floor to see her.

"Oh, Mom, I'm so glad you're here." Jill began to sob when she saw her mother. Marie hugged her and patted her cheek. "My dear, dear girl, what else are you going to have to endure?"

"Mom, I don't want to talk about it. Please just sit here with me; it's a comfort just having you here. Johnny, did you check on the boys?"

"Yes, honey, they're fine. Mom is picking them up after bit and taking them to her house and they'll spend the night with her. She'll make sure Mark gets to school on time."
"Then I'll be staying with you for as long as you need me." Marie could hardly keep from crying herself. She felt so sorry for Jill; she looked so pitiful lying there. This is going to be a real struggle for her to overcome this; her other problems are minute in comparison. Some women never recover from rape; she hoped Jill wouldn't be one of the unlucky ones.

Jill was able to sleep with the help of a sedative, but awoke in a cold sweat. She was shivering and burning up at the same time. When the nurse came in to check her vitals, she discovered Jill was running a high fever. She left the room quickly and phoned the doctor. He prescribed a heavy dosage of antibiotic to be taken through an IV. By Noon the next day, Jill's fever had broken, but there had been another day tacked onto her stay, due to the infection.

Her therapist had come by and advised her to stay in for a few days to heal, both physically and emotionally. She told Jill the most important element in her recovery was to feel safe again. Once her body healed, she should venture out a little bit every day, increasing the length of time daily until she began to feel more secure. She told Jill to expect an uneasy feeling at first, but eventually, her fears would subside. Jill couldn't imagine ever feeling safe again.

Dianne was the first of her friends to find out about the rape. She had dropped by to see Jill and instead found

Marie, who told her the grisly details. Dianne was stunned; "How could this happen in Creviston, of all places? Should I go visit her, Marie; do you think she'd want to see me?"

"I think Jill would be extremely glad to see her friends; the moral support you girls give her might work wonders." Dianne immediately called Janet and Teresa and together, they made plans to go to the hospital during visiting hours that evening.

CHAPTER 40

After learning of Jill's rape, Dianne opened the store and began her daily routine. She couldn't stop thinking about her friend and how she must be suffering. She immersed herself in work, opening new shipments, hanging garments, checking the items against the packing slips to make sure everything had been shipped, but nothing seemed to distract her. The problems with Mike and his infidelity seemed small in comparison to Jill's rape. She hadn't allowed Mike to return home yet; his behavior was absolutely unacceptable. The infidelity was almost unbearable for her, but combined with his pattern of sitting at the tavern every night instead of coming home, plus his inability to communicate, all added up to an intolerable situation and she wasn't sure he'd ever change. She wondered if he even wanted to change.

The bell on the door rang and she went out front to greet her first customer of the day. Maybe selling something will lift my spirits; she thought, it generally gives me a high. But it wasn't a customer; it was Teresa.

"Dianne, I can't believe what's happened to Jill. What else does that poor girl have to go through? Do you suppose they'll catch this guy? What a disaster!"

"Teresa, slow down. I'm overwhelmed this morning. I realize it's hard to grasp the reality of this, but when we go see her tonight, we have to be positive, no negative thoughts. I'm afraid she's in for a long road of recovery; with the problems she'd been having and now this to boot, I'm worried about her. The only thing we can do right now is to be there for her, whatever it is she needs."

"Yes, I see what you're saying. Do you think we should take a box of chocolates? You know how she loves them."

"That's a great idea! Maybe we could take her a pair of these cute house slippers I just got in. She loves pink and these are so pretty. I'll spring for these if you'll get the chocolates. Janet will want to get her something too; I'll give her a call and let her know what we're doing."

"I have some good news to share. I went to my sister's for the weekend with the girls and when we got home; what a surprise! Ted had completely redone my kitchen, new tile, cabinets, added an island with a built-in cooktop, new refrigerator, the works. The only thing I have to do now is pick out the paint and get some new curtains. It is absolutely beautiful. I can't wait for you to see it."

"Teresa, you have it all. Why on earth do you insist on continuing this affair with Doug? Do you have any idea how much this would hurt Ted? I just found out that Mike has been seeing Vicki Grey, the girl who sat at my table the night of the Halloween party at the club. The way I found out was weird. She came in here to buy some things and ended up looking at jewelry, mentioning a jade earring she'd lost some time back. Do you remember that? Anyway, he didn't come home on Friday night, so I drove by her house; lo and behold, there he was. I knocked on her door and had it out with the both of them. He followed me home, but I threw him out and don't know if I'll ever take him back.

"Oh, my God, Dianne, that was the earring you found beside your bed. How did she react to that? We all thought she was so nice; I guess first impressions aren't always right, are they?"

"I hate to defend her, Teresa, but she was taken in by him too. She thought he was single and lived alone. Being new in town, she didn't know any different. When she found out the night of the Halloween party, she quit seeing him. He had stopped in unexpectedly on Friday night, hoping to make up with her. If we stay separated, she may change her mind, who knows?"

"I understand completely what you're saying about Doug. I do love Ted and we have a comfortable life. It could be a lot worse. Being bored and fantasizing about a long-lost love is no excuse for what I've been doing. I've been trying to justify it in my mind; but it's getting a lot harder to do. Doug and I have plans to spend the night together in Indianapolis the week after Thanksgiving. Maybe I'll break it off with him then, or just not go. I feel like I'm on a roller coaster of emotions. I know it would hurt Doug, but which is worse, hurting Doug or Ted? I'm just unsure about building a life with someone based on a bunch of lies."

"Those are truly the most sensible thoughts I've heard come out of your mouth for a very long time. Hip, Hip Hooray for you! I only hope you have the courage to follow through. I know when you're with Doug; all reason seems to fly out the window."

"I know, but I am going to try to break it off. I'll see you tonight in the lobby at the hospital.

"Sounds good to me." She watched Teresa leave and

couldn't help but compare her to Mike. Is he truly sorry or just trying to get back in my good graces?" Right now, she had things to do; she couldn't spend any more time thinking about him.

CHAPTER 41

After seeing Robert, Linda awoke on Monday morning determined to find out what her husband was doing. She had actually thought of confronting Teresa, but decided that would likely backfire on her. What about Ted? She nixed that idea also; if he didn't suspect, there was no point in upsetting him right now. Her biggest hope was Robert. She wondered if he had ulterior motives for giving her this new information. She planned on going for a walk this evening and stopping to use the phone at the drugstore. She needed to stick his mother's number in her pocket along with a dime for the pay phone.

Beth was finally getting over her colic. The doctor had said three months and he was right. She had been feeding her rice twice a day and was now starting her on fruit. Beth loved the peaches. She hated to wish her baby's life away, but she couldn't wait to get rid of the sterilizer. Fixing those bottles was time consuming, not to mention expensive. Dextra Maltose, Carnation canned milk and corn syrup added up on her weekly grocery bill, not to mention Diaper Sweet. Boy, was that a joke! Whoever thought that name up had, obviously, never had to deal with a diaper pail. Having babies was not for anyone with a weak stomach.

While Beth was taking her nap, Linda took a shower and washed her hair. She got dressed in a pair of black slacks and a red V-neck sweater before tackling her hair. She got out the "Dippity-Do" pink gel and combed it through her hair. She then proceeded to roll her hair on huge brush rollers, minus the brushes. Long ago, she had figured out that the brushes caused her hair to tangle and frizz. She secured the rollers with long clips and then drug out the portable hair dryer, which had been a Christmas present last year from Doug. This dryer is pretty nifty, she thought, it has its' own little case and I can use it anywhere. She sat down in her favorite chair, positioned the hood on her head and turned it on. It was chilly in the house and the heat of the dryer felt nice. After about an hour, her long hair was dry. She teased it on top to make it full and used her Aqua Net hair spray to hold it in place. If she didn't use these products, her hair would be as limp as a rag. Beth began to fuss after her nap; Linda sighed, having timed that just right. After she fed and diapered her, she applied her makeup and thought, now I'm ready for whatever comes my way today.

CHAPTER 42

Janet stopped off at the florist to pick up some fall flowers to take to Jill. She hoped they'd brighten her mood, even if it was just for a moment. Walking into the lobby of the hospital, she saw Dianne and Teresa already there, waiting for her. "Sorry I'm a few minutes late" she said, "I had to stop by and pick these up." They exclaimed how pretty the flowers were and headed for the elevator.

Janet asked, "How should we handle this? Should we encourage her to talk about the rape or pretend it didn't happen?"

"We can't pretend. We'll tell her how sorry we are that it happened; that whatever she needs we'll be there, and let her lead the way" said Dianne, always the voice of reason. She was amazed that Janet could even suggest such an approach.

They walked into Jill's room and were immediately taken aback at how pale she looked. Apparently, the fever she had was caused by a urinary tract infection, a common occurrence in rape victims. But, the antibiotics seemed to be taking care of it. Jill explained to them that she had some stitches, plus the infection and would be spending another couple of days in the hospital. The doctor wanted her to be infection free when she went home.

Teresa asked, "But otherwise, you're going to be okay, right?"

Jill smiled at her, a welcome sight. "Physically, I will be fine, but mentally and emotionally, that remains to be seen. I will need some serious therapy to work through this. I still have the shakes and when I close my eyes, I relive it in my mind. Johnny has been wonderful, but I have to consider how this will end up affecting him. The therapist told me I could experience nightmares, trouble sleeping, anxiety, panic disorder, issues with sexual relations, and a whole litany of other issues. She said all or any of those would be completely normal and that I will need to replace any negative thought with positive thought. She told me I may also be angry or irritable. That, of course, wouldn't be anything new."

They all laughed, glad to see that she hadn't lost her sense of humor. Teresa told her about the new kitchen; Dianne related the events of the weekend with Mike; Janet confirmed to them that she was involved in a relationship with Dave Powers and they were both divorcing to be together. No one was shocked at that revelation.

Jill opened up her box of chocolates and they all indulged in at least one piece. She thought the flowers were beautiful and loved the slippers, trying them on immediately. Visitation was only for one hour, so soon it was time to say goodbye. They told her to let them know as soon as she got home and they'd be over to help, however they could.

Jill cried when they left; Johnny came back in and tried to comfort her. She told him he needed to get home to the boys and relieve her mother; there was nothing more he could do here. She'd try to get some rest. After he left, she laid there for a long time trying to go to sleep, until finally the nurse came in and gave her sleeping pills. She wondered if she'd ever feel like her old self again, whatever that was. With the postpartum depression and now this, she could hardly remember ever feeling good. Finally, she fell asleep, only to wake up a short time later with a nightmare. She could feel his hands on her and she was screaming. The nurse came running in to see what was wrong and Jill tried to fight her off. After she woke up, she apologized to the nurse, who in the meantime, had called the doctor. He ordered a sedative to relax her and soon she was out like a light.

CHAPTER 43

As soon as the evening meal was over and she had the dishes cleaned up, Linda told Doug she needed to get some air and would he mind tending to Beth for a little bit. "Of course, I will" he answered. "Why wouldn't I?" He did wonder why she was venturing out so late; it was after dark and cold outside. But she bundled up and took off.

As soon as she got to the drugstore, she called Robert. "Hi, it's me. Did you find out anything?"

His mother was sitting nearby and he didn't want to talk in front of her; so he asked if he could meet her in five minutes.

"Sure, I'm at the drugstore. I'll be standing outside in five. Don't be long." She picked up a couple of things she needed, paid and went outside to wait. He was punctual; she'd have to give him that.

Hopping in the truck, she asked: "Why couldn't you tell me over the phone?"

"Linda, I love my mother, but she was sitting right there by the phone; we don't have an extension. Anything I said would be common knowledge by tomorrow; or maybe even later tonight. Anyway, I ran into a guy who works for Ted last night at the tavern and he said Teresa was going to some kind of a seminar in Naptown the week after Thanksgiving.

He also told me that Ted was surprising her with a new kitchen; that would have been yesterday, apparently, they installed everything in the last two and a half days, while she was at her sister's place over in Ohio."

"Wow, lucky girl, to have a brand new kitchen. When you say Naptown, you're talking about Indianapolis, right?"

"Yeah, it got that nickname a few years back because it's such a boring town, puts you to sleep."

"Well, interestingly enough, Doug is going to be there the week after Thanksgiving for three days, some kind of insurance convention to kick off a new method of handling claims. What a coincidence. Did the guy happen to know what days?"

"No, he only heard it in passing. He did say though that Ted wasn't thrilled about it and that he doesn't like his wife working."

"I would bet anything they have something planned. I could find out from Joanne where he is staying; she always makes his reservations. Hey, do you have a cigarette? I could really use one." He handed her his pack and she took one. He held the lighter for her and looked into her eyes.

"I would never treat you like this, Linda. He's such a fool." Robert pulled off on a side street and reached for her. She went willingly; grateful that someone cared about her. He kissed her deeply and they necked for several minutes until she told him it was time for her to get home. "Why," Robert asked, "does he have a timer on you or something? We were just getting started."

"No, but until I get this mess straightened out; I don't

want to complicate things and that would be very easy for you and I to do. I need a clear head to handle this."

He nodded, "You're the boss, just remember, I'll be here if you need me or just want to talk." He pulled away from the curb and slowly drove her toward home. She got out a block away, waved goodbye to him and quickly walked the rest of the way to her house.

When she walked in, Doug remarked, "You look flushed; is it so cold outside that it turned your cheeks red?" She didn't comment, just picked up the baby and went upstairs. She changed Beth's gown and diaper, then, laid her in bed while she went back downstairs to warm up her bottle. She felt very impatient waiting for the water to heat and the bottle to warm. It seemed to take forever. Checking the milk on her wrist, and satisfied that it was the right temperature, she started back upstairs to feed Beth. "What's wrong with you tonight", hollered Doug; "you've had nothing to say since your walk. Has the cat got your tongue?"

"No, I'm just trying to get Beth ready for bed. What is there to talk about? Do you want to tell me about your day or listen to me talk about mine? I didn't think so; why don't you go back to Gunsmoke or whatever it is you're watching." He couldn't figure her out; sometimes she was nice as could be and other times, like tonight, she was as cold as ice.

When she got back upstairs, she picked up the bedroom extension and called Melanie, her sister, asking if she could stop by on her way to work the next morning. Melanie asked if something was wrong, but Linda told her they'd talk about it when she got there. She promised she'd have the coffee pot on, hoping Doug would be gone when Mel arrived. His office opened at eight, so he probably would be.

Melanie showed up a little after eight the next morning and sat down at the kitchen table for her usual coffee and cigarette. "Okay, sis, what's up? You sounded anxious when you called last night and I suppose Doug was nearby so you couldn't talk."

"You're exactly right; I ran into Robert the other night when I was leaving the drug store and he gave me a lift home. He mentioned to me that the rumor around town is that Teresa and Doug are a hot item, seeing each other one afternoon a week at some out-of-the-way motel. Then I saw him again last night and he'd found out that Teresa is planning a trip to Indianapolis the week after Thanksgiving; which, coincidentally, so is Doug."

"Hmmm, how interesting! The plot is thickening; so how do we find out more? I am assuming you'll want to venture down to Indy that week, right? Doug should be telling you what hotel he's staying in; what if you had an emergency? It's not as though it's just you now; you have a child. So, we can find out in some manner what day Teresa is out of town and that's the night we'll go. Mom will keep Beth for you; she'd come over here if you ask."

"Okay, but how do we find out about Teresa? Do you know George Ross very well? Obviously, he would know or perhaps the agency secretary for sure. What is her name? Bonnie or Connie, something like that."

"Yes, Bonnie Frazier, I went to school with her, I haven't seen her for some time, but we were good friends for years. I'll come up with some excuse; I could have a friend moving to town and looking for a rental property.

"I knew you'd have a solution, you always do."

"What I want to know is this: what happens if you find them together? Have you considered that? It's akin to catching a fish; are you going to filet it or throw it back? You'll need a plan of action. Hopefully, if we find them together and it looks like that could be a distinct possibility; are you going to go hysterical or stay calm? Are you going to tell him he has to make a choice and if so, are you prepared to accept his decision? Do you still want to stay married to him if he is with her? Linda, these are all questions you need to be asking yourself. Do you love him enough to forgive him and move forward? You've got some decisions to make and quickly."

"I know, Mel. I'm not sure how I'll feel; I know it hurt when Robert told me what he'd heard. I've been heartsick ever since. I'll find out where he's going to be. Do we need to know if she is staying at the same place or not? She may not even get a room. This whole thing is bizarre; I have to know. Whatever we find out, it will be a relief."

"I would imagine she'd stay at the same hotel, but we'll figure that out later. Right now, I've got to scoot. I'll call you later in the week. Chin up, sis."

CHAPTER 44

Wednesday morning, Jill was chomping at the bit when the doctor came in. She was ready to go home to be with her family. He actually agreed with her; telling her that her fever had subsided and by continuing on the antibiotic after she went home, the infection should go away completely. She asked about the stitches and he told her to get some Witch Hazel and apply it four times a day with a cotton ball; they would soon stop bothering her and eventually melt away. He advised her not to have relations for three to four weeks, thereby giving everything a good length of time to heal. She couldn't imagine having sex at all, even in three weeks. Dr. Morgan wanted her to make an appointment with his office for a follow-up visit in ten days. She thanked him for his kindness in this awful episode and said she'd make the appointment. She then got on the phone and called Johnny. He answered on the first ring; he must have been expecting her to call. "You can come get me", she said and he flew out the door.

Jill was glad to get home; Mark was at school but Charlie and Gary were at home with her mom and they were thrilled to see her. She held both of them on her lap and kissed their cheeks. They giggled and laughed, happy to have her home. They wanted to know if she was still sick and the little one, Gary, asked her if she was going to die like Grandpa. "No,

Gary, I'm going to be right here for a very, very long time." That satisfied him and he jumped down to play with his toy trucks. Her mom was fussing over her, asking if she wanted a cup of coffee or something to eat. "No, Mom, I'll be fine; I'll eat when I'm hungry and I'm just not there yet."

She seemed to be alright, but Johnny wasn't convinced. The therapist had told him that she might be in denial for a period of time. "Mom, when I get to feeling better in a few days, what is our next step at the B & B?"

"The carpenters have been working on the bathrooms, finishing up after Johnny did the plumbing. The wallpaper in there is beautiful. I can't wait for you to see it. The carpets have been laid upstairs and the wallpaper has been hung in the bedrooms. Now, we need to select bedding and accessories to complete the look. Plus, we will need towels, plus, new sets of dinnerware and flatware that serves at least twelve. We will probably need juice glasses and water glasses. The list seems to never end."

"Oh, Mom, let me help you with those things; I love doing things like that, plus I need to start my Christmas shopping soon too." She winked at Johnny, who just nodded and smiled. Maybe I will recover sooner than anyone expects, she thought, I feel good today.

"Jill, we'll want to wait until the January white sales to get most of the things we need. We can save a lot of money by waiting, maybe as much as fifty percent on some items. I don't mind buying discontinued items either; that could really save us some cash. One thing you could be working on right now is the brochure for distribution. We can get the wording done; I'd like to give each bedroom a name and include photos in the brochure with their descriptions."

"Mom, that's a great idea; when they look at the brochure, they can decide which room they want and make their reservation accordingly. I'll start on it tomorrow; that might keep my mind busy. That is one of the things my therapist recommended I do, keep busy."

"Jill, please don't push yourself" Johnny pleaded. "You were just released from the hospital today. Why don't you rest and after your follow-up appointment with Dr. Morgan, you can get started then. We need to be thinking about our Thanksgiving dinner too. Do you want to have it here or at your mom's? Marie, what do you think? This will be our first Thanksgiving without Harold; maybe you want to give that some thought." They decided to put off the decision for a couple of days and see how Jill was feeling.

CHAPTER 45

Teresa and Doug were scheduled to meet at their regular place at two this afternoon. She hurried through her last showing to get there on time; however, Doug hadn't arrived yet. A half an hour later, she was still sitting in her car, fuming. Always punctual, she hated to be kept waiting and she was getting angrier by the minute. Fifteen minutes later, he pulled into the parking lot, got the key and came around to her side of the car.

"I'm sorry, Teresa. A claims adjuster stopped in at the last minute and I had a hard time getting away from him. I would understand if you're upset with me, but it couldn't be helped."

"Doug, I have been sitting here for forty-five minutes and waiting on anyone is not my strong suit. Yes, I am upset. You could have told the guy you had another appointment, or did that even occur to you?"

"Like I said, I'm really sorry. Can we just forget about it and make up? I don't want to spend the time we have left arguing."

"I want to be with you; but right now, I don't think I can. I'm just too upset. Ted never makes we wait."

"Oh, so that's the way it is. Look, maybe we just need to take a break. Linda is getting very suspicious; I think she knows something is going on with us; she just can't prove it. The holidays are coming and we both need to spend time with our families."

Teresa began to cry. "It's just like it was back in high school; you'd rather take the easy way out. Are you saying we're through?"

"I don't know, Teresa." He tried to comfort her, but she pulled away from him. He didn't know what to do; he wanted to continue to see her, but Linda was really putting the heat on him. He couldn't afford a divorce right now; it would ruin him financially. He didn't want to tell Teresa about that; she would know he was choosing his business over her, which, in essence, he was.

"I'm leaving, Doug. I've got to accept the fact that we're over. Deep down, I knew it would happen eventually; but I didn't think it would be before we went to Indy. Maybe it's for the best, but right now, my heart is breaking."

"Teresa, please know that I love you and always will. There are too many obstacles standing in our way. Hurting so many people would not be right and we both know it. Maybe at some point in the future, we can finally be together; it's just not going to be now." He walked over and hugged her, holding her close one last time. "I'll never forget you, kid."

She walked out the door and hurried to her car, wondering how she was ever going to get through this heartbreak. An unusual, early snowstorm had begun while they were in the motel room and it was coming down hard.

Driving back toward Creviston, she could hardly see the road. The next thing she knew, her car was sliding sideways down the highway with another car headed her way. The crash seemed to happen in slow motion; she saw the other vehicle coming and it hit her car on the passenger side, pushing her into the ditch. She came to in the floorboard of her car, wedged between her seat and the steering wheel. Someone was outside the car, trying to get her door open. Finally, the door sprung free and other motorists were there, trying to help.

"Are you okay?" someone was saying. "The police are on their way; the other driver is already out of his car and is alright." Teresa, with their help, managed to climb out of the car and thanked God she wasn't hurt. The snow was falling fast now and accumulating on the roadway. Someone threw a blanket around her shoulders and walked her to his car to warm up and wait for the police. Once the officer arrived, things happened fast. A report was made, insurance information was exchanged and tow trucks were dispatched. The officer offered to drive her home and she accepted. Oh my God, she thought, what am I going to tell Ted? He'll want to know why I was clear out here. Should I tell him about Doug? I can't do that, it would kill him. I'll just tell him I had an accident on the highway; he doesn't have to know where.

They arrived at her house; the officer walked her toward the door and Ted came rushing out. "What happened, are you okay?"

The officer relayed to Ted the details of the accident, including where it happened. He looked at Teresa and she just bowed her head. He knew something was up. Ted thanked the officer for bringing her home and he and Teresa went inside.

"Now that I see you're okay, would you mind telling me why you were out there by yourself? Where had you been? I want the truth, Teresa, no excuses."

She started to sob. "Ted, I've been such a fool. Doug and I have been seeing each other and we broke it off today. That's why I was out on the highway; I was coming home after talking to him. Please believe me, I am truly sorry. I don't expect you to forgive me, maybe you'll never be able to forgive me, but I do love you. I've realized that in the past few days; that's why I wanted to end it."

"Teresa, I'm glad you weren't injured, but I need some time to digest this. I knew something was going on, but never did I think it was to this degree. Right now, I feel blindsided." With that, Ted turned around and walked out of the room.

He was distraught and didn't know where to turn. What do I do now? Should I stay or leave? How can I ever look at her in the same way? She's my wife and now she's been with another man, laid with him; how can I handle this? Am I the fool or is she? I've known she wasn't happy, that's why I did the kitchen. I just never knew it was this bad. He put his head in his hands and wept. He loved her, but how could he forgive her?

Teresa knew better than to bother him right now. He needed time and maybe she did too. Her heart was breaking over Doug and Ted's heart was breaking over her. How ironic; neither Doug nor I deserve anyone feeling heartbreak over us. She hated hurting Ted; now that he knew, would he be able to forgive her? Her body was aching almost as much as her heart; how do you mourn the loss of an illicit love? If she wanted to keep her marriage intact, she'd have to be careful not to show any sadness over Doug. She decided to take a very hot bath before the girls arrived, they'd probably be home sometime in the next hour. Her mother had picked them up earlier in the day, something she did twice a week. Would they sense the tension?

Doug passed the accident shortly after it happened, but didn't stop. It looked as though there were plenty of people already there. The car in the ditch looked like Teresa's, but he nixed that thought right away; I'm just being paranoid, he thought. How could I have let her go again? Maybe we're just not meant to be together for more than short spurts of time. Can I be satisfied with Linda? I don't want to lose my family and that means staying with Linda and giving Teresa up. I've got to go home; begin my life again with my wife and try to be a better husband. Can I do that? At least, I don't have to go home to another confrontation. One a day is enough.

He pulled into the drive, noticing that more than three inches of snow had already fallen. There would probably be a lot of claims come out of this storm. The first one of the year always caused a lot of accidents; people had forgotten how to drive on snowy roads. It happened every year.

Linda was in the kitchen, warming up a bottle and balancing a crying baby on her hip. Dinner was on the stove, Chili, which he liked. He kissed them both, got a bowl and dished up his food. "Where are the crackers, Linda?" She motioned to the pantry and magically, there they were. He poured a big glass of milk and sat down at the kitchen table. She sat down next to him and started feeding Beth, who seemed to be starved. "She acts as though she's not eaten for hours", he commented. Linda gave him a dirty look and said, "Yeah, I've been withholding food from her lately.

She's growing, Doug, her appetite is stronger. I need to start her on vegetables this week and continue her on fruit and cereal twice a day."

"I'm sorry, Linda. I didn't mean you weren't feeding her, I can see she's growing. Maybe she's going through a growth spurt right now. I know my sister's kids were always doing that. When they did, they'd eat you out of house and home. How was your day?"

"The only interesting thing that happened today was on "As the World Turns". Lisa and Bob had a fight and he left her. Other than that, it was pretty much a dull day."

"Did you see how much snow we've gotten? I'll be busy tomorrow with all the fender benders; hopefully, nothing any more serious than that. By the way, I've changed my mind about the insurance convention the week after Thanksgiving. I've decided I don't need to attend that. If you've been to one; you've been to them all.

She tried to hide her dismay. What's happened, she thought. Maybe Teresa couldn't get away or, could it be they broke up? No, that would be too good to be true. She asked, "What made you change your mind, other than what you said?" She was trying to sound indifferent, but finding it difficult.

"I suppose it doesn't interest me as much as it used to, those things tend to cost money and we don't need to be spending any more than necessary. I've not had much new business coming in for a few months; I need to be working on that. Plus, this way, I don't have to leave my family alone for three days."

"For what it's worth, I'm glad you're not going. I was

apprehensive about being alone with Beth for three days in a row and I sort of like having you around too." She winked at him and raised Beth to her shoulder for a burp. As she patted her on the back, she was thinking about Teresa. She'd have to make a point to run into her sometime during the next few days in order to gauge her reaction.

CHAPTER 46

The word had gotten out around town about the rape. Ed Bates was getting tips right and left about who could have done it. Some he discounted; others seemed legit. The most credible tip he had gotten was from, of all people, Robert Steele. He had seen a guy fitting the description at the tavern on Friday night. The guy had gotten into a scuffle over a pool game and the bartender had thrown him out. Later, Robert had seen him passed out in his truck parked along the street beside the tavern. The truck was dark blue. Robert hadn't seen him since and the bartender didn't know his name. Now the problem was how to find him. Did anyone at the tavern know who he was? That was what Marshal Bates had to find out.

The women around town were justifiably scared. They were afraid to go out alone, even during the day, because broad daylight was when the rape had occurred.

During his patrol, Ed noticed a group of guys going into the Legion to play cards. He stopped and went in. They hadn't dealt yet, so Ed asked the group if they knew anyone with a dark-blue pickup. One of the guys stepped up and said his neighbor had a truck like that, an older one with lots of rust. "What can you tell me about the guy?" Ed asked.

"He's just an old, dumb hillbilly. He works odd jobs and lives with his sister."

"What does he look like?"

"Well, average height, I guess, brown hair, nothing special."

"Okay, tell me where you live and which house is his? I'll go have a talk with him."

The guy gave Ed his address and said the house he was looking for was to the North of his. He also told Ed "Hey, don't tell him how you found out about him; he's kind of weird. I'd just as leave he not know I ratted him out."

"Yeah, sure, I wouldn't have said anything: I never reveal my sources, so rest easy." Ed was guardedly optimistic about this tip. He felt like this could be something. He headed out to pay the guy a visit.

Pulling up to the house, he noticed the truck and the rust along the fenders. He rapped on the door and a woman answered. "I am Marshal Bates, mam, here to talk to your brother for a few minutes. May I come in?"

"Sure, Marshal Bates, I'll get him. Arnie, where are you? The marshal wants to see you about something."

"Hello, marshal, what can I do fer ya?"

"First, give me your full name."

"Sure, it's Arnold Simpson."

"Arnold, I have several questions for you. I can either ask them here or we can go down to the station. What'll it be?"

"I can answer em here. No need to go nowheres."

"Where were you this past Monday morning? Say around eight o'clock?"

"Hmm, I had a job just east of town. That's probably where I was. I don't remember for sure, marshal."

"Do you own a Cincinnati Reds ball cap, or a blue-flannel plaid shirt?"

His sister asked "What's this all about, marshal? Do you need to see those items?"

"It's about the rape, mam; does he have items of clothing that match those?"

"Yes, Arnie, get those and bring them out here." Arnie went into the bedroom and brought a black cap and a flannel shirt out to the marshal.

"Okay, Arnold, I'm going to have to arrest you on suspicion of rape. You'll have to come with me to the jail. Mam, you can stop in tomorrow and we should be able to give you a date his arraignment. We'll also need to take that shirt and cap along."

Ed cuffed him and put him in the back seat of the patrol car. He radioed the station and informed the officer on duty that he was bringing in a suspect. The officer was happy to hear that; the whole town was in an uproar over this. Now, maybe things would settle down.

CHAPTER 47

When Ted got up the next morning, his back ached from sleeping on the couch and his heart ached with the realization when he awoke of what Teresa had done to him. Now, he had to go and deal with that bastard because he carried their insurance. He made coffee, fixed a cup and left before anyone else got up. He couldn't face her this morning. He didn't trust himself not to do or say something he'd regret. What the hell, I don't have any regrets, but I sure as hell hope she does. He was angry, with her, with Jones, with himself for not seeing this sooner. How could he not have known?

He stopped off at Millie's for breakfast and ran into Robert. Oh man, misery loves company, he thought. Robert was in about the same boat, only they were getting a divorce. He sat down next to Robert at the counter and asked, "How's it going?"

Robert looked at him and said, "I think I'm better than you; you look like hell, man; didn't you sleep last night?"

"No, I didn't. I slept on the couch. It just seemed the right thing to do, under the circumstances. Teresa wrecked the car yesterday afternoon out on Highway 3 and I've got to go turn in a claim this morning. Thankfully, she wasn't hurt, at least we don't have to worry about that."

"Was she showing a house in that awful snowstorm?

Who'd be desperate enough to look at a house in that kind of weather?

"No, nothing like that, she was taking care of personal business. So, what's been going on with you, Robert? Are you still at your mom's?"

"Yeah, for now, I'll probably be there until after the holidays. I need to get some money together, so I can get my own place. Janet sure did a job on me."

"Sorry to hear that, man. I guess I'd better get going. Talk to you later."

Robert watched him leave, wondering if Teresa had been with Doug; was that her personal business? She was lucky she wasn't hurt, but if she had been with Doug, why wouldn't he have been there to help her out? Probably the cowardly son-of-a-bitch bailed on her; being a gambling man, he figured that was a sure bet.

Ted drove downtown and saw that Doug was in his office. Good, he thought, maybe his secretary isn't there yet. That would be perfect. He walked in and Doug came out into the reception area. "Hey, Ted, what can I do for you?"

"Well, for starters, Teresa wrecked the car yesterday; it's probably totaled. You need to get the adjuster to settle with me and then, I want to cancel all my insurance."

"But, Ted, why would you do that? I've carried your policies for years. Is Teresa okay?"

"That's none of your business. But, this is from me." Ted hit him square on the jaw and it made a loud pop. Doug fell against the desk and rubbed the side of his face.

"I guess I deserve that. I'm sorry things had to work out like this. I do love her, Ted, but I don't want to give up my family. Did she tell you that? She was pretty upset when she left me yesterday; that could be why she had the wreck. Man, I feel terrible about this. You have every right to hate me and I'm sure you do. Teresa is a good woman and I know she loves you and the girls. Please don't turn your back on her."

"What are you afraid of Doug; if I left her, she'd cause trouble for you? You are such a selfish bastard; I'm sure that's what you're thinking, how to save your own hide. Does Linda even know about any of this?"

"No, but I'm sure it won't be long before she hears about it. When things get started in this town, everyone knows before the day is over."

"Well, she won't hear it from me. I like Linda and I don't want to be the one to hurt her; but, of course, you've already managed that." He turned around and left, slamming the door in the process.

Doug went back into his office and sat down, still feeling the effects of Ted's fist. I probably need to tell Linda, but I'm going to take my chances she won't find out. I'll tell her I slipped on the ice today, fell and hit my jaw on the sidewalk. She'll believe anything I tell her. He wondered how Teresa was feeling, but he couldn't call and find out. That had been her car I'd seen in the ditch. Why didn't I stop? What was I thinking; that I didn't want to be caught there? What an asshole I've become! Damn, I want to call her, but that would be opening up a new can of worms. For the first time, he wished he'd never started this affair; he felt like it was going to haunt him for a very long time.

Linda picked up the phone on the second ring; it was Robert." Hey, sweet thing, have you got a minute?"

"Sure, what's up?"

"I had coffee with Ted this morning and Teresa wrecked her car late yesterday afternoon out on Highway 3 coming back into town. I asked him if she was showing a property and he said she was out there on personal business."

"Doug got home a little after four yesterday; one of the first things he told me was that he'd cancelled his trip to Indy after Thanksgiving. I bet they broke it off."

"Could be, or at least had a fight. Ted was on his way to see Doug about the claim; I'd sure liked to have been a fly on the wall at that meeting. So, Doug didn't say a thing about Teresa having a wreck?"

"No, not a word; but maybe he didn't know. However, he'll definitely know by this evening and then I should be able to detect some reaction. Thanks Robert, for giving me a heads up on this."

"Yeah, like I said before, if you need me, call. You did hear about the rape, didn't you? Be careful when you're out; I don't want anything happening to you. I'll talk to you later."

Linda hung up the phone and sat down, lit a cigarette and smiled to herself. Well, little miss Teresa wrecked her cute, navy Tempest. AAH, such a shame and to such a nice girl. HA! I can't feel too bad for her. She's nothing more than a home wrecker; whatever she gets, she deserves. As for Doug, I need to make him suffer. He doesn't realize how much I know about his affair; best I keep it that way for now.

She called Melanie and shared the news; it wouldn't be necessary now for her to visit the realty office. Mel also thought the whole thing was rather amusing.

CHAPTER 48

Ed Bates continued to grill Arnold Simpson after reading him his rights. He found him to be a little slow, similar to what Jill had described. After a couple of hours, he admitted to the rape and signed a confession. Fortunately, for Jill, she wouldn't have to face him at this time. Maybe she would be stronger by the time he went to trial. The arraignment was scheduled for later today and he assumed the judge would set the bail high enough that he would remain in jail until the trial.

Ed left the jail and drove over to Jill's house. Her mother came to the door and invited him in. "Marshal Bates, what a surprise. I hope you have some good news?" she asked as Jill entered the room.

"Hi Jill, I hope you're feeling better, and yes, Marie, I do have good news. We've arrested the rapist and he has confessed. His arraignment will be this afternoon and I don't expect him to be released on bail. You were right, Jill; he doesn't have much of an education. He might not be playing with a full deck either, if you know what I mean."

"Does that mean he may get off? He was obviously smart enough to do what he did and get away with it for a few days. I would hate to think he'd do that again; if he's done it once, what would keep him from repeating it?"

"Well, that's up to the courts to decide. They will have a

doctor perform a psychiatric evaluation of him, appoint a public defender and then proceed to trial. I did want to prepare you for that; you will be called to testify against him. But, that will be months down the road."

"Thanks, Ed. This is a huge relief. I've been afraid to venture out, not wanting to run into him. Now, perhaps I can face the world again."

"Okay, ladies, I'll let myself out. You two have a good day now."

Jill and Marie were ecstatic that the guy had been arrested. Jill's therapist would be pleased as well; she had mentioned this as being one of the steps toward her recovery. She wouldn't be looking over her shoulder at every turn. Johnny would be happy too, although he would have enjoyed being the one to take him down.

CHAPTER 49

Dianne was preparing for the Christmas season at her store. She still couldn't believe it was actually hers. Ordering Christmas wrap, boxes and ribbon were on her list, as well as an advertising plan. Molly had never done much advertising, but Dianne had opted to make some changes. She was meeting with newspaper representatives from two of the nearby cities today and the local radio rep tomorrow. She was hoping to draw some business from the neighboring towns. She wondered if Jill would feel up to helping her out during the Christmas rush. It might take her mind off the rape and the ensuing consequences. If not, she would have to hire someone; she just didn't know who.

Dianne hated artificial Christmas trees, but for safety reasons, she decided to go in that direction. Molly had lots of decor and she busied herself this morning unpacking all the ornaments and garland. Business had been spotty, mostly due to the early snowstorm. Molly had warned her to expect weather to have a large bearing on her business. She had mentioned that a woman will venture out to buy bread or milk, but she can usually wait on a new blouse. New shipments were still arriving, although they had slowed down. This was the season to move merchandise on hand, bringing in only off-price or holiday glitz to freshen up the look. She knew the club was planning a big New Year's gala and she had purchased a number of individual dresses in preparation for this event. They were arriving today; she only hoped they would sell.

The bell attached to the door jingled and she dropped what she was doing and went out front. "Oh, it's you", she said, when she saw it was Mike.

"Dianne, would it be possible if I came by tonight to see Phillip? I really miss the little guy and I'd like the opportunity to talk to you, if you'd be willing." It had been ten days or so since she'd made him move out and they hadn't talked since. He felt like it was time they made some decisions about their future.

"I'll talk to you. Why don't you pick Phillip up when school is out. You can spend the evening with him and bring him back in time for homework and bed. We can talk after he goes to sleep. I'll let Mom know you're picking him up."

"Great, thank you, Dianne. I guess I'll see you tonight."

After he left, she admitted to herself that it was good to see him. She had missed Mike, as had Phillip, but she was still very angry over what he had done. How could he have been so selfish? She wondered what he wanted to say; she was anxious to hear it. She returned to sorting Christmas decorations and then customers began arriving. Thank God the snow was melting!

When things slowed down, she called Jill. "I have a question for you and I don't need an answer for a couple of days. I'm sure you'll want to discuss it with Johnny and your mom. Would you like to come in and help me out at the store during the Christmas season? It would mean working from the day after Thanksgiving until shortly before New Year's Day. I am planning an after-Christmas sale, so I would still need you until then. I can't afford to pay you a lot, but, you'll get a nice discount."

Jill was astounded. "Dianne, do you think I could sell clothes? Seriously? I would need to talk to Johnny, of course and maybe even to my therapist. She is still going to want me to maintain regular appointments. Would that be a problem? Oh, some good news: Ed arrested the guy who raped me. Isn't that wonderful? He is now off the streets."

"Jill, your therapy has to be a top priority and we don't open until ten, so perhaps you could schedule your sessions early and then come to work. I'm sure we can work around that; talk to her and Johnny and let me know in a couple of days. It sounds like you're feeling better."

"Yes, I am; I have good days and bad days. Physically, I am healed. Now, I need to work on the mental and emotional aspects. This job might be a good thing. I'll let you know as soon as possible. Thanks for thinking of me."

Dianne thought Jill might accept her offer. She sounded more relaxed; maybe she was turning the corner. One of the newspaper reps arrived and interrupted her musings, back to the business at hand.

Mike dropped Phillip off, promising him he'd be back before bedtime. Dianne finished up the dishes while Phillip did his homework. She had told him that he could stay up long enough to say "good night" to his dad and then it would be off to bed. Of course, he was disappointed he couldn't stay up longer, but he knew better than to argue with his mom. When Mike came back, he gave Phillip a big hug and the little boy, satisfied for the moment, scurried upstairs.

Mike was noticeably uncomfortable and sat down on the sofa instead of his old recliner.

"Now, Mike, what is it we need to discuss?"

"Dianne, we've stayed married through a lot of strife and I don't want to throw away what we've accomplished together all these years. I still love you and if you still have any feelings for me; could we take that and build on it, plus not to mention our son; he needs both of us on a full-time basis."

"Mike, that scenario sounds good in principle, but will it work in reality? The problems we've had are huge, the drinking, the womanizing, infidelity, abuse. How can you change all that?"

"I know I've been a terrible husband; I've only thought of myself. There are a lot of things I have to fix in order for this marriage to ever stand a chance of working. The important point I want to make now is that I finally recognize what I've done wrong and want to make it right. I've not had that incentive in the past, or at least been smart enough to realize it. What I'm asking you, and I don't expect an answer tonight, is could we could try again?"

"You're right about one thing; I can't give you an answer without a lot of thought; what actions would you take to better our marriage?"

"Well, for starters, I'd come home after work and not frequent the tavern. I know that has been a big source of our problems. Counseling for my anger issues would be another solution and perhaps marriage counseling for both of us. I always thought it was beneath me, but now I think I need it. Phillip needs more of my time; there are lots of things I can teach him and utmost, you need me to be a better man. I can be that man, Dianne, if you'll only give me a chance. That's all I'm asking, is a chance. If, it doesn't seem to be working, we'll look at a separation or divorce."

"Mike, I don't know if I can get past the fact that you had another woman here, in our bed, showing a total lack of respect for me or even for her. That taints our private area, don't you see that? We can't afford to move, so we're stuck. Can't you imagine that every time I lay down in that bed, I think of you lying there with Vicki? What do you think that does to me? I don't even need to mention the abuse and ridicule I've endured over the years. All of it has taken a toll on me and I don't know if I'll ever be able to forgive."

"Dianne, do you still love me?"

She looked at him for a long time. "Mike, I really don't know. I have felt numb for so long, I cannot tell you what's in my heart; I don't even know myself."

"Are you saying there's no chance; that you'll never take me back?"

"No, that's not what I'm saying; I just need time and I can't even tell you how much time. Let me get through the holidays at the store; if you want, you can spend Thanksgiving and Christmas with us. Maybe that would be a start, but I'm not making any promises."

"That's more than I hoped; at least, it's not an outright "No". I'll call you this weekend and we can make some plans. Will that work?"

"Sure. Now, I need to say good night. It's been a long day." He leaned over, kissed her on the cheek and left. She sat there, reflecting on their conversation, wishing he would have said those things a year ago. Was it too late for them?

CHAPTER 50

Teresa was trying to establish some sense of normalcy in the household. Ted was due home anytime; the girls were watching television and she was cooking dinner. Her mother had dropped in, but thankfully, had not noticed her distress. She hadn't wanted to answer any of her probing questions.

She heard Ted's truck in the driveway. How do you act toward your husband when he's discovered your affair? She was at a loss, willing to let him lead the way. He walked in the door, looked at her and asked how she was feeling?

That's a start, she thought, at least he's talking to me. "I am really sore today, every muscle in my body aches. I suppose that's from being thrown around the car."

"Probably so. I turned in your claim today; I also gave your boyfriend a black eye."

"Ted, he's not my boyfriend. That's over, but I really wish you hadn't done that. Now, Linda will end up knowing and soon, the whole town. I won't even be able to hold my head up. I'm sure it'll have an effect on my realty business."

"Teresa, you should have thought about that before you jumped into bed with him. I just don't know how we're going to get through this. I don't know if I can handle it. Do you love him?"

"I thought I did, but I do know I love you. We've had a

good marriage until this happened. I'm going to make it up to you; I don't want to lose you."

"How can I trust you again? Every time I see him, I am going to be reminded of this; I honestly hate the man."

"I understand that; I really do." She walked over to where he was sitting and touched his arm, looking down at him. "I want this marriage, Ted. I want you and the girls. I didn't realize what I stood to lose; I've been so foolish and selfish."

"I can't make any promises, Teresa. We can only go on from here. I still love you, God help me, but I've got to work this out in my own way." Just then, the girls came running in and jumped on his lap. The giggling, hugging and kissing took precedence over any further conversation.

Doug walked into his house, dreading for Linda to see his jaw and black eye. Would she believe his concocted story or should he just be straight, for once, and tell her the truth?

Linda saw his face and said, "My God in Heaven, what the hell happened to you? Is that courtesy of Ted Farris?"

"How did you know? Who told you? I didn't want you to find out; I didn't want to hurt you."

"Hurt me?" She screamed at him, causing the baby to cry. "Doug, since when has that been a priority to you? For your information, I've known about it from stories around town; but I couldn't confirm it. I've already suffered through the hurt and humiliation. Now, I'm just angry. Is it over? For good?"

"Yes, Linda, please believe me; it's over for good." He sat there with his head in his hands, sobbing. "I couldn't go on deceiving you any longer. I can't look at Beth and not feel guilty toward her. The feelings Teresa and I shared weren't real; they were a fantasy of times past. We were trying to relive our teenage years, our youth. We finally both realized that, but I was the one who made the decision to break it off. I don't know if that makes any difference to you now, but I had to end it. I don't love her, Linda; I love you and Beth. Do you think you can forgive me? I know I don't deserve it; but I'm begging you to forgive me."

"I'm not throwing you out; I don't want a divorce, not with a new baby, but you have a lot to prove, buster. It's not going to be easy for you around here. You may end up wanting to leave; it's now going to be my way, not yours."

"I'll do anything; if you'll just let me stay, Linda, anything at all."

"Quit groveling. It's not flattering; actually, it's sickening. You're going to have to toe the line; it's that simple. Help me out with Beth, treat me like you used to, don't lie to me; those are just some of the things I want. Nothing major; just be a model husband." In reality, she didn't think he would ever measure up; he was too much of a narcissist, but for now, she'd let him squirm. It would be good for him and she was going to enjoy it.

CHAPTER 51

Jill accepted Dianne's offer of a job and loved it, flourishing in the constant flow of business and conversation with local people. She was thoroughly enjoying the camaraderie of the store and wasn't looking forward to her seasonal position ending. However, she and her mother had a lot of loose ends to tie up on the future bed and breakfast inn, which they had decided to name "The Hoosier Hospitality Inn". Jill had brochures and business cards printed and had been handing them out to Dianne's customers as they were leaving the store. There was a good deal of excitement over the coming of the inn amongst the townsfolk. Jill and Marie had decided to have an evening meal for the general public, by reservation, on Saturday nights. They wanted to test the market for that night and if it was well received, they might expand the service. There would be a limit of twelve for each dinner. They were also entertaining the idea of doing some catering; however, they wanted to get the business off the ground before they ventured into anything else.

Jill's therapist was amazed at her progress. Apparently, Dianne had been right in her assessment of the situation; working was just what Jill needed. She had little time to dwell on the rape and her depression was lifting. Johnny was thrilled; even their sex life had improved of late. Unbeknownst to Jill, he had undergone counseling for his feelings after the rape. He had worried about his performance, wondering if he would still have the desire to make love to her, knowing some other man had violated her. The therapist helped him view Jill as a victim, not a willing partner, in the rape. He had already accepted this fact on a mental level; it was the emotional level which was giving him problems. But, after a few sessions of seeing the therapist and talking his way through it; he felt like he could again be a husband to Jill. She, on the other hand, was afraid Johnny would no longer find her attractive, that he would not desire her sexually. She feared he would be thinking about her with the other man every time he tried to make love to her. The first few tries at sex were awkward for both of them, but through the combination of their love, communicating their feelings to one another and lots of patience; they managed to come out unscathed. Things were looking up for the Hines' family.

Dianne asked Jill to stay through the first of the year to help out with the After-Christmas Sale and to assist customers who were shopping for the big New Year's gala at the club. Dianne had stocked several full-length dresses and skirts, along with sequined tops and shawls. Jewelry and small evening bags were also must-have items with these looks. Dianne had her fingers crossed that most of these items would sell for this event.

CHAPTER 52

The first week of December, the friends got together at Millie's for dinner. They had a lot of catching up to do; since this was the first time they'd been together in over a month. Everyone was so busy and with Jill's dilemma, it just didn't seem appropriate. Now Jill was working for Dianne and life had settled down for the other two.

"Okay" said Janet, "who wants to talk first?" Habitually, they took turns relating recent events and regaling the group with their outlandish activities.

"I will" popped up Jill. "I've started working for Dianne and I love it! My therapist says I can cut back on my Valium, the kids are behaving as well as can be expected, the brochures have gone to print and Johnny is great. Life after rape can be mastered; if you have a loving family and friends." The other girls responded with "AAH" and were delighted that she had come so far. Someone asked if she would have to testify and she shrugged "I assume so, a trial date has been set for early April; around the time we open the inn. Bad timing, but we'll work it out."

"I'll go next" said Janet. "Dave and I have been spending a good deal of time together and our divorces will be final in mid-January. After that, we're going to make plans for our future." "OO-LA-LA" said the other girls. Teresa asked "Are you inviting us to the wedding? We definitely want to plan a shower. You need to let us know as soon as the date is set." They all agreed.

Dianne was next. "You may be disappointed in me, but I've let Mike move back in on a trial basis. He wants to be a better husband and he's really trying. Now, the problem is me; I still have feelings for him, but I'm not sure I love him any longer. Phillip is glad he's home, of course." Janet asked if the sex was any good between them. "It is okay, no earthquakes. It used to be wonderful; I miss that." Teresa told her to give it time; right now, it's all new and different, you'll settle in and perhaps things will get better.

The last girl to speak was Teresa. She smiled and said "Girls, all of you tried to tell me; now you can say "I told you so" because you were right. Doug is a jerk; once a jerk, always a jerk. I'm not sure he ever loved me. My car is totaled and I'm driving a rental piece of junk. I have a suspicion that he saw my wreck that afternoon and drove on by. Not only is he a jerk, he's a scoundrel. Ted has been a rock; at first, he was livid with me, but now he is trying. Did you know that he gave Doug a black eye? I wonder what Linda had to say about that. Anyway, we took our insurance elsewhere and I haven't seen Doug since the day of the wreck. He's broken my heart twice and now, I'm finished with him. There is one thing on which I need your advice and I promise, this time I will take it. My period is two weeks late and I'm never late. I'm afraid I'm pregnant. The bad part is I don't know who fathered the baby. What do I do? I am scared to death to tell Ted and I don't want Doug to even suspect it might be his. I am going to hide it as long as possible. I can just see Linda; she'll be sure it's Doug's. I can't believe my luck. I have a doctor's appointment in two weeks; I'm taking my calendar in and maybe he can figure out who the father is. If not, we'll have to do a blood test. Then, if it belongs to Doug, how will Ted feel about that? Will he be willing to accept it and will Doug want to be a part of its' life?"

Janet chimed in "You may be borrowing trouble; first of all, you don't know for sure yet. You need to make a calendar while it's still fresh in your mind, if you can remember when you and Ted had sex. Since your periods are so regular; it should be simple to figure out for yourself."

"Do you need to tell Ted that it might be Doug's?" Dianne asked.

"Yes, I do. I've lied to him so many times and I made a promise to him that there would be no more lies, about anything. I have to tell him. I want it to be Ted's baby, and legally, it will be, since we're married."

"You need to relax and trust your husband" Jill told her. "Believe me; I've had to learn to do that. I don't think I would have ever made it through this rape without Johnny. He's been my rock."

After hearing their support and advice, Teresa felt better about her situation. She told them they'd be the first to know, on everything. Jill said "Aren't we always?" and they all laughed. The remainder of the dinner was spent talking about Christmas shopping, the upcoming New Year's Eve party and clothes. Soon, the checks arrived and the girls said good night, hugging and encouraging each other.

CHAPTER 53

Teresa and Ted were coming to terms with their marriage. Now, she was forced to face her new problem. She had visited the doctor, who confirmed she was almost two months pregnant. Embarrassing as it was, she told her doctor she wasn't sure if her husband was the father. She hadn't told Ted yet and she certainly would not be telling Doug. Whoever had biologically fathered this child didn't matter; Ted would be the baby's real father.

Her thoughts began to wander. Recently, she had run into Linda at the Five & Ten Cent Store and Linda had snubbed her. Apparently, she knew about the affair. What did she expect Linda to do? Embrace her? She noticed, from time to time, women she knew whispering behind her back. Were they talking about her? Ted was beginning to act more like his old self; she was afraid this pregnancy would be a setback for him. But, he might also be happy about it. He had talked often about them having another child, so she prayed he'd accept this. She hadn't seen Doug since the last day at the motel. She missed him, but in another way, she'd lost respect for him. Her heartache was finally beginning to subside. She could now see him for what he was, a selfish, self-centered person. Would she describe herself in that same fashion? She knew she had behaved selfishly, but she had been blinded by her feelings for him. Teresa wondered if Doug had ever had true feelings for her, or was it like Janet had warned her, simple sexual desire.

She supposed she'd never know and as time passed; it was becoming less and less important to her.

Ted came in the back door and kissed her hello. He looked tired and she told him so. He commented "I've had some long days lately; it will be nice to have a few days off over Christmas."

"I bought a nice ham for Christmas dinner. Would you like to invite your parents and I'll invite mine? It would be nice to have a family dinner with both our parents and it would also be a good time to make our announcement." He looked up at her, wondering what she was talking about. "Ted, I have something important to tell you. I went to the doctor today and we're going to have another baby. It will be born in late July."

He jumped up and hugged her, asking "Do the girls know?" Then, it was as if a shadow passed over his face. "Is the baby mine?"

"Ted, after talking with the doctor, I believe it is. There is a very small possibility that it's not, but because of the timing; he thinks you're the father."

"How will we know for sure? Is there a way to find out?"

"If you insist on knowing, once the baby is born; a blood test can be done. The test can exclude a man as being the father, but not confirm it; so it's not a sure thing. As far as I'm concerned; this child is yours and mine and that's the way it will be raised."

"Teresa, I have a strong feeling that it's ours. I do love you and I love our family. You and the girls are the most important part of my life. Nothing is more precious." He had tears in his eyes and when she saw them, she realized how much she loved him.   Yes, she thought, this will be our baby, no doubt.

CHAPTER 54

Dianne had reluctantly allowed Mike to come home. She knew she had to give it one more chance; she'd never forgive herself if she didn't. She owed that much to her son.

Their lives together were moving smoothly; he was coming home after work; they were sharing their evening meal and behaving as a normal family. This was what Dianne had always wanted, but it seemed like they were only going through the motions, that their hearts weren't in it. Phillip was happy, but it was going to take time for his parents to adjust to this new way of life. Their lovemaking wasn't what it used to be either; she wasn't the least bit enthusiastic about it and Mike knew it. She thought she'd give this a few more months, not necessarily put a time limit on it, but she would know when the time arrived.

Janet and Dave continued to see one another almost every day. She was acclimating herself to the canning factory and becoming well versed in all aspects of the company. It was a much more exciting business than she had imagined. The salesmen coming in, the part-time workers and their families, the people on the line, the different products the company produced; all this combined to make a fascinating environment in which to work. Dave was spending longer hours at the bank, preparing for the bank examiners to return the first week of January. Both divorces were due to be final the following week. She couldn't wait for all of it to be behind them. Robert had kept his distance and she had heard, via the local gossip mill, that he was dating Vicki Grey. Things had a strange way of working out, she thought.

CHAPTER 55

The month of December flew by. Dianne's store had a record-breaking season. Her advertising had paid dividends with new customers coming in from nearby towns, old customers returning and lots of younger women stopping by and snapping up her new looks. All the ladies in town who were planning to attend the country club's party stopped in to look at dresses and separates. Most found something they couldn't live without, a few bought only jewelry, but Dianne was satisfied. She knew she couldn't be everything to everyone.

The New Year's Eve Gala at the country club promised to be the biggest event of the season. Everyone with any status in town was planning to be there. The ballroom was decorated with gold streamers, red tablecloths with centerpieces made of gold-flaked pine cones, greenery, gold ornaments and candles. The tables were set with white dinnerware and gold napkins; place cards had been set, by couple for this event. Apparently, the place settings at the Halloween party had not been well received by the membership. There had been seventy-five tickets sold, one per couple, so a large crowd was expected.

Jill and Johnny, along with Marie and a long-time male acquaintance named John, were attending. Jill and her mother had purchased dresses from Dianne; Jill wore a turquoise, full-length dress with a halter top. With her red hair, she looked terrific. Marie's dress was a basic black dress with silver beading and a matching scarf.

Janet was stunning in a long, pale blue, scooped-neck dress with an empire waist accented by a large bow. The skirt portion of the dress was embroidered in white. She was wearing her hair in a stylish French roll and as an accent, had chosen pearl accessories.

Teresa wore bright blue, similar to Janet's with an empire waist and full skirt. This dress was chosen primarily to hide her pregnancy, which was just beginning to show. She had selected a sterling silver necklace and earrings which looked spectacular against the blue of the dress.

Dianne looked gorgeous in a green satin, full-length sheath which hugged her body. The dress sported a boat-neck, one of the newest looks for 1968. She had accented the dress with gold jewelry from her store. She was certainly a great model for her business.

All the men were in their "monkey suits", as they called them. Actually, the guys there looked quite dashing in their tuxedos.

As Teresa looked around she saw Robert and Vicki, quite the surprise couple of the season; Doug and Linda, when they saw her, immediately turned away; Kris and Toni had set a wedding date for June; and Debbie and Jake, the second surprise. The chemistry in the ballroom was volatile. With the combination of people, their respective entanglements and alcohol, anything could happen.

This was a "coming-out party" of sorts for Dave and Janet. They had kept their relationship under wraps until recently.

Most of the guests had been unaware of their relationship; consequently, it stirred up a lot of conversation. They weren't being ostracized; however, the situation tended to make most people uncomfortable and they weren't sure what they should say. Teresa had picked up on this and hurried over to greet them. "Hi," she said "have you located your table yet?"

"No," Dave answered "we only just arrived ten minutes ago and the shock on people's faces is interesting, to say the least."

Janet added "It is funny, but they'll get used to it. Debbie and Jake are also here; I saw them when we first came in, so people shouldn't be too surprised."

Teresa suggested "Let's go find our tables; hopefully, we'll be sitting together or be able to communicate with the others at our table, unlike the Halloween Party where I ended up next to Linda. What a disaster that was! Oh, here we are. You are sitting with Mike and Dianne and Toni and Kris. That should be a fun table and you'll be comfortable there."

"Here is yours, Teresa. The two of you are sitting with Linda and Doug. There is also another couple who I don't know. Maybe we could trade your names for Toni and Kris."

"Yes, let's do that. This would not work." They quickly exchanged the place cards and no one seemed to notice. "This is great; all of us at the same table. I wonder where Jill and Johnny are sitting, probably with Marie and her friend."

Everyone began to find and take their seats. Dinner was due to be served soon. The menu was filet mignon, baked potato with butter and sour cream and an arugula salad.

Hot bread was served with the salad, followed by the entree and then, the dessert, Whiskey Bread Pudding with coffee. Red wines were brought around by the wine stewards during dinner and chilled bottles of champagne were standing by for the upcoming celebration. The three-piece combo played soft music during dinner, but was now beginning to pick up the beat for dancing.

Linda was keeping an eye on Doug, watching to see if he was looking at Teresa. She hadn't caught him, as yet, but felt sure she would eventually. The band was playing "Chances Are" an old Johnny Mathis tune and the dance floor soon became crowded. Doug asked Linda to dance and they joined the throng. He hadn't wanted to attend this event, but because of his business and Linda's insistence, he had little choice. Lately, he had little choice in anything. Linda was being true to her word and making his life a living hell. She hadn't said that in so many words, but that was her intent. The atmosphere around their house was like a war zone with an armed truce. He felt as though he was walking on eggshells all the time. Knowing he deserved it was one thing; living with it was another. He wasn't sure how long he would be able to stand it.

Ted was feeling much the same as Doug, not wanting to be there, but finding it a necessary evil. Looking around, he saw Doug and Linda and thought about the baby Teresa was carrying. How he hated that son-of-a-bitch! Too bad he hadn't punched his lights completely out; then he wouldn't ever have to look at him again. He held Teresa closer as they danced and she smiled up at him. How she melted his heart.

Janet and Dave loved dancing together. He was such a good dancer and she was almost as tall as him, so they made quite a pair on the dance floor. "Just think," he said "in approximately two weeks, we'll both be free, free to do whatever we choose; what do you choose, young lady?"

"I choose you, Mr. Brown, for the rest of my life. I am enjoying being with you tonight, even if we're getting some odd looks. One of these days, we'll be old news and they'll be talking about someone else." The song ended and as they turned around, they ran into Debbie and Jake. Pleasantries were exchanged and each couple proceeded to their table.

Robert had been watching Janet with her new guy, thinking about their divorce, which would be final in a couple of weeks. She was still his wife and she was out flaunting this relationship, embarrassing him and making him look like a fool. He picked up his third glass of Jack Daniels and downed it. Vicki was hanging onto him like he was going to disappear or something. She was very clingy and he wasn't sure he liked it. She was okay, but she wasn't Janet. He was only now beginning to realize that maybe he had loved her after all. He sure did miss her.

Mike was being very attentive to Dianne, telling her how gorgeous she looked, what a great figure she had, really laying it on thick. She was paying very little attention to him; she'd heard it all before and it meant next to nothing. At least, he was saying those things to her and not to Vicki or some other woman. Wishing she could respond to him; she took his hand and held it. "You know I'm trying, Mike; it's not easy to trust you again. But, I do appreciate the effort you're making. I'm glad we came tonight; I see that Vicki is here with Robert Steele. Did you see her?"

"Yes, I saw her, Dianne. I haven't talked to her and don't intend to. Are you trying to needle me?"

"No, but I have to wonder how you feel when you see her?"

"I don't feel anything; unless it would be a little bit of discomfort. I never felt anything for her, so why should I now?"

"I just wondered, Mike. I suppose a man's feelings are a lot different than those of a woman. If there was a man here with whom I'd been involved, I'd feel sad. But, let's change the subject and dance."

Teresa stole a look at Doug; she couldn't help herself. Ted was at the bar waiting for his drink and she was sitting alone for a few minutes. She thought Doug looked guarded, as though he was being held against his will. She hoped he was suffering; he deserved to suffer after the way he had treated her. Knowing she only had herself to blame; it still hurt. Thinking about the baby she was carrying made her shiver; hoping Ted was the father and not this man. She didn't want her baby to have such a father. How could she have been such a fool? She wondered how both their marriages would turn out; his couldn't be any easier than hers. It might even be harder; Linda didn't seem like the forgiving sort. She even felt a little sympathetic toward Linda; her life couldn't be very easy at the moment either.

Jill had refrained from drinking tonight; Johnny had agreed she could have one glass of champagne at midnight, no more. She was okay with that; another concussion was not on her agenda. Her mother, Marie, was having fun, dancing with John. It was good to see her mother enjoying herself again. Life is for the living, she thought. She glanced over at Johnny and he winked at her; what a lucky girl I am, she thought. The only thing affecting her happiness adversely was the upcoming trial. She was dreading the day she'd have to face her rapist.

At 11:45 PM, the stewards began to pass out bottles of champagne and glasses to the guests. Hats and streamers were already on the tables and were being donned by many of the revelers. The countdown began at two minutes before twelve. At midnight, the bells rang, balloons were released from the ceiling and couples celebrated with the first kiss of the New Year. The fire siren could be heard in the distance, along with gunfire. Champagne was uncorked and glasses were raised in celebration. Soon afterwards, the party began to break up.

As Dave and Janet prepared to leave, Robert approached them. "Oh no", she thought, "is this going to be trouble?"

"Hey, Brown, you know she is still my wife?" Robert was clearly drunk and Janet was frightened. "Our divorce won't be final for another couple of weeks and here you are, out with her already?" He grabbed Dave by his shirt collar, getting into his face as he yelled at him. "Don't you have any respect, for her or your own wife?"

"Take your hands off me, Robert, or I'll have to do it for you." Dave pushed him away and he staggered against a table. He then dove at Dave and the fight began. They were on the floor, fists were flailing and lots of punches were being thrown. A group of guys broke them up, pulling Dave off Robert and holding each of them at bay. Security guards arrived and told them both to get out immediately.

Robert took Vicki's arm and strode away. Janet put her arms around Dave and told him how sorry she was.

"You have no reason to be sorry, Janet. He's not your

responsibility now. Fortunately, nothing was broken here at the club and he's gone." They got their coats and left the party, wondering if they should have waited before appearing in public.

CHAPTER 56

Dave went into the bank early, knowing the bank examiners would be in today. He was sure he'd been able to cover up the phony transactions he'd made, but he didn't know what methods the examiners would be using. He hadn't diverted that much money, around $20,000, but he knew the feds wouldn't look kindly upon any amount. In advance of their visit, he had met with his attorney, Fred Waters and informed him of what could be transpiring at the bank. He was extremely anxious about this; he had tried to return some of the money, but with Debbie's incessant spending and the tuition bills pouring in; it had, thus far, been impossible. His thoughts turned toward Janet, how disappointed she would be in him if she knew he was involved in such a scheme and his dad; how he would suffer from the shame if it was discovered. As the morning progressed, he tried to keep himself busy and keep his mind off the activities of the examiners. They were currently looking at the transactions within the Trust Department, where he had made changes to some of the accounts. This was an area of which he had sole control. Being a small bank, the president had more obligations; where, in a larger bank, he would be delegating these tasks. Consequently, if they found discrepancies; it would point directly at him.

By lunch time, they were still auditing transactions. He

was getting more and more nervous; they should be finished with that area by now. Have they discovered the trail? What were they finding? Am I now in trouble? Why did I do this; he thought. If I'm caught; it could ruin my life, or at the very least, my career in banking would be done. Then what would I do? Would I have to spend time in jail? Janet called and asked if he wanted to have lunch, but he begged off; telling her the examiners might require him to answer questions. Indeed, his prediction materialized.

Walt Langley, the Chief Auditor, stepped into Dave's office. "Mr. Brown, we'd like to go over some of these transactions with you. Would you have an hour or so to spare?"

"Sure, Walt, come on in. What can I do to help?"

"We have found several discrepancies, totaling $19,860.00. These items involved various accounts, but appeared to be mishandled in much the same manner. This leads us to believe that the same person committed all the thefts and then initiated a cover up. Can you explain this?"

"I'd have to look them over myself, Walt. I have no explanation; are you sure your auditors have not made an error?"

"I'm sure of that; I have reviewed these findings using different auditing methods and the results have turned out the same. Is it true that you have sole responsibility for these accounts?"

"Yes, I'm the only one who handles these accounts."

"That's what I thought. There are no checks and balances in your position; therefore, if funds are missing, the onus would be on you. Have you misappropriated these funds, Mr. Powers?"

"Before I answer any further questions; I will need to have my attorney present."

"Very well, Mr. Powers; we will have to report this discrepancy to the FBI, who will then consult with the county prosecutor and most likely, you will be charged with a crime. Do you understand that?"

"Yes, I do." Langley left the office and Dave sat back in his chair, wishing the floor would swallow him up. He called his attorney and asked him to come by the bank; the matter they had discussed earlier had been discovered.

Within three hours, a warrant for his arrest had been issued and Marshal Bates came by to enforce it. "I'm sorry to have to do this, Dave, but you're under arrest. Ed read him his Miranda rights and they walked out to the patrol car. The Head Cashier had been informed of the embezzlement and would move into a supervisory position at the bank on an interim basis. Dave's attorney, Fred Waters, was already on the phone trying to arrange an emergency hearing with a judge to set bail. If he couldn't accomplish this, Dave would be spending the night in jail. Luckily for Dave, Fred got the job done by pulling in favors owed; the bail was set at $20,000 and Debbie was called to bail him out.

When Debbie arrived, she was in total shock. "How could this have happened to you? What the hell is going on?"

Dave told her "Just wait, I'll explain everything when we get in the car. Let's get out of here right now." They walked out to her car, got in and he told her to take him to his car, which was in the bank parking lot. "Debbie, I've screwed up.

Funds are missing from the trust accounts and I'm at fault. These accounts are completely my responsibility."

"What are you telling me Dave, did you embezzle this money? How much was it and why on earth would you do that?"

"I did embezzle the funds; we needed money for Dave Jr's Ivy League school. That was my only resource. I didn't want to disappoint you and my son; now I've done that in a far worse way. I'm morbidly ashamed of this; I will end up paying for it, in a supreme fashion. My banking career is finished; who knows what kind of a job I'll be eligible for now."

"I'm sorry, Dave. I wish you'd come to me; Dave Jr. could have gone to a state university; he didn't need to attend Yale. He'll have to drop out now anyway; we won't be able to afford to send him there. Well, here you are; please keep me posted on what's happening."

"I will, Debbie, thanks for coming through for me." He stepped out of her car, got into his and drove away. How am I going to tell Janet? What is she going to think? Will she even want to stay with me? I'll have to tell her tonight; I can't wait and take the chance of her finding out elsewhere. He was terrified to tell her.

CHAPTER 57

Janet was already home, having freshened up for her dinner date with Dave. He was picking her up around six and she was very anxious to see him. Her divorce would be final on Friday and tonight they were celebrating. Dave was taking her out of town to a quaint restaurant known for its' Italian specialties. For the occasion, she had chosen a red long-sleeved dress with a black and white hounds-tooth jacket. Dianne had told her it was the latest thing.

As soon as Dave walked in, Janet knew something was wrong. He looked wrung out and haggard. She'd never seen him look like this; it frightened her. "Janet, we need to talk. I'm not sure we'll be going out for dinner. We can decide later."

They both sat down on the sofa and he took her hand and held it for the longest time before he said anything. "Janet, this is the hardest thing I've ever had to do. There is something about me that you need to know and it will affect our future together. I was charged with embezzlement today; obviously, I've lost my job at the bank and I may end up in jail for this. I took the money to get David Jr. enrolled at Yale; it helped smooth the application process. In retrospect, I was obviously not thinking ahead. Now, he'll have to drop out and go to a state university, if I can even afford to send him. Debbie was spending money like water and every time I would get in a position to replace it; some other expense would arise. But, I'm not blaming her. She bailed me out today or I'd be sitting in the county jail right now waiting on my hearing. I've contacted my lawyer and he says that due to the fact this is a first offense and a white-collar crime, I probably will not do any time for it; just probation and restitution. I can live with that. The big question in my mind is: can you live with it?"

"Oh my God, Dave, this is too much to absorb. I am floored; that's all I can say. You know I love you; what you've done doesn't change that. But, it shakes my belief in you; I was always of the opinion that you were a straight arrow. Now, to find out different; it's hard to comprehend. My first reaction is to stand by you and support you; but my second reaction is to wonder if I fell in love with a man who isn't real. The values I thought you held dear aren't there. I really need time to think; our future is in jeopardy and I'm not sure it can be fixed. I'd like to be alone tonight and process this on my own. Can you please understand?"

"Of course, I understand. Being the woman you are; I wouldn't expect any less from you. Can I call you tomorrow and we'll go from there?"

"Yes, tomorrow evening, after I get home from work, would be best." He leaned over and kissed her on the cheek. As he left, he wondered if this would be the last time he'd be leaving this house. He was unable to read her reaction tonight. As well as he knew her; this was not what he'd expected. He had thought she'd listen, chastise him for what he'd done and put her arms around him. She only listened. A sense of foreboding crept over him.

Janet sat there dazed and confused after Dave left, trying

to sort out her thoughts and feelings. As though in slow motion, she went to the bedroom, undressed and prepared for bed. Was I wrong in what I said to him tonight? Should I have been supportive, but supportive of what, a crime? How could he be so devious; he's not the man I thought. Should I stay with him, not knowing if this is a one-time occurrence? Will he use bad judgment in the future when it comes to our lives? Then, thinking about that, what kind of a life can we have together now? I have to stay in Creviston; my family business is here. He won't want to stay here; what would he do in this area now? The only job he would ever get in this town is one I might provide him at the plant and who would respect him? What would my dad say about that; or the board of directors; probably a big fat NO. In Creviston, we don't have a future together and since I'm tied to the town; that makes my decision very simple. I love him dearly, but maybe I was just in love with a facade. Her heart breaking, she turned off the lights and hoped she'd be able to sleep.

As Dave drove toward his dad's house, he was thinking how disappointed his dad would be. My dad has always been so proud of everything I've accomplished; in sports, business, my golf game, my family. Now, those things will all be wiped out by this one disastrous decision. I made a very bad choice for what I thought was a good reason, but that reason doesn't absolve me of guilt. I may end up in prison; Fred could be wrong about a plea agreement. Janet might decide she doesn't know who I am and dump me. I've lost my job, possibly my freedom and the woman I love, the respect of my dad; my kids will not be able to hold up their heads in this town; what else is there to lose? As he drove aimlessly, he found himself at the lake, a place he had loved dearly as a child. He and his dad would come out here;

they'd swim, fish and canoe. They even camped out a few nights. It was dusk and he could see lights twinkling in the distance; but with it getting darker and no big city lights to interfere, the stars were blanketing the sky. He could pick out the big dipper and even the little dipper; what a sight. "How could I have been so stupid" he said aloud, but there was no one there to reply. Never having been a man of faith; he couldn't even pray. He knelt down and tried, but no words came out, only the sobs of a broken man. There's only one answer for me, he thought. He went back to his car and opened the glove compartment. Several weeks ago, when Robert had begun threatening Janet, he had put his Smith & Wesson 38 automatic in the car for protection. He slowly removed the gun from the holster and walked to the edge of the water. Unceremoniously and without remorse; he raised the barrel to his temple and pulled the trigger.

The next morning, Dave's father looked in his bedroom and discovered his bed had not been slept in. He must have stayed in at Janet's last night, he thought. He had not been making a habit of it, but it was only a few days and they'd both be divorced; they're adults, what difference does it make at this point.

He went into the kitchen and put the coffee on to perk. It looked like snow was coming in; the sky was gray and the wind was whistling through the trees. It was a normal, blustery January day in Indiana, he surmised. He was trying to decide what to have for breakfast when someone knocked at the door. Hurrying to answer the door, he glanced out the window and saw the police car parked outside. Whatever does the marshal want?

Ed was standing on the porch, despising this part of his job. Notifying a family member of a loved one's death was, without a doubt, the worst part of this position. "Hello, John, may I come in?"

"Sure, what can I do for you this morning? I just made a pot of coffee; can I get you a cup?"

"No, no, can we sit down, please; I've come to deliver bad news." Before they could sit, he said "John, we found your son out by the lake this morning, shot to death. It was apparently self-inflicted. There was no evidence of foul play and the gun belonged to him.

"Oh, no, you must be mistaken; why would he do such a thing to himself? I've got to sit down, Ed; I feel like I'm going to collapse."

"John, if you didn't see Dave last night; you are probably unaware of the embezzlement at the bank. Apparently, he had diverted funds from trust accounts into his own account. The bank examiners discovered it yesterday and Dave was arrested. Debbie bailed him out of jail yesterday afternoon and we don't know where he went after that. It was his first offense, so it was unlikely he would have seen any prison time, but he obviously wasn't prepared for the consequences, whatever they would be. He didn't leave any kind of note; although it's highly unusual for suicide victims to do that. We can only imagine how he was feeling, the despair and the shame. Is there anyone I can call to be with you?"

"Yes, call my other son, Steve and he'll come right over. Thank you, Marshal Bates, for being so kind. I'll be fine until Steve arrives. Do Janet and Debbie know yet?"

"No, I plan to go see Debbie next and as a professional courtesy; I will notify Janet. She is going to be devastated."

Ed was thinking about Dave and his life on the way to his family home. This was a permanent solution to a temporary problem. The ones left behind are always the ones who suffer; the deceased only leaves behind misery, while escaping his own. What a tragedy. One of the daughters came to the door; he asked for her mother to step outside. "Debbie, I am afraid I have bad news for you and your family. We found Dave out by the lake. He shot himself."

"Ed, is he alive?" He noticed the trembling in her hands.

"No, Debbie, I'm sorry. It was instant; there would have been nothing anyone could have done if they'd been there. According to his dad, he didn't come home last night, so we're assuming that is when it occurred. The coroner will be able to tell us a more exact time of death when he does the autopsy. That is necessary whenever a person dies alone, especially under these circumstances. Is there someone you want me to call? I'd be glad to stay with you while you tell your daughters, if you'd like."

"Ed, thank you, but I'll do that myself. It's the least I can do for Dave now. This is so terrible; he just couldn't face these charges. Some may say it was the easy way out, but for his family, it won't be. This was a very selfish thing to do. He wasn't thinking about his kids, only himself. I hate him for doing this. I appreciate your kindness, Ed. Right now, I'd like to be alone."

Ed dreaded his next stop almost more than the first two. He had known Janet for most of their lives and had some idea of how this would affect her. She would be getting ready for work this morning and he hoped he'd catch her before she left. When he arrived at her house, he was relieved to find her car still in the drive. He knocked on her door and when she opened it, she immediately saw from the look on his face that something was terribly wrong.

"Ed, what's wrong? Is it Daddy or Mother?"

"No, Janet, they're fine as far as I know. Can I come in and sit down for a few minutes? I need to talk to you." They sat down at the kitchen table and he proceeded. "We found Dave this morning out by the lake with a self-inflicted gunshot wound to the head. He's gone, Janet, a suicide." She looked at Ed, unbelieving at first; then she became hysterical.

"Ed, this is my fault. He was here last night and I made him leave. I couldn't accept what he'd done. I told him I had fallen in love with a man who wasn't real. I caused him to do this; he had no hope, nothing to live for." She was sobbing, totally out of control. Ed put his arms around her.

"Janet, you can't blame yourself. No one knows what goes through a person's mind prior to a suicide. We can only speculate. There are a lot of men whose self-worth is measured by their career and by their position in the community. He probably felt he had no future; that he had nowhere to turn. His dad knew nothing of the debacle at the bank; maybe Dave did this instead of going home to face his dad. We'll never know. The one thing I do know is you can't take responsibility for this act. Only he can do that."

"But Ed, if I'd only been supportive, he might have had some hope for the future. I couldn't give him any support at that moment; what else could I have done?"

"You did what any normal person would do; you questioned his motives and his values. He gave you a lot to think about and he was willing to give you whatever time you needed to figure it out. I can totally understand that. Now, you need to accept the fact that it's not your fault." She continued to sob. He knew he couldn't leave her alone.

He picked up her phone and called Teresa. "This is Marshal Bates. Could you come to Janet's and be with her this morning? Dave Powers killed himself last night and she can't be left alone."

"Oh, Ed, that's awful. Of course, I'll be right there."

"Janet, Teresa is coming over here. I'll stay with you until she arrives. Can I get you a glass of water, a cup of coffee or a couple of aspirin?"

"No, I don't want anything. I just want to die. I can't believe he's gone. I can't stand it." He went to the bedroom, retrieved a blanket and told her to lie down on the sofa. He covered her with the blanket and picked up the phone once again to call her parents. Her dad made plans to go to the plant to take care of Janet's duties while she was out. He assumed she'd be off work for several days. Her mother was coming right over.

Teresa and Janet's mother, Kate, arrived at the same time. When she saw the state of mind her daughter was in, she promptly called Dr. Nelson. He prescribed a sedative and Kate left to pick it up. Teresa sat down beside Janet on the sofa, telling her "Janet, I'm so very, very sorry. This is a tragedy for you and a loss for our town. I know what happened yesterday at the bank, but everyone would have forgiven him. I suppose he couldn't face what he'd done. There is nothing I can say that will make you feel any better. It may have been a spur-of-the-moment decision on his part. He didn't take the time to think it through. We'll never know what he was thinking; we can only imagine the despair he must have felt to commit such an act."

"Teresa, I didn't give him any hope; I made him leave so I could think. How could I do that?"

"Janet, you did what you thought was best; no one can fault you for that. How could you have known he'd do this? It doesn't even seem feasible for him. Never in a million years did you dream this would happen; you can't blame yourself. Dave would not have wanted you to feel this way. He'd want you to try to understand." Kate had returned from the drugstore and gave Janet the sedative. Because she had not eaten, the drug took effect immediately and she soon fell into a deep asleep.

"That's the best thing for her right now," said Kate. "She will need to rest up for the days to come. There are going to be some extremely difficult times ahead." Teresa nodded in agreement. Kate said she would stay with her daughter, so Teresa decided to go back home to her family.

Debbie paid a visit to the funeral director and planned his memorial. Dave had expressed to her at one time that he wanted to be cremated and Debbie had decided to follow his wishes. There would not be a funeral, only a private memorial service for family and a few friends. She planned on including Janet; she knew Dave would have wanted her to be there.

The day of the memorial service was very cold and dreary. Janet equated the conditions with her feelings. As she walked in the funeral home, the first person she saw was Debbie, who smiled and came toward her. She started to reach out her hand, but hugged Janet instead. The two women felt the bond, both having loved him. Dani came up and hugged her too, telling her how sorry she was and saying she wished he could have lived to be her husband. She was mature beyond her years. Debbie and Janet proved to be a great consolation to each other in the days ahead and against the odds, became close friends.

CHAPTER 58

By early March, Jill and Marie were putting the finishing touches on the inn. Food had been stocked in the pantry; clean linens were on the beds and menus had been planned. Blueberry pancakes, which were a specialty of Marie's, along with sausage links, would be the star of the breakfast menu. Guests could opt for bacon and eggs, oatmeal, croissants with cream cheese or dry cereal. Coffee, tea and juices along with fresh fruit in season would complete the menu. They both considered these entrees plentiful and should satisfy even the pickiest guest. There would be cookies, coffee and soft drinks on hand during the day if someone desired a snack. Newspapers and magazines would be available for perusal. A guide to local sights, including a map of the area, would be placed in each room. A fan, iron and extra blankets would be placed in the closet of each guest room. Their weekly Saturday night dinners were scheduled to begin the first week of May. Getting their first month behind them was crucial to their success. The inn was booked for every weekend through the end of June and both Jill and Marie were ecstatic.

Teresa was hurrying to the drugstore to pick up a prescription for Rose, who had developed a nasty sore throat. The weather is beautiful for this time of year, she thought; I wish she wasn't sick. She picked up her medicine and on the way out the door, bumped smack into Doug, who was coming in to buy a pack of cigarettes. She wasn't wearing a coat and was noticeably pregnant.

"Oh, my gosh, I'm so sorry; I almost knocked you down" then she looked up and saw who it was. "Oh, hello, Doug."

"Teresa, are you okay? I was in such a hurry; I wasn't paying any attention either. It's obvious you're expecting a baby. May I ask when it is due?"

"The baby is due the end of July and before you ask, the baby is legally Ted's, and morally too, I might add."

"But there has to be a possibility it's mine. If it is, I want to be a father to it."

"Doug, we cannot have this discussion right now; the baby will be Ted's and that's that. I have to hurry home; I have a sick child."

"Teresa, it was nice to see you. Be well." She quickly disappeared from sight. Now, how will I ever know if I'm the father; apparently, Ted has reconciled himself to the fact that it will be his child. But, what if it is mine? I want to know; I need to know; the question is how? What would Linda think if it was mine? She would have a cow! I wonder if she knows about this. I'll just have to ask her.

He did just that and just as quickly, he wished he hadn't. At home that evening, he asked Linda "Did you know that Teresa is expecting? According to the due date, the baby could be mine. Of course, she is going to deny it; she told me that legally the baby is Ted's, no matter what. Do you think I should pursue this?"

She looked at him as though he had two heads. "Are you out of your freaking mind? You are truly a dumb ass; if you think for even one minute that I'm going to be a step-mother to your love child; then you'd better think again, because it would have to be a cold day in hell for me to fill those shoes. How did you happen to derive this tidbit of information from her?"

"Linda, I literally bumped into her as she was leaving the drugstore; it's a warm day; she wasn't wearing a coat and her pregnancy was very visible. I had to ask if it was mine; I needed to know. She denied it, for the most part. I don't think she is sure, but she definitely wants the baby to be Ted's."

"Well, let's review this. If you know what's good for you; you'll forget it. I won't put up with this; Doug, I'm warning you right now. That baby, whoever it belongs to, needs to stay with Ted and Teresa, end of story. Don't you dare think that you can lay claim on it. We're not paying support or having visitation rights or any of that bullshit. Now, just put it out of your mind. Don't ever bring this subject up to me again." He cowered under the onslaught, but vowed to himself he'd find out, whether she liked it or not. He knew a blood test was available; apparently, for either he or Ted to be named the father, their blood type would have to match that of the baby. If it did not match, that person would be ruled out. The obstacle in knowing for sure would be if he and Ted shared the same blood type; then there would be no definite answer. How he wished there was something more definitive; maybe at some point in the future there would be a better system.

CHAPTER 59

Dianne called Jill and Teresa, wanting to meet for dinner on Thursday night. It would be Janet's birthday and they didn't want her spending it alone. Jill suggested they meet at the inn. Her mother would prepare the meal, excuse herself and leave them to enjoy it. Both the girls agreed. Now, how would they entice Janet to the inn? Jill said she would call and invite her to stop out for the evening; an open house was being held and as a local businesswoman, her presence would be appreciated. They thought this might work. Marie would bake a cake and all the girls planned on buying her a gift. Marie was fixing beef stroganoff with home-made noodles, mashed potatoes and broccoli. Her special Parker House Rolls were also on the menu. They planned on meeting at the inn around five-thirty. Janet was expected at six.

The friends were excited about this surprise dinner. They had all been like a mother hen to Janet during this mourning period, hovering over her. It had been two months and she still found herself crying, especially when she was alone at night.

The table was set, candles were lit, a bottle of red wine had been opened for the occasion and gifts were placed on the buffet. Janet rang the doorbell and Jill went to answer the door. She walked in and the girls sang "Happy Birthday" to her. She was in disbelief. "You girls, you are so devious. I can't believe you pulled this over on me."

"Come on in. We'll have a drink; you can open gifts and then we'll have dinner, which Mom is cooking as we speak. It's your favorite, beef stroganoff. This is our first event at the inn. Isn't that exciting?" Jill was very enthused about throwing this party for Janet, especially here.

Teresa fixed their drinks, a Manhattan for Dianne, gin and tonic for Jill and a sweet old-fashioned for Janet. She poured herself a glass of iced tea. They sat down in the living room of the inn and Janet opened her gifts. The first one was from Dianne, a beautiful silk scarf in black and white to wear with a jacket or a simple dress. The next gift was from Jill, a pair of sterling silver earrings and a simple chain with a little bird in flight. Then came Teresa's gift; a photo album with several pictures of the four of them in various stages of their life. There was lots of remaining space yet to be filled. It was obvious a great deal of thought had gone into each gift. Janet hugged and thanked each of her friends and told them how much she appreciated all the support they had given her over the years and especially during the last two months.

Marie came and told them dinner was served. She excused herself and gave them their privacy. The meal was delicious and Jill assured them she would pass their praise on to her mom. The cake was brought in, a three-tiered chocolate masterpiece covered with twenty-five candles. The girls raved about the cake to Marie, saying it was far too pretty to cut. Janet blew out her candles and Jill did the honor of serving. Then it was time for their customary talk.

Jill offered her opinion. "Since it's Janet's birthday, she should go first." They all agreed.

"Well, I suppose I can do that. I want to thank all of you for the party, the gifts and everything you've done for me over the past couple of months since Dave's death. Things are getting a little easier for me; you all know how much I loved him, but the worst part, other than his death, is my inability to judge men. First, it was Robert and we all know how that turned out, then Dave. I thought he was the most upstanding, decent guy I'd ever met; then to find out he was capable of such deceit. How blind could I be? As you know, Debbie has been a very good friend to me through all this. We share a common bond; even though I started seeing him before they were divorced. She has forgiven me for that and I am eternally grateful. Robert has come back around, wanting to make up with me; but I told him that would never happen. I can be his friend, but no more than that.

Teresa said to her "Janet, it wasn't only you that Dave fooled; he had the whole town fooled. He wasn't a bad guy; he was guilty of bad judgment by making that one decision. Apparently, he did it for a good reason; it's too bad he didn't take advantage of his banks' ability to loan money or ask his dad; he would have loaned him the cash. We don't think you're using bad judgment; you've just been unlucky in love. The third time should be the charm."

"I know what you're saying, but it has definitely shaken my confidence. I am planning on traveling during the next six months on behalf of the company, visiting regional sales offices, other facilities and touching base with our customers. This will be therapeutic for me, getting away from Creviston and the memories for a period of time."

Jill added "Janet, traveling sounds great. We all need a change of scenery occasionally. I assume I can go next. You all know what my life has been for the past year or so. Ironically, I'm looking forward to testifying at the trial of my rapist and putting that chapter of my life behind me. My depression has lifted with the help of medication, counseling and my loving husband." Jill raised her arms and looked around the room. "This place has been and will continue to be, a wonderful project for Mom and me. We are booked through the end of June and we're so excited to see how it goes. The boys are getting older and take a little less work, so the timing of this business is perfect for me. Actually, for real this time, we are planning an open house for the last weekend of March, before our official opening in April. If any of you would like to act as hostesses for the event, I'm sure we could use the extra help. I can't wait till opening day."

All the girls jumped at the chance to be a hostess for the open house. "What fun will that be", exclaimed Dianne. "It's wonderful to see you excited about something again; you've had more than your share of traumatic events to deal with, from the depression to the death of your dad and the rape. It takes a hell of a woman to overcome all that." They clapped and gave her hugs, each friend congratulating Jill on her progress.

"Dianne, we all want to hear about the store and what's going on with Mike," said Jill. "It's your turn at the podium."

"Gee, where do I begin? Let's start with the store. My Christmas season was over the top in sales, beating last year's figures by eight percent. Since the first of the year, we have been holding our own; the weather has thrown us some curve balls, but, I am very pleased. Spring has arrived in the store, even though it is yet to arrive on the calendar. Surprisingly, lots of women like to shop early in the season for their wardrobe. I suppose they like getting the first choice of the latest styles. Summer goods will start coming in mid-April and we'll be having a sale around Mother's Day.

I expect to see all three of you in the store soon."

"As for Mike, the jury is still out on that situation. We've been married since I was sixteen; it's hard to give up that investment in time. He has been working hard to be a good husband; Phillip is enjoying the time Mike spends with him, but as crazy as it sounds, I may have liked the old Mike better. The dynamics of our marriage have changed and I'm not sure it can survive. For now, though, I am going to maintain the status quo. I am not miserable, but I can't say I'm satisfied, either. I had not shared that with any of you prior to tonight; what do you think?"

Teresa was the first to speak. "Dianne, you sound like me a year ago. I wasn't unhappy, but I wasn't ecstatic either. Let that be a warning; look what that feeling did for me. Sometimes, we're happy and don't have the sense to recognize it."

Janet agreed. "I had a ton of issues in my marriage and I knew he was wrong for me; therefore, there was never any question in my mind as to was I happy or not. It just took the incentive of a future with Dave for me to have the courage to end a bad situation. Perhaps, you should ask yourself if this is the man you want to spend the rest of your life with and go from there."

Jill spoke up. "Dianne, you have shared most of your problems with me over the years and what I see now is you have no problems. Could that be it? Maybe you need a crisis to feel alive."

Dianne replied "That's certainly a new slant on things. Maybe you're right; what I need is another challenge. I could open more stores. I've been thinking about doing that. Wouldn't it be wonderful to have a store in each of the bigger cities in the area?" Dianne was glowing as she expounded on this idea. "Back to my marriage, I appreciate the advice and I'm going to give it another year or so and put as much effort into it as possible. Mike is certainly putting his all into it and I will too. At the end of that period of time, if I still feel the way I do now, I'll get out of it. But, in the meantime, I'm going to become the owner of a clothing store chain."

All the girls applauded; why not look into that? The economy was good, women loved to shop; it sounded like a great idea to them. Expand your business. Dianne felt exhilarated, "It always helps me to get your feedback. This encouragement was exactly what I needed."

Teresa said, "You've left it to me to finish up the evening. How can I follow what's come before me? One news flash; I ran into Doug a few days ago, the day it was so warm, and I wasn't wearing a coat. He noticed the pregnancy right away and asked when it was due. I told him the baby would be born around the end of July and that he didn't need to ask if he was the father; the baby belonged to Ted. He wasn't convinced; I'm afraid. I may have problems with him once the baby arrives. I don't want him to be the father; I want it to be Ted. I was so stupid to have ever had that affair. I should have listened to all of you; you had my best interests at heart. My husband has been an absolute saint, much better than I deserve. He's convinced the baby is his and he's so excited, as are the girls. They want a baby sister and naturally, he wants a son."

"I spent months mourning the death of this affair; in a proper society, there is no viewing or funeral for this type of loss. You knew I was hurt, but I never let you know the depth of pain I was suffering. I hid it from you, as well as my family, but I've battled my way back and I'll never go there again. I value my family and my husband now more than you can ever know and I will do whatever is necessary to protect them."

The girls sat there quietly, each waiting for the other to say something. This had not been the normal birthday party; it was more like a therapy session. Hopefully, it would have a lasting effect. Everyone hugged, promised to stay in touch, and said good night.

CHAPTER 60

The morning of July 22 dawned with Teresa waking up in labor. She roused Ted, telling him it was time to go to the hospital. They dropped the girls off at his mother's and by the time they arrived at Labor & Delivery, the pains were only two minutes apart. The nurses wasted no time getting her into the delivery room; bypassing the standard labor room. It was way too late for that. One of the nurses said to her "Your husband should have gotten a wheel chair; you could have dropped this baby in the parking lot." Teresa was horrified at the thought. Even though she already had two children, she hadn't known that could happen. Twenty minutes later, her son was born, weighing in at eight pounds, one ounce. He was twenty inches long with a mass of dark hair. Ted was thrilled beyond words. They had decided to name him Benjamin Alan Farris.

Later that day, after Ted had gone to his mother's to tell the girls and the rest of the family, things settled down. The baby was brought to her for his first feeding. She held him, examining his little body, making sure he was perfect and concluding he was. Holding him, she looked into his eyes and whispered "Ben, my sweet, sweet boy; you have your Daddy's eyes."

The End